SECURING CAITE

SEAL of Protection: Legacy, Book 1

SUSAN STOKER

Edited by Kelli Collins
Cover Design by Chris Mackey, AURA Design Group
Manufactured in the United States

DEDICATION

For Lee. You might be gone, but your cartoons will live on forever.

CHAPTER ONE

"Hot enough for ya?" the naval officer asked as he held open the door for her.

Caite McCallan gave him a friendly smile but internally rolled her eyes. Intellectually, she knew the Middle Eastern country of Bahrain was going to be a lot warmer than she was used to feeling back in San Diego, but she hadn't been prepared for exactly *how* hot it was.

"Thank you," she told him after she quickly walked through the door and headed for the elevator. She was running late this morning, otherwise she would've taken the stairs. She wasn't an exerciser. She'd rather be sitting in a chair on the beach with her toes in the water, drinking a margarita, than going to the gym, taking a jog, or playing volleyball for "fun."

But since she'd been in Bahrain, she'd started taking the stairs to her third-floor office because her lack of movement was almost embarrassing. There was no way she was going to take a run out in the heat, and she very rarely left the safety of her apartment, except when on the American naval base southeast of the city of Manama.

She impatiently hit the button and sighed in relief when the doors opened almost immediately. Caite slipped into the elevator and hit the button for the third floor.

Just as the doors were closing, a large hand caught them and they reopened.

Resisting the urge to sigh in irritation, Caite moved to the back of the small space, giving the three men room to enter.

She looked up at them with wide eyes. She'd been working in the country for four months now, and had seen her share of good-looking men in uniform, but these men, who seemed to take up every inch of space in the small elevator, were hands down the hottest men she'd seen yet.

All three had dark beards covering the bottom half of their faces, but it was the first man who'd entered who Caite couldn't take her eyes off of. "Lush" was the only way she could describe his dark hair. It was longer than his friends' hair, and she had the sudden urge to run her fingers through it to see if it was as soft as it looked. All three men were taller than she was, but that wasn't saying much, as she was only five-five.

He had dark eyes that seemed to latch on to hers when he entered the elevator. His nose was a bit

2

crooked, but it gave his face character. He was muscular, and had a larger build than the other two men with him. He wasn't only taller than them, he was bigger in every sense of the word. He made her think of late nights and cuddling on the couch.

"Morning," the man said in a deep voice. His lips were quirked upward, as if he found something amusing, and Caite knew she was blushing.

"Hi," she mumbled and looked down at the briefcase in her hands.

The elevator lurched as it began its upward trajectory, and Caite held her breath as she pressed her lips together. She wanted to flirt with the man. Wanted to have the confidence to look him in the eye and smile. But that wasn't who she was.

She wasn't exactly shy, but she didn't have confidence when it came to men. She was much more comfortable fading into the background and observing people. She found out a ton of information that way. Like the time she'd learned that her supposed best friend in high school secretly asked out the boy Caite had a crush on. Or when she'd overheard one of her TAs in college telling a girl in the class, who he'd been dating, what was going to be on the final exam...which subsequently helped Caite pass the class.

And when she'd heard a naval officer back in San Diego bitching to a coworker about how much contractors made when they volunteered to work overseas, when stateside employees didn't get the same bump in pay.

Hence, why she was in Bahrain at the moment.

"I swear this place gets hotter with every trip," one of the men grumbled.

"Global warning and all that," another said, more to himself than his friends.

The third man didn't comment. Caite kept her eyes on her fingers and willed the elevator to move faster.

"Is it always this hot in here?" the first man asked.

Knowing she couldn't exactly pretend she hadn't heard him, Caite finally looked up. The man who'd asked had a closely cut beard and his hair was almost shaved on the sides, while longer on top. He should've looked silly, but somehow, with his brown camouflage uniform, the style made him look handsome.

He was much leaner than the man who'd immediately caught Caite's eye, and it was easier to see his lips as his beard was cut much closer. He was the shortest of the bunch, probably only a few inches above her height, but somehow she still felt as if he towered over her. Maybe because of the air of confidence surrounding him.

She nodded. "The AC doesn't seem to work much in the elevators so it's always hotter in here."

"It could be worse, Ace," the man she'd been secretly admiring said. "We could be doing PT out in the sun."

"True," Ace said and shrugged.

Just then the elevator made a loud clanging noise and shuddered.

Caite put out a hand to brace herself on the wall next to her and sighed in frustration.

"What the hell?" Ace exclaimed.

"Shit!" the second man said, as Ace let out another low curse.

Without fanfare, Caite placed her briefcase on the floor. She then leaned against the wall and lowered herself to sit. She was grateful she'd worn a comfortable pair of loose black pants today. She brought her knees up, clasped her hands around them and settled in to wait.

She knew all three men were looking down at her in surprise. Before they could ask what was going on, she said, "This happens at least twice a week. You might as well get comfortable. The last time, I heard it was an hour and a half before they were able to get it running again."

"Are you kidding?"

Caite looked up at the man she'd been ogling. "No."

Sighing, he eased himself to the floor near her. With one leg stretched out in front of him and the other bent at the knee, he smiled and held out a hand. "I'm Blake. Blake Wise. Rocco to my friends."

Caite stared at his calloused hand for a beat before reaching out. "Caite McCallan."

"Hi, Caite," Rocco said in a husky voice that made goose bumps race up and down her arms.

"Rocco, you can't seriously be thinking about sitting here and waiting for them to get us out? We can just—"

"Sit, Gumby," Rocco interrupted. He was still holding her hand, and Caite knew she was blushing once again.

"But—"

"We'll just hang out here with Caite until help gets to us." Rocco turned to her. "Do they know the elevator is stuck? I don't see an emergency phone or anything in here."

Caite swallowed and nodded. "I'm pretty sure they know. The last time, one of the people I work with was in here. He said within a few minutes, someone called down—or up, I don't remember which—to him and the others stuck inside, and told them maintenance was working on it."

Why was he still holding her hand? Caite had no idea. It felt good, but awkward.

Finally, he ran his thumb over the back of her hand and slowly let go. She clasped her hands together in her lap nervously.

Ace and Gumby finally sat on the other side of the small space.

"Not the way I thought we'd start our tropical vacation," Ace quipped.

Caite's lips twitched. Bahrain wasn't her idea of either tropical or a vacation.

Obviously having seen her amusement, Ace said, "Hey, it's warm, by the ocean, and we didn't have to run five miles in the sand this morning. Sounds like a vacation to me."

She looked at him and said, "But there aren't any alcoholic drinks. How can it be a vacation without sipping a blue drink with ice cubes, sliced fruit, and a cute little umbrella?"

"I'll never understand why chicks like that crap. I mean, what's wrong with an ice-cold beer?" Gumby muttered.

"It's gross," Caite said without thought, then mentally smacked her forehead in exasperation. "I mean...it's fine...if you like that sort of thing."

The man next to her chuckled. "I take it you're not a beer drinker."

She glanced at Rocco and shook her head. "No."

"It's an acquired taste," Ace said.

Caite nodded, but couldn't take her eyes from Rocco. His dark brown gaze hadn't left her face, and it felt weird to have a man pay such close attention to her. She'd gotten somewhat used to having guys stare at her since she'd arrived in the Arabic country, but the way Rocco was looking at her was different than how the locals stared. She always felt as if they were judging her, and finding her lacking in some way, but that wasn't the vibe she got from Rocco.

It was as if he could read her mind. Could somehow sense how attracted she was to him.

The thought flustered her, and Caite looked back down at her hands in her lap.

"Hey! Anyone in there?" a muffled voice called out from below.

"Yes! There's four of us!" Ace yelled back.

"They're working on getting you guys out of there. Just hang on!" the voice said.

"Will do!" Ace bellowed back.

After a long silence, Gumby said, "So, we might as well get to know each other. And I know *these* yahoos, but I don't know you..." His voice trailed off.

Caite shrugged. "I'm Caite."

"You said that," Rocco replied, clearly amused. "Where are you from? What do you do here? How long have you been here and how long are you planning on staying? Got any plans for dinner?"

At his last question, her eyes swung up once more and met his. She expected to see him smiling at her, letting her know he was teasing, but she saw absolutely no humor in his gaze. She looked over at Ace and Rocco. *They* were smiling, but their amusement seemed to be aimed at the man at her side, rather than her.

"Um...I had an apartment in the San Diego area. I've been here a few months and my contract is for a year, with the option to renew for a second if I want. I haven't decided yet whether I will or not." She purposely ignored his last question.

"What do you do?" Ace asked.

Now that, she could answer. "I'm a secretary. An administrative assistant."

"How did you end up all the way out here?" Gumby

8

asked.

Caite shrugged. "I needed the money."

Silence met her response. It felt awkward, so she hurried to explain. "I majored in French in college. My mom told me I was making a mistake, but I ignored her. I fell in love with Paris in high school, and wanted to be go there to live and work more than anything. I took French as my foreign language requirement in high school and decided to continue it in college. I loved every second of it, but after I graduated, I realized Mom was right. It wasn't like there were that many jobs for a French speaker in the San Diego area. Spanish, yes, but not French.

"I started working as a secretary for a friend of my dad, and he suggested I apply for a Department of Defense contract position. So I did. I got hired and worked there for several years, but I was buried in debt. From college expenses, my car, my credit cards...I couldn't seem to get ahead, and living in San Diego isn't exactly cheap. Overseas positions pay more, and when the job out here came up, I applied." She shrugged. "I got it and...here I am."

"Do you like what you're doing?" Rocco asked.

Caite shrugged again. "I don't hate it," she said after a beat. "But who loves their job? We work because we have to eat."

"I love *my* job," Rocco told her.

"Me too," Ace echoed.

Gumby nodded. "Me three."

Now Caite was embarrassed. "Right. Of course. Join the military and see the world and all that," she said. "Well, it's too scary to wander around Manama by myself. Women aren't as persecuted around here as they used to be, but I'm just not the risk-taking type. And it's hot. I hate the heat."

Rocco grinned. "But you live in San Diego. It isn't really cold there."

"I know, but it's also not a hundred and ten degrees either. If I wanted to be that warm, I'd move to Phoenix."

"It's good that you don't wander around. It's not safe," Rocco said, getting serious.

"The crime rate isn't exactly low here," Gumby added.

"Bahrain is one of the most tolerant countries in the Middle East when it comes to dress code, and women finally got the right to vote in the last twenty years or so, but there are still no laws to protect them against domestic violence," Ace informed her.

Caite nodded. "I know. I did my research before I accepted the job, and it was also part of the orientation. Why do you think I don't get out much? I mean, besides the heat. I'm not willing to go alone. Everyone around here is busy, and the younger naval guys are too interested in partying than hanging out with me or showing me the sites. Besides, it's frowned upon to frat-ernize with the military employees."

Rocco grimaced. "It doesn't sound like much fun

working here," he observed.

Caite shrugged. "I'm making it sound worse than it is. I like most of my coworkers and there are always interesting people coming in and out of the office. I've met a ton of people from around the world. For instance, this week, my boss is meeting with some men from Gabon."

"Hmmm."

Her smile dimmed. He didn't sound all that impressed. "What about you guys? Where are you from?"

"Interestingly enough, we're also from San Diego," Rocco told her.

"Really? Cool! How long will you be here?"

The three men exchanged glances that Caite couldn't interpret before Gumby said, "We're not sure. It depends on how long our mission takes."

"Ah. Well...I hope you'll be able to get out and see some of the country between your official stuff," she said, somewhat lamely.

Silence fell over the group once more and Caite searched her mind for something else to say. "So... Gumby and Ace? Those aren't...those aren't your real names, are they?"

All three chuckled.

"No, darlin'. I'm Decker," Gumby said.

"And I'm Beckett," Ace told her.

"Is Caite short for Katherine?" Rocco asked.

Caite could've sworn he'd moved closer to her when

she was looking at his friends, but it was hard to tell. She shook her head. "No. It's just Caite. Spelled C-a-i-t-e. I guess my mom wanted my name to be different, but not impossible to pronounce or weird."

"It's beautiful," Rocco replied.

Caite knew she was blushing again, damn it, but she hoped they would misinterpret her flushed cheeks as a result of the heat. The air in the elevator wasn't exactly cool, and she knew it would only continue to get warmer until they were rescued.

"Where are you staying?" she asked, simply for something to talk about.

"Housing on the base," Ace told her. "Where do you live?"

Not even thinking that it wasn't smart to tell strangers where she lived, Caite said, "There's an apartment complex right outside the gate. I was too chicken to get a place too far away from here. I don't have to drive to work, I can just go right out my apartment building and walk here. I've only gone into Manama once, and I was with three other DOD employees."

"Maybe if we're here long enough, we can show you some of the city," Ace said.

Caite blinked. She hadn't been fishing for them to escort her anywhere, but it probably *had* sounded like she was. "That's okay."

"How about dinner?" Rocco asked. "I was serious about that."

He was staring at her so intently, she shivered. He

couldn't be asking her out, could he? She'd never, in her entire life, been asked out. She'd gone on dates, and had even had one long-term boyfriend, but they'd all been set up by friends.

Caite had long since come to terms with who she was and how she looked. She'd never be called beautiful. Her nose was a bit too big and her features were simply too plain. She liked her hair, but it didn't stand out in any way. The light brown locks were thin and if she tried to grow them out too long, they broke off at the ends and looked straggly. She'd never been the kind of woman that anyone took a second look at. She wasn't hideous, but she wasn't model beautiful either.

It had been her experience that men simply overlooked her. She wasn't pretty enough, interesting enough, or skinny enough to deserve a second glance. Especially since she tended to keep to herself in social situations. There were always women around who were more interesting, outgoing, and pleasing to the eye.

But Rocco was looking at her as if she was the most fascinating person he'd met in his entire life. If she was being honest, it was discomfiting. She wasn't used to being the center of attention.

Knowing she'd been silent too long and things were getting awkward again, she quickly said, "Um...yeah, I can join you guys in the cafeteria one night if you want."

"Not what I meant, Caite," Rocco said. And once again, the husky, low tone of his voice did weird things to her insides.

She glanced at Ace and Gumby, and they were both smiling once more at her and Rocco. Not in a "my buddy's gonna get him some" way, but in a genuinely pleased way. She licked her lips and looked back down at her hands. "Oh, um...okay."

"I don't know when, though," Rocco went on to say. "I wouldn't mind if it was tonight, but I'm afraid we have to check in with the base commander and get the lay of the land. Not to mention we have to get a job done while we're here. But I'd like to make the time to get to know you better. If that's all right with you."

All sorts of things were swirling around Caite's head. Big caution signs, for one. This gorgeous man couldn't really be interested in *her*. Maybe it was a joke. Maybe he thought she'd go to bed with him because she'd been here so long and obviously didn't get out.

But...she didn't get those kinds of vibes from him. She was pretty good at spotting players. And Rocco seemed more mature and above those kinds of games.

Deciding that this was the most exciting thing to happen to her in months, besides getting stuck in the stupid elevator, Caite nodded. "I'd like that."

The smile on his face widened. "Good. Tell me where you work so I can find you later this week."

She did—and noticed his smile dimmed a bit.

"What?"

The emotion immediately cleared from his face. "Nothing."

Caite shook her head. "No, it's something. What?"

"It just so happens that you work for our temporary commander," Ace volunteered.

"Oh."

"And he doesn't approve of work relationships," Gumby said.

"This isn't a work relationship," Rocco grumbled. "It's dinner. We aren't going to go off and get married or anything."

Caite smiled at that. The thought popped out of her mouth before she could recall it. "Right. But if we *did* get married, he couldn't do or say anything about it, could he?"

Ace and Gumby chuckled as she looked up at Rocco, horrified. "Not that I think you'd want to! I mean, it's just dinner and... Oh shit," she said, and closed her eyes and rested her forehead on her knees. "I'll shut up now."

She felt Rocco take her hand in his and she reluctantly looked at him. "Relax, *ma petite fée*, I know what you meant."

Caite blinked. Had he really just called her "my small fairy" in French?

"Did I say it wrong?" he asked, smiling gently at her.

"What did you mean to call me?" she asked.

"Small fairy."

She shook her head. "You didn't say it wrong."

"Good. I'm fluent in Turkish, but have picked up a bit of French here and there."

Caite wanted to ask why he'd called her that, but

was too embarrassed. She was all too aware of his friends sitting there staring at the two of them, and the last thing she wanted was to hear him say it was because she reminded him of a child in some way.

"You're fluent in Turkish?" she asked instead.

"Yes."

He didn't elaborate, and Caite felt awkward all over again. She wasn't used to being the center of attention. She liked listening to others talk, not having to carry a conversation all by herself.

Just then, the elevator lurched and immediately fell about three feet before stopping once again.

Caite screeched in fear and reached out to grab ahold of something, anything. Her hand encountered Rocco's camouflage-covered thigh and she gripped him —hard. She hadn't been wrong about how muscular he was. It almost felt like she was holding on to a rock rather than a human being.

Rocco immediately moved closer and put his arm around her shoulders, pulling her into him. His beard brushed against her cheek for an instant before he looked at his friends. "We're done." He lifted his chin as he said the words.

As if they'd been waiting for his say-so the entire time, Ace and Gumby leaped up and immediately got to work on the hatch in the ceiling.

Caite's attention was brought back to the man at her side when he looked down at her and murmured, "Easy, *ma petite fée*, we'll be out of here in a few minutes.

Caite barely heard him. She was tucked against his side and she'd never, *ever* felt safer. If the elevator suddenly plunged to the ground, she had no doubt she wouldn't feel a thing.

Somehow, even in the overly warm small space, Rocco smelled delicious. Not like cologne; no, a man like him would never be caught dead splashing that stuff on. But like soap and...man. She couldn't explain it. But if someone found a way to bottle it, they'd make a fortune. She wanted nothing more than to snuggle up against him, tucking her head under his chin and resting it on his chest, but she forced herself to loosen the death grip she had on his pants and try to straighten. But he wouldn't let her go.

"I'm okay," she said quietly.

"I know you are. Just hang tight for a few more minutes." Rocco sounded completely calm.

And just like that, things clicked in her brain.

He and his friends were SEALs.

She should've figured it out way before now, but she'd been distracted by his looks. He was all muscle under his uniform, and the fact that he and his friends were here for a "mission" was a big giveaway. She'd met several different SEAL teams during her tenure, and they all had a certain aura about them.

But it was the way he and his friends handled the situation in the elevator that clinched it for her. Without any fuss or discussion, Ace and Gumby had the hatch in the top of the small space unlatched and

Gumby disappeared through the hole as if he did this sort of thing every day.

"We aren't even very high," Rocco reassured her. "Even if the car did fall, we'd only fall a story or two. But Gumby will figure out how far we are from the next floor and he'll get us out. Don't worry."

Caite could only nod, and that made his beard brush against her shoulder. She couldn't feel it through the long-sleeve blouse she was wearing, but her nipples didn't seem to care. They puckered, and she hoped like hell her slightly padded bra was doing its job. She sneaked a glance downward, relieved to see that she wasn't giving Rocco and his friends a peep show.

"Still okay?" Rocco asked, sounding concerned.

"Yeah," she said immediately. "Thanks. I was just startled there for a second."

"Can't blame you," Rocco told her.

"Good news," Gumby said from above their heads.

Caite looked up and saw him staring down at them through the hatch.

"The car's just below the second floor. The doors are right here. We can pry them open and climb out from up here."

Rocco nodded and removed his arm from around her shoulders and stood. Caite immediately felt chilly, which was ridiculous, as it was at least eighty-five degrees inside the elevator. He held his hand out to her. "Ready to get out of here?"

Caite nodded and reached for his hand.

As his fingers closed around hers, and he helped her up, she never wanted to let go.

Apparently, he felt the same way. Once she was on her feet, he intertwined his fingers with hers and held on tightly.

Feeling giddy and like she was a teenager on her first date, Caite stood there while he discussed the safety of what they were about to do with Ace and Gumby.

"Ready?"

Caite forced herself to pay attention. "What?"

Ace smiled down at her. "I asked if you were ready."

Caite shook her head and said at the same time, "Yes."

The men all grinned once more at her contradictory word versus her head movement. She wasn't all fired up to climb on top of the elevator and crawl out onto the second floor. There were bound to be others around who would gawk at the four people climbing out of the elevator shaft. She hated being the center of attention.

"You got this, *ma petite fée*," Rocco said, then squeezed her hand.

She nodded and took a deep breath. "How am I going to get up there?" she asked no one in particular.

"I've got you," Rocco said.

"Give me your briefcase," Ace said, and Caite let him take the bag from her.

Rocco kneeled in front of her and held his hands up. "Step up onto my shoulders. I'll lift you. I won't let you fall."

Caite said the first thing that came to mind. "It's a good thing I'm not wearing a skirt today or you'd get a show."

All three men chuckled again, and Caite blushed furiously.

"I'm actually more relieved you're not wearing heels," Rocco told her. "Those would hurt like hell digging into my shoulders."

"Can't stand the things," Caite said. "They hurt my feet, and it's not like two or three inches would make that much of a difference in my height. I'd still be smaller than just about everyone." She tried to think of something else to say that would delay the inevitable, but Rocco obviously read her body language.

He looked up at her from his crouched position and patiently continued to hold his hands out to her. "I'm not going to let anything happen to you, Caite."

"I'm heavier than I look," she blurted.

His eyes quickly darted from her face down to her chest and hips, before coming back up to meet her gaze. "You're perfect," he said. "Besides, I carried this guy," he used his head to indicate Ace, standing nearby, "for more than a mile once. In full combat gear. Compared, you weigh next to nothing. Come on, *ma petite fée*, trust me."

How could she not when he called her his little fairy in that adorable, horrible French accent? She wanted to hear more about when and why he'd had to carry his friend, but knew asking would be just another stalling tactic. Without further delay, she reached for his hand and lifted her leg to step up onto his shoulder.

Within seconds, she was standing on his shoulders, bent over and clutching his hands for dear life.

"Easy, Caite. I got ya," Rocco told her as he rose slowly until he was standing under the open hatch.

"Let go of one of his hands and reach upward," Gumby ordered from above her head.

Caite took a deep breath. She didn't want to be a wuss, but damn, this was *so* not something she was enjoying. It took a few seconds, but none of the men rushed her. Ever so slowly, she loosened the fingers on her right hand and blindly reached upward.

She immediately felt her hand grasped by Gumby's large warm one.

"Now the other one," he said softly.

Carefully, she let go of Rocco's other hand. Even as Gumby was grabbing hold of her, she felt Rocco's hands grasp the back of her calves, steadying her, holding on and making sure she was secure.

The elevator wasn't all that tall. By the time Rocco was standing up straight with Caite on his shoulders, she was practically out of the elevator already. All it would take was a small step up and she'd be standing on top of the metal box next to Gumby.

"That's it," Gumby said. Clearly this wasn't a big deal for him...or the other two men. He'd leaped right up and out of the elevator as if he did it every day of the week. When she glanced at their clasped hands, she saw that the sleeve of his uniform was pushed up, and she caught a glimpse of tattoos around his wrist.

They fit him. She could totally imagine him riding a motorcycle wearing nothing but a leather vest as he raced down the road. She'd been obsessed with *Sons of Anarchy* when it had been on, and Gumby could totally fit right in with all the characters on the show.

"Caite?" Gumby asked. "I've got you. You aren't going to fall."

Mentally chastising herself for not paying attention, she said, "I know." She shifted her weight and picked up her right foot.

Within seconds, and without much effort on her part, she was standing on top of the elevator car next to Gumby. The entire process took less than a few seconds and was so smoothly executed, she knew for a fact that they'd definitely done this before. She wondered how many other damsels in distress they'd had to rescue from broken-down elevators.

Gumby left his hands on her waist for a second, making sure she was stable. "Okay?" he asked.

"Yeah."

"Good. Now let's see about getting the hell out of here, shall we?"

Before she could blink, Ace and Rocco appeared. With all four of them on top of the elevator, things were a bit crowded. Rocco stood behind her and replaced Gumby's hands on her waist with his own. He pulled her close, until she could feel his chest against her back. "Let's give them some room to work," he said.

Caite wanted to tell him to be careful. To not back up too far. The last thing she wanted was for him to fall, or for the stupid elevator to suddenly start up again and have him get caught in the cables or get scraped against the walls of the shaft, but she kept her mouth shut and watched Ace and Rocco make quick work of forcing open the doors on the second floor.

Ace hopped up and out of the elevator shaft and placed her briefcase on the floor. Then he turned and held out his hand.

Rocco walked her forward until she was standing in front of the elevator doors. On her, they were at about chest height. "Up you go," Rocco said softly, and tightened his hands on her waist. She reached up and grabbed Ace's hands just as Rocco lifted her off her feet as if she weighed no more than a sack of potatoes. Once out, she hurried out of the way and watched as Gumby and Rocco hopped out of the elevator shaft as if they did it regularly.

The air conditioning felt awesome, but it also made her shiver.

Something struck her then, as she watched the three men talk with one of the maintenance workers who had shown up.

They could've gotten out of that elevator at any time, but they hadn't. They'd sat on the floor and chatted with her instead. It hadn't been until the elevator had lurched and scared her that they'd gone to work on the hatch in the ceiling.

She wasn't sure why they'd waited, but she didn't have time to think about it as Rocco came toward her. "Ready?"

"For what?" she asked stupidly.

He smiled. "To go to work."

Caite wrinkled her nose and Rocco grinned. "Come on, we'll go with you and make sure you don't get in any trouble."

"I'll be fine," she told them honestly. Her boss could be an ass, but it wasn't like she could help the fact that she'd been inside the elevator when it had gotten stuck. Everyone who worked in the building knew the thing was persnickety.

"We're headed the same way you are anyway," Gumby informed her.

"Oh. Right." Caite felt stupid. They hadn't pushed any other buttons when they'd gotten inside the elevator. Of course they were going to the third floor. Reception for all temporary employees and sailors was on her floor and her boss's boss was their temporary commander.

"The stairs are this way," she told them, and gestured toward the end of the hall. Ignoring the stares from the other contract employees and military personnel, Caite held her head up and acted like she climbed out of an elevator shaft—with three of the most gorgeous men she'd ever seen—every day of her life.

CHAPTER TWO

By sheer force of will, Rocco kept himself from looking back at Caite as he and his teammates continued alone toward a door down the hall. There was something about her that had immediately snagged his attention. The second he'd seen her standing against the back wall of the elevator, his protective instincts had almost overwhelmed him.

She was shorter than him by nearly a foot, which for some reason intrigued him. The top of her head came to about his shoulder but when he'd put his arm around her in the elevator, they'd fit together perfectly. Her light brown hair was smoothly styled and just brushed against her shoulders. She had a cute little pixie nose and her cheeks had pinkened every time he'd stared at her a beat too long.

She'd made reference to being too heavy, but there was nothing about her that turned him off. She had plenty of curves, and from what he'd felt when she was leaning against him, she was soft in all the right places.

He'd already been mentally plotting a way to get to know Caite better when the elevator had stopped working. He'd prevented Ace and Gumby from finding a way out of the situation, despite knowing they hated to sit around and wait when they could be taking action themselves. Rocco knew his friends were more than amused by his obvious attempts to woo Caite, but like true wingmen, they hadn't interrupted or given him shit about it. *Then*. He knew the second they were alone, they'd be all over him about her.

It was unfortunate that their temporary commander was her boss's boss, but, as he'd pointed out, it wasn't as if they were going to get married or anything. They'd only be in the country for a week or so, not enough time to really get to know her well or start any kind of relationship.

The thought irrationally bothered Rocco.

The way she'd flat-out admitted that she'd taken the job for the money also struck a chord in him. He'd joined the navy for the same reason. He hadn't planned on joining the SEALs or making the navy a career. But after basic training, he'd been placed in a unit with Ace, Gumby, Bubba, Rex, and Phantom. The bond they'd formed was immediate and intense. They'd decided as a group to try out for the SEALs. The experience had made them even closer. Luckily, their superiors had seen how well they worked together and made them a team.

Now, Rocco couldn't imagine *not* being with his friends and teammates. They'd saved each other's lives several times over, and the men were like blood brothers to him.

Caite had been nervous and unsure in the elevator, but she'd loosened up as they'd spoken. She'd actually said she'd go to dinner with him—but then the elevator had lurched. The nickname *ma petite fée* had just popped out. She looked like a little fairy compared to him. Next to him, she was tiny.

"How much time do we have before the goods are moved?" Gumby asked quietly as they walked toward the commander's office.

Rocco forced himself to concentrate on the mission at hand, and not the intriguing woman they'd left at her desk. "According to what the commander said, there's a tight timetable," he said. "We're not sure what the reasons are for the speed of the transfer, but it should be within a few days."

"And we're sure the Bahraini government isn't involved?" Ace asked.

Rocco shrugged. "As sure as we can be about anything."

"Why are we even here?" Gumby wondered. "It seems to me if the commander has a suspect in mind, and has an idea on when the tablets are going to be moved, there's no need for us. They could use some of the naval investigation folks stationed here to track them down."

Rocco shrugged. "I'm assuming that's what the commander will be talking to us about." And with that, he smiled and nodded at the man sitting at a desk in front of what was obviously the commander's office. "Sorry we're late. We had the misfortune to be stuck in the elevator this morning."

The man chuckled. "That damn thing. One of these days, they're going to just shut it down and force us to use the stairs all the time. Commander Horner's ready for you. Go on in."

The three men headed into the large corner office and stood at attention.

"At ease, men. Sit. I appreciate you coming out here. I had a long talk with Storm and he had nothing but good things to say about your team," the commander said.

Rocco nodded. Commander Storm North was in charge of their team back home in San Diego. He was forty-seven, around the same age as Commander Horner, and Rocco knew the two men had served on the same Navy SEAL team once upon a time.

"Thank you, Sir," Rocco said respectfully.

"I'm sure you're wondering why I only requested three of your team rather than have all of you come out here."

"The thought did cross our minds," Rocco admitted. It wasn't that he, Ace, and Gumby couldn't get the job done, but generally when they traveled overseas for a mission, Bubba, Rex, and Phantom were included.

"Frankly, we're also wondering why a SEAL team was called in the first place."

"Right. This is a somewhat delicate situation. The King of Bahrain has gone on record to claim his country doesn't condone smuggling. But in the last year, there've been more goods smuggled over his borders than ever before. It's embarrassing for him, and he wants it stopped. His own security force hasn't been able to prevent it, so he asked for assistance from the United States. We've got a team on it, but it seems every time we get close to making a move, shit goes sideways."

"You think you have a mole?" Ace asked.

The commander nodded. "Yeah. And it pisses me off. It's taken months of surveillance and research, but we've finally identified one of the lower-level players here in Bahrain. I could send some of my guys out to intercept him, but given that we haven't discovered the mole, I have a feeling the outcome will be the same... the goods will be gone and we won't have any evidence to hold this guy."

"So this is completely on the down-low?" Rocco asked.

"Yes. No one knows why you're here or even who you are, except for me. There's an Archaeology and Museums Conference the base is hosting this weekend. The story is that you're with Naval Criminal Investigative Services and you're here for the conference. Bringing in all six members of your team would've looked even more suspicious than it already does, so I requested North only send three of you."

"Makes sense," Gumby murmured.

The commander went on. "We've invited representatives from the communities around Manama, as well as soldiers from Iraq and various African countries. We want to educate people that taking these artifacts is damaging to everyone's culture. Not only that, but it's illegal—and the United States Navy is willing to do what it takes to prevent the smuggling of such artifacts out of the Middle East."

"So we're here to take down one smuggler?" Gumby asked.

"Yes. He's not the only small-time player, and taking him down isn't going to end the problem. But I'm hoping it'll at least slow it down and result in leads. I've also disseminated false information in the hopes that we can figure out who the mole is. We've got it narrowed down to a few people, but until we know for sure, our hands are tied. So while you guys are tracking down the smuggler, we'll be running a separate side operation to try to find the mole."

Rocco nodded. Having the SEALs come in seemed a bit like overkill, but he understood why the commander had resorted to that option. "So, who's the smuggler?"

"His name is Jeo Bitoo. Fifty-three years old, and he's been in country about fifteen years. He's got a store outside Manama. We think it's where the goods are stored before being moved out. He's currently visiting relatives in his home country of Gabon. His luggage was searched before he left the country, and he didn't have the cuneiform tablets with him that are on deck to be smuggled out. We think he stashed them and will make the drop when he gets back."

"Why would he leave them behind? I mean, I'm assuming he's getting paid a pretty penny for them, so it doesn't make sense that he'd just leave the country before offloading," Ace said.

"His mother is dying. He didn't have a choice but to leave right now," the commander said.

"Wait," Rocco said, remembering something Caite had mentioned. "Does he have children?"

"Yes, five sons. Why?" Commander Horner asked.

"Just something that someone said today. Are they coming to the conference?"

"Actually, yes."

"I'm confused," Gumby said with a shake of his head.

"Keep your friends close and your enemies closer," Ace said with a smile. "Smart."

The commander grinned. "Evidence is pointing to the patriarch, but just in case, we want to keep the boys busy."

"Boys?" Gumby asked.

"Not literally. Oldest is thirty-five and the youngest is twenty-five. They were supposed to keep their dad's store open and running while he was gone, but apparently they're more interested in drinking than working."

"Are they involved in the smuggling?" Ace asked.

"Not that we know of."

"Why do they think they were invited to the conference?" Gumby asked. "If they aren't in cahoots with their old man, they wouldn't be interested in an archaeology conference, would they?"

"No," the commander said. "But on Saturday, there's a huge job fair being held in conjunction with the conference. And we made sure Jeo heard about it. He's been on his sons for months to get jobs to help support the family. Legitimate jobs. We believe he thinks it'll make the money he's earning by smuggling a little less obvious. Not only that, but if one of his sons gets a job working for a museum or for a curator of antiques, it'll make it easier for him to conduct business."

"So what's the plan for us?" Ace asked.

"You need to check out Jeo's store. Since that's where we think he's storing the tablets, we need someone to get in there and find them before he gets back from Gabon. His sons haven't bothered to open it since he's been gone, so it should be an easy task to get in and out without detection. Especially for you guys."

"And if the sons suddenly decide they'd better do as Daddy told them?" Ace asked.

"They won't," the commander said with confidence. "Seriously. These guys are lazy as fuck. Every night since their dad left, they've gotten drunk and hung out at their house. We've got some insiders who are keeping an eye on them. By six o'clock every night, they're already hitting the bottle. They haven't been near their dad's store since he left."

"You've got people watching them?" Gumby asked.

"Yes. Well, not all the time, but enough to be nearly certain they're not part of the smuggling ring."

"Hmmm," Rocco said. Something was bothering him about the whole situation, but he couldn't put his finger on it. He'd talk to the guys later and see if they could figure it out.

"So we're here to stop the latest smuggling attempt," Gumby said. "What happens then? You said yourself that this Bitoo guy is small time in the smuggling ring. Why go after a low-level middleman and not the big players?"

"Oh, we're going to go after the big guys," Commander Horner said, "but the first thing we have to do is figure out who the traitor is in our department. Someone is leaking information about everything we've planned faster than we can make a move. Catching Bitoo could result in leads, and it'll at least be enough to allow the king to say he's doing everything possible to stop the smuggling. He wants to catch someone, anyone, and show Israel and Iraq that he's doing his part in stopping the thieves. While you guys are searching for the ten missing tablets, NCIS will be watching an alternate location on the other side of the city that they've purposely leaked. Whoever shows up to try to get the tablets will be interrogated. We're gonna find the mole if it's the last thing we do."

Rocco nodded. The job sounded interesting. It was nice to have a mission that wasn't simply all about guns and brute strength. This would be more about stealth than anything else.

The only problem was that it sounded too easy.

Commander Horner looked at his watch. "If you'll excuse me, gentleman, I'm running late. There's a gathering for some of the participants of the conference. I'm supposed to give the welcome speech before the morning program." He handed over a folder to Rocco. "That's the info we have on Jeo Bitoo."

Rocco reached for the folder, eager to start looking into their assignment.

"Oh, and all five brothers will be here on base today."

At that, Rocco's eyes met the commander's. "Today? I thought the job fair thing was on Saturday."

"It is. But everyone who participating is supposed to attend the opening ceremony. The men and women who're attending the job fair will receive information on which organizations are hiring so they can plan their strategy for Saturday. They'll check in with one of the admins, and then head up to the ballroom on the top floor for the program and lunch."

Rocco immediately thought about Caite and felt uneasy. He knew instinctively that she was probably the one checking in the participants for the conference. She said that she worked with the foreign visitors, and even as they'd left her at her desk, he'd seen several men hanging around the lobby area.

He tried to tamp down his worry for the diminutive woman, but wasn't exactly successful. "Is it safe to have Bitoo's sons on the base?" he asked.

The commander nodded. "We believe so. They've been thoroughly checked out. Now, if you'll excuse me. Feel free to use my office as long as you want. It's secure." He then stood and straightened his uniform jacket before striding out of the room.

Rocco heard him telling the admin outside that his guests were not to be disturbed and they could use his office for as long as they wished.

"Let's go," Rocco said as soon as the older man had left.

"What?" Ace asked.

"Seriously?" Gumby echoed. "We need to review the information we just got."

Rocco stood, lifted the back of his button-down and tucked the folder into the back of his pants, then dropped the shirt, covering the folder. "The last thing we need is to be seen hanging out in the commander's office. No one will believe we're here for some random visit."

"True," Ace mumbled.

"And I want to make sure those assholes don't harass Caite," Rocco added, even as he headed for the door.

"You really like her," Gumby said.

Rocco stopped with one hand on the doorknob and

turned to face his friends. "I do. I don't know why."

"Maybe it's because you're horny," Ace quipped.

"Shut the fuck up," Rocco warned, glaring at his friend. "That was uncalled for."

Ace looked surprised. "Shit, you're serious. Roc, we're only here for a week or so, probably less. She's here for another eight months, at least. You can't seriously be thinking about starting something with her."

Rocco sighed and tamped down his irrational anger at his friend. Ace was right, he knew he was, but something wouldn't allow him to let this go. Wouldn't let *Caite* go. "I just...there's just something about her that got to me."

Ace and Gumby eyed him silently for a moment before Gumby nodded. "Let's go make sure she's okay. Then we'll find a place to hole up and look at the information the commander gave us and go from there."

Rocco nodded, feeling lighter just knowing he'd get to see Caite again. It was crazy. He'd just seen her twenty minutes ago. But knowing she'd be anywhere near five brothers who—regardless of what the commander said—could be neck deep in smuggling precious artifacts out of the country, was enough to make his protective instincts sit up and take notice. He couldn't stand by her desk with his arms crossed, glaring at anyone who approached, but he could make sure, for now, that all was well.

Ace slapped Rocco on the back in support and the three men left the office.

Caite felt off-kilter. She hated being late, especially today when she had over three hundred people to check in to the Archaeology and Museums Conference the base was hosting. It wouldn't be bad if it was just the conference, but since someone had decided it would be a good idea to hold it in conjunction with a job fair, she had easily twice as many people to deal with as she might otherwise.

As the administrative assistant in charge of foreign visitors, it was her job to make sure everyone had the necessary documents in order to receive their visitor passes and hand out the registration packets for the conference. She'd been slammed for the last twenty minutes, quickly moving people through the check-in process.

It wasn't exactly in her job description to be in charge of welcome packets for the conference, but her boss hadn't seen anything wrong with assigning the job to her anyway. She *did* have to make sure everyone had proper paperwork for the visitor passes, but how that had turned into her being the go-to person for the archeology conference, she didn't know. It actually would've been fine if she only was handing out packets —but she was also answering questions, organizing meals, and making sure the rooms were set up properly. It was annoying.

Unfortunately, she knew complaining to Joshua

Mullen would get her nowhere. Her boss had been a DOD employee way longer than Caite. Complaining about the extra work would be an excellent way for him to get rid of her, something she was well aware he wanted to do. He'd told her more than once that her job was supposed to go to one of his buddies back in Virginia. Caite had no idea how she'd gotten the job over his friend, but now that she had it, she wasn't going to do anything stupid to lose it.

She'd only been in Bahrain for four months, but she'd already made a big dent in her credit cards and was working on her other debt now.

"Hey," a deep voice said from next to her.

She'd been so lost in her head—which wasn't exactly unusual—she'd completely missed Rocco and his friends walking up to her desk.

"Oh. Hi," she said shyly. "Everything okay?"

"That was going to be my question to you," Rocco said.

Caite's brow furrowed. "Why wouldn't it be?"

"No reason," he was quick to say. "I just wanted to let you know we're headed out."

Caite was thoroughly confused. It wasn't as if she and Rocco had an appointment. And she'd thought they'd already said their goodbyes when leaving her at her desk. "Oh. Okay."

He grinned down at her. "I'm assuming this is where you can be found during the weekdays?"

"Uh...yeah."

"I don't have a phone, since Bahrain isn't covered by my cell company. But I wanted to make sure I knew where you'd be so I could find you to set up dinner."

"Oh!" She finally clued in...and immediately blushed. "Yeah. This is my desk. Most of the time I feel like I live here, but of course you know I have an apartment just outside the gate. I've got a cell, but it's work-issued. I went ahead and canceled my personal one to save the money. But I guess that doesn't help, since you don't have one, huh?" Caite knew she was babbling, but it was such a surreal experience to have a guy actually want to take her out. "I don't know what your schedule is like, but I'm usually here until six or so."

"Six? You don't go home at five?"

Caite shrugged. "Officially, yes, but most days I stay late because it's not like I have anything else to do. It's easier to do stuff when no one is around to interrupt me."

"Like I'm doing," Rocco said with a slight frown.

"No, it's just—" Her phone rang, and she smiled apologetically at him. "Wait just a second?"

"Of course," he responded.

Caite picked up the phone—and immediately wished she'd let it ring.

"You aren't getting paid to flirt with the visiting sailors, Ms. McCallan. Do you have that report done yet that I asked you for this morning?"

She sighed. Her boss was an ass. "No, sir. I've been busy checking in the visitors for the conference." She wanted to say, "for the conference you set up and didn't ask me if I'd be willing to help with," but figured she'd be pushing her luck if she did.

"Right. So how about you put away your googly eyes and get to work?" Joshua said haughtily.

"Yes, sir."

He hung up without another word.

Caite hated that her desk was in direct line of sight from her boss's through the window of his office. Knowing she was poking the bear, and not caring that she'd most likely piss off Joshua by not immediately getting to work, she stood and held out a hand to Rocco. "It was good to meet you, Rocco. I'd love to go to dinner with you. At the risk of sounding lame, I never have any plans, so whatever works with your schedule will work with mine."

He smiled at her and took her hand in his. He brought it up to his mouth and kissed the back. "Friday?"

Caite nodded and couldn't take her eyes from his mouth. The beard tickled the skin of her hand, and she wondered what it would feel like on other parts of her body.

"If I'm in the area, can I stop by before then?" he asked.

"I...I'd like that," she got out. It was time she stopped being so damn shy and said what she meant. It wasn't as if men were falling out of the sky at her feet. She was almost thirty, and if she wanted to ever settle down, she needed to work on being more outgoing. Not that she was going to marry Rocco. She was just saying.

"Me too," the man in front of her said. Then with the kind of perception she imagined all SEALs had, he said, "And now I'd better get out of your hair so your boss doesn't have another reason to yell at you."

"He doesn't need a reason," Caite blurted. "He's not a very happy man."

"Hmmm." Rocco dropped her hand almost reluctantly.

"It was good to meet you guys too," Caite said politely, looking around Rocco to Ace and Gumby.

"You too," Ace said with a wide grin on his face.

"It was a pleasure," Gumby echoed.

"Thanks for knowing what to do in the elevator," Caite told Rocco, prolonging their goodbye.

"Of course. I'm looking forward to getting to know you better, *ma petite fée*," Rocco said.

Caite knew she was blushing, *again*, but managed to keep eye contact with him.

"Be safe out there," she told the trio.

"Be safe in *here*," Rocco returned mysteriously.

Before she could ask him what he meant, he nodded at her and turned to head down the hallway toward the stairwell with his friends.

Despite knowing she was going to be reprimanded by her boss, Caite stood there for a moment longer, staring at Rocco's ass as he walked away. The view was worth every harsh word she'd receive later.

CHAPTER THREE

Two days later, on Friday, Rocco was standing outside the barracks they were staying in with Ace and Gumby. They'd spent the last two days researching the info Commander Horner had given them. They'd also enlisted the assistance of their good friend, Tex. The man was tight with the SEAL teams back home and was an absolute computer genius. Rocco had seen his work firsthand when the man had single-handedly figured out where Dakota and Caroline—the women of two fellow SEALs—were being held after being kidnapped a couple of years ago. Rocco had kept in touch with Tex, and the man had offered his assistance whenever and wherever Rocco and his team needed it.

The other SEAL team they'd assisted to rescue Dakota Cutsinger was legendary. They'd been successful on so many of their missions, they'd been called "unbeatable."

Of course, Rocco, and even that team's renowned leader himself, Wolf, knew that was bullshit. All it took was one bullet to fuck up an entire mission. The last Rocco had heard, Wolf and his teammates were retiring at the end of the year. They were all happily married and only too willing to transition out of active duty to the training side. Rocco was thrilled they were staying to share their knowledge with teams like his, as well as the younger SEALs. Everyone could learn from Wolf and his crew.

Tex had no intention of retiring though. He'd told Rocco in no uncertain terms that the day he quit helping his country fight against terrorists, hoodlums, and general assholes, was the day they put him in the ground. He'd confirmed the information commander Horner had given them, that Jeo Bitoo was currently visiting his family back in Lambaréné, a small town near where Albert Switzer had built his famous hospital. He also confirmed that his sons all lived together in a small hovel about ten minutes from the store owned by the elder Bitoo. When Jeo was in town, he and his wife lived in a room above the store itself.

The parents were booked on a flight back to Bahrain on the following Monday. Which gave the SEALs plenty of time to search the store for the tablets. They had to find them before Jeo got back and could pass them off to be shipped out.

Rocco, Ace, and Gumby were heading out that afternoon to scope out the store. Their hope was that they'd stick out less if they were wandering around in the daytime than at night. Their plan was to get in, hopefully find the tablets, and get out with no one being the wiser. The fact that the sons hadn't bothered to open their dad's store while he was away made things a bit easier, as they shouldn't have to worry about anyone interrupting them. The SEALs didn't have any leads on the mole Commander Horner had eluded to, but that wasn't their mission. Finding the artifacts and preventing them from leaving the country was the goal.

Despite the mission keeping him busy, Rocco had been…unsettled…the last couple days.

Gumby called him out on it. "Go see her," he ordered.

"Who?" Rocco asked, knowing full well who his friend was talking about.

Gumby simply raised an eyebrow. "Look, whatever connection you two have could be the real deal. I may not have found my woman yet, but I'm not an idiot. You aren't concentrating fully, and you won't if you don't go see Caite. Talk to her."

Rocco ran a hand through his thick hair. "I don't know why she's gotten under my skin so fast. I don't even know her."

"Doesn't matter. You saw it happen to Wolf and his team time and time again. Why should we be any different?" Ace asked.

"Because I'm not them," Rocco said. "I don't get worked up over women. And like you said, we're leaving as soon as this mission is over. It wouldn't be fair to start anything with her and then leave. Hell, we all know that being with a SEAL isn't easy. And I can't even tell her I *am* a SEAL." He shook his head. "What a clusterfuck."

"Stop thinking," Gumby ordered. "Go see her. Confirm your dinner. Then *afterwards* you can worry about all that shit. You might find out she chews with her mouth open. Or she orders a salad when she really wants a steak. Or she has some other annoying quirk that you can't deal with. We need you completely focused on what we're doing, and you can't do that if you're worrying about her as much as you are right now."

Rocco nodded. "You're right. And I admit that I want to see her. Need to make sure she's okay. Knowing she's been around anyone we're investigating hasn't sat right with me the last two days."

"She's fine," Ace reassured him. "You watched her walk home the last two evenings."

"I know, I know," Rocco said. And he had. He'd hidden in the shadows and followed her to her apartment building both nights, just making sure no one hassled her. She'd been fine, and had no clue whatsoever that she was being followed—which also bothered him—and she'd gone straight home both nights. But he still worried about her and what was happening inside the building. Was her boss still giving her a hard time? Had the brothers been clued in that their father was being investigated and if so, would that put her in danger?

He had no idea if seeing Caite again would make him worry less or more, but there was no doubt he wanted to see her. "Fine. I'll just head up there and see if she can take a ten-minute break or something. I'll meet you back here at the barracks and we'll head out."

Gumby nodded. "Tell her we said hello."

Rocco was about to tell his friend to fuck off when he realized he was serious. He narrowed his eyes at him.

"Hey! I like her," Gumby said, holding his hands up in capitulation. "Not like *that*, but she was pretty calm when we had to go out the top of the elevator. She wasn't happy about it, and she was obviously scared, but she held herself together. That shit goes a long way in my eyes."

"Yeah, she was nice," Ace added. "She seems like she has her head on straight. She's not looking for a free ride by marrying a military man. And you deserve a nice woman who isn't constantly eye-fucking you and doesn't just wants to get in your pants." Ace smirked.

Rocco rolled his eyes. There'd been a time when all of them had been more interested in what was under a woman's clothes than what was between her ears, but they'd all learned over the years to appreciate being more than a piece of meat themselves—and no longer treated women the same. "I'll send your regards," he said with a hint of snark. "I'll be ready to go in thirty."

The other two men nodded and headed for the door

to the barracks. Rocco turned and walked quickly across the base to Caite's building. He strode inside and headed for the stairs. He was actually glad to see an "out of order" sign on the elevator. From what Caite had said, it sounded like it was about time, as often as the damn thing kept breaking down.

He headed down the hallway toward her desk and smiled when he saw her. She had her head bent over some papers and was mumbling to herself.

"Do they ever talk back?" Rocco asked as he stood right in front of her desk.

She startled badly and looked up at him.

"Crud, you scared me!" she said, holding a hand to her chest.

Rocco couldn't help but follow her hand movement with his eyes. He could see her chest moving up and down with her quick breaths as she tried to regain her equilibrium. Her tits were small, but they fit her frame perfectly. She'd claimed she was too heavy for him to lift the other day, and he'd thought it ridiculous then, just as he did now. He couldn't see her legs since they were hidden under the desk, but he remembered that she was the perfect blend of curvy and lush without being fat.

What women didn't understand was that ultimately, most men didn't care how big their tits were. Men just loved boobs. All sizes and shapes. And if they were attached to a woman they were interested in, they were absolutely perfect.

Besides, what *he* cared about was what kind of

person she was. He didn't know Caite yet, not really, but he'd talked to a few others on the base who did. He'd overheard a sailor who had moved into a room on their floor in guest housing talking on the phone, telling someone how much of a help Ms. McCallan had been. He'd just missed her in the food court one day, arriving in time to see her helping an elderly person get his food to a table before she headed out the door. He'd even asked Commander Horner about her, and he'd had nothing but good things to say about how helpful, efficient, and pleasant she was. Those things went a long way in his eyes.

"Sorry I scared you," he said softly.

"It's okay," she said immediately, letting him off the hook. "I was just trying to figure out what the heck my boss wrote. His handwriting is atrocious. He took off and won't be back until Monday, and he left me a bunch of directions for the conference."

"He left? I thought he'd organized the thing?" Rocco asked.

Caite shrugged. "He did. But everyone knows that it's the grunts like me who *actually* run and organize stuff like this."

She had him there. "Right, so since Mr. Grumpy isn't here...can you take a break?"

She immediately looked concerned. "Is everything all right?"

"Of course," he soothed, liking how she seemed worried about him. "I just haven't seen you in two days and wanted to catch up...and make sure we've got our schedules coordinated for dinner tonight."

"Oh. Although I'm not sure how we can 'catch up' when we don't even really know each other in the first place."

He chuckled. "Point made. Fine. I missed you and wanted to say hello. Is that better?"

Rocco was fascinated by the way her cheeks turned pink at his confession. It had been a long time since he'd made a woman blush with such innocent words.

"Oh."

"So...can you take ten minutes?" he pressed.

Caite nodded. "Of course. Let me put some things away..." She started shuffling papers around on her desk, and he was impressed that, even though she was only stepping away for a few minutes, she knew the importance of making sure everything was secured. She locked her top desk drawer and her computer screen and stood.

Today, she was wearing another pair of loose black pants with a short-sleeved white shirt. He could just see the outline of the camisole she wore under the blouse, but not enough for it to be indecent when she walked around outside. The norms of the country frowned upon anything see-through.

"There's a break room down the hall. We can go there," she said.

Not wanting to be where anyone might overhear

them, and wanting her all to himself, Rocco asked, "Do you mind if we step outside?"

"Outside?"

He chuckled, remembering her dislike of the heat. "We'll be fast. I'm not a fan of enclosed spaces," he told her. And it wasn't a lie. Thanks to a stint as a Taliban prisoner a few years back, he now preferred being outside rather than in. Not to mention he had no idea who the mole was in Commander Horner's department, and didn't want to risk him, or her, overhearing anything he might say.

"Oh! Of course. That's fine. No problem," Caite said quickly, falling all over herself to apologize.

Rocco gestured for her to precede him and took the chance to check out her ass as she passed. He hadn't been with anyone in a very long time, but that didn't mean he wasn't appreciative of a good-looking woman.

And Caite McCallan had a perfect ass. He guessed maybe she'd been thinking about that particular body part when she'd mentioned her weight. But her bubble butt was incredible. His fingers actually twitched with the need to squeeze the generous globes.

She looked over her shoulder and gave him a shy smile. "Coming?"

"Right behind you," he said automatically, mentally reprimanding himself.

They walked down the stairs and out into the heat. It was at least one hundred degrees already, and as much as he wanted to spend time with Caite, he didn't want her to suffer in the heat either. He gestured to a small bench placed under a grouping of trees. It was shaded and, more importantly, empty.

They sat on the bench, their knees angled toward each other.

"So..." she said after a moment.

"So," he echoed with a grin. "How are you?"

"I'm good. You? Everything going okay with your thing?"

"My thing?"

"Yeah. The reason you're here. Mission. Job. Thing."

Pretty and considerate. "Yeah. My thing is good. We're headed out right after this to get more information," he told her.

Caite frowned. "Is it safe?"

He would've blown off the question, but her genuine concern touched him deeply. "It's safe," he said. "Not everything we do is, but as far as *things* go, this one is relatively harmless. Just some recon at a local shop."

"Good."

Rocco wanted to ask her if she'd seen anything weird going on at work. Wanted to see if he could find out who the mole was that Commander Horner talked about, but one, he didn't have time, and two, he preferred to learn more about *her* in the short visit he had with her. "How's the conference going? Any problems?"

Caite shrugged. "Nothing more than usual. People are the same all across the world."

"What do you mean?"

"They think rules don't apply to them. They 'forget' the papers they were supposed to bring with them. They want more than they're entitled to receive. They feel as if they're more important than everyone else around them. They're rude. They talk too loud and say inappropriate things."

With every word out of her mouth, Rocco got more and more pissed. "Someone was inappropriate with you?" he asked in a hard tone.

"Rocco, people are *always* that way to me. I'm just a secretary. I don't have any rank on my shoulder *and* I'm a woman. But I don't think anything of it."

"You should complain."

She gave him a dubious look. "To whom? Joshua? He'd just tell me if I can't handle the job, I should go home. In case you haven't noticed, there aren't a lot of female contractors here. I guess it's because we're in the Middle East. I've met some amazing people, but I've also had way more side eyes than I can count. Again, I'm just a secretary and I'm a woman. That's two strikes against me here."

Rocco clenched his teeth. "It doesn't make it right."

"No, you're exactly right, it doesn't. But some dude from Iraq refusing to speak to me because of my gender isn't the end of the world. Neither is a group of men loudly discussing how I might perform in bed when—"

"No, they fucking did not!" Rocco interrupted,

furious on her behalf. "This is the twenty-first century. They can't talk to you like that!"

"Calm down," Caite said, putting her hand on his thigh. "They weren't talking *to* me, and they were speaking amongst themselves in French and didn't think I could understand. And I almost *couldn't*, even though I'm fluent, because of their accent."

"That doesn't make it any better."

"You're right, it doesn't. But you're not getting my point."

"You have a point?" Rocco asked.

"Yes. I know I don't belong here. The military has always been a man's world. I knew that when I accepted the job. But like I said, I needed the money."

"You don't have to put up with this shit for money."

"I don't?" She smiled. "I don't know anyone else who's going to pay off my student loans for me. Or who'll pay the exorbitant rent in the San Diego area. Or who will pay for food, gas, and everything else I need. All I'm saying is that I have thick skin. As a woman in a man's world, I've learned a lot by sitting back and not rocking the boat. Listening. You'd be amazed at the things I've found out by fading into the woodwork and not getting up in people's faces when they're rude."

"Like what?" Rocco asked tightly. He wanted to continue to argue, to tell her that if she'd let him, he'd help her out, but now wasn't the time or the place.

Caite smiled again and looked around furtively, as if making sure no one was lurking before imparting some big secret. "Like there are three new guys living in the barracks who are 'wicked hot.'"

Rocco blinked. Was she being serious?

"Word on the street—okay, with the two women sailors I overheard talking in the cafeteria—is that you and your friends haven't been to the club yet, and they've been there every night, just in case. And if you, Ace, or Gumby gave them the slightest sign that you're interested, they'd be more than willing to," she cleared her throat and blushed slightly as she continued, "make you breakfast in the morning before you left their apartment."

Rocco shouldn't have been shocked, but he was. "We're here for work," he said seriously.

Caite giggled. "You asked what I've overheard. I'm just telling you."

"You're kidding, right?"

She shook her head. "Nope. I also know that there's a petty officer first class who's cheating on his wife with an officer in the Australian Navy, and a chief warrant officer 4 who was busted for having child porn on his work computer, and the public relations department had to scramble to cover up the scandal when a rear admiral who was visiting the base was caught in a prostitute sting by the local police."

Rocco could only stare at her.

Caite sat back and looked extremely proud of herself. "Don't look so shocked, Rocco. You'd be surprised at the things people say when they don't think anyone is around to hear them. I've just learned to stay quiet and listen. It's crazy what people will say to each other or on the phone when they don't take the time to look around and see who might be listening. I already blend into the background, and people only tend to notice me when they're *really* looking." She shrugged. "It's easier, and safer, to lay low and not make a fuss than try to rock the boat."

Rocco shook his head. "First, you do *not* blend into the background. I have no idea why you think that."

"Because it's true," Caite insisted. "It's fine. I don't mind. I wouldn't know what to do if men hit on me all the time or if women were constantly trying to talk to me."

"I saw you the second we walked into that elevator," Rocco said. "And I don't just mean because you were the only one in there. You were flushed from the heat and irritated that I'd dare force myself into *your* elevator."

She stared up at him with huge guilty eyes.

He went on. "You were surprised we'd even bothered to say hello, and when the elevator stopped, you weren't fazed, you just plunked yourself down on the ground without a word of complaint."

"I told you that I hate to complain because it never does any good," she said, blushing harder.

"I'm thinking the people you've known in your life are blind," Rocco said. "Either that or they're so narcissistic, they never take the time to look around and notice anyone else. I'm sorry others are assholes to you, especially my fellow navy peers. I'm sorry that you have to put up with rude behavior. I'm sorry that you haven't found anyone you feel safe enough with to explore Bahrain. It's an amazing country, with wonderful people. Yes, their culture is very different from ours, but that's what makes it so wonderful. If I was going to be here longer, I'd absolutely give you a tour. I'd show you what areas to stay away from and how to navigate the city. I'd show you how delicious falafel and machboos are and take you to Tariq Pastries, so you could try their chocolate-dipped baklava."

Caite licked her lips as she stared up at him, and the longing on her face was almost painful to witness.

Rocco raised a hand slowly and brushed the backs of his fingers against her cheek. He stared into her dark blue eyes and said, "Don't sell yourself short, *ma petite fée*. And don't think that no one sees you. I do. Those assholes sexually harassing you in French saw you too. And I bet your boss is threatened by you, so he sees you as well. You're an adult. You can do what you want, all I'm asking is that you're careful. Staying quiet is often a good idea, except when it's not."

"I don't understand," she whispered.

"There's a time to be silent, and there's a time to yell as loud as you can at the top of your lungs. You'll know the difference when the time comes."

Caite took a deep breath and straightened. Rocco forced his hand back to the edge of the bench. Her skin was soft, and he'd wanted nothing more than to shove his fingers in her hair, tilt her head back, and see if her lips were as soft and sweet as the rest of her.

Clearing his throat, Rocco said, "So... tonight...dinner?"

Caite nodded.

"Please tell me you don't want to go to the Taco Bell here on the base," he quipped.

She smiled. "No."

"Good. There's a place in Block 338 that I think you'd like."

"Block 338?"

Rocco looked at her in surprise. "Yeah. Some of neighborhoods around Manama are labeled in blocks. For instance, the naval base is closest to Block 338, and the Ritz-Carlton is north of here on the other side of the island in Block 428. And there are some areas that you just plain shouldn't go to, no matter what. Like Block 404 and 424. They aren't safe."

She nodded. "I got the briefing when I arrived. The US embassy puts out maps of places that are off limits. I don't remember anything about blocks, but they gave us a map of the city with some areas marked in red where we shouldn't go."

"Good. Anyway, Block 338 isn't too far from the base. There's a restaurant inside a hotel that's really good. It's called Kolors, and it's got just about every kind of international food you could ever want. But if nothing appeals, Miz Natasha will let us special order anything you want, even if it's not on the menu. I didn't think you'd be comfortable going way off base, but maybe you could trust me enough to go just a bit farther than you've been so far."

Caite nodded immediately, which made him feel good. "I'd like that."

"Then it's a date." Rocco couldn't stop smiling when she blushed again. He could see a sheen of sweat on her forehead and knew it was time to get his girl inside.

He stilled at that thought. His girl. The very idea was irrational, and way too soon, but it didn't feel wrong.

He stood and held out his hand. "Come on. Time for you to go inside before you melt."

"It's hot out here," she said in her defense even as she stood.

"You don't know hot until you've been in the Iraqi desert, in full uniform, including bulletproof vest and helmet, in one-hundred-and-twenty-degree temps in the glaring sun, tracking down insurgents," Rocco said without thought. "This feels like a nice spring day in comparison."

She stopped him with a hand on his arm. Concern was written all over her face. "Thank you, Rocco."

"For what?"

"For what you do. For your service to our country. For having to trek through the one-hundred-and-twenty-degree heat to keep people like me safe. Our way of life. Just...thank you."

His heart melted. "It's words like yours that make it all worthwhile."

And without thought, he did what felt right. He leaned over and gently brushed his lips against hers.

It was a short, chaste kiss, but the effect on Rocco was as intense as if he'd been hit by lightning.

He watched as she licked her lips, as if to have the taste of him on her tongue. Rocco himself felt tongue-tied, which he *never* was. To cover his surprise at the depth of emotion he was feeling, he took hold of Caite's hand and draped it over his arm. They walked side by side back to the front door of her building.

"I'll meet you here at five when you get off work. I'll walk you to your apartment so you can change, then we'll catch a taxi to the restaurant. Sound okay?"

She nodded and stared up at him.

Rocco took her in for a brief moment. She really was tiny compared to him. At six-three, he was taller than most people, but with Caite, it felt right. He was big enough to stand between her and anyone or anything that might threaten her. It was an odd thought, but he'd been full of those lately.

"I'll see you tonight then."

"Promise?" she asked with a small grin.

He returned it. "Nothing would keep me away," he vowed, doing what he'd wanted to do since the second his lips left hers. He leaned down once more. This time she came up on her tiptoes to meet him halfway.

The kiss was once again short and sweet, but the promise of it was oh so dirty.

It was Rocco who licked his lips this time. "Later, *ma petite fée.*"

"Later."

He turned and somehow resisted the urge to look back one more time, and made his way to the barracks, where Ace and Gumby were waiting for him.

They were right. Even though he was looking forward to tomorrow more than he'd looked forward to almost anything in the last year and a half or so, his mind was clearer.

Caite was fine. She could hold her own. She was smart, and as a woman working in a male-dominated field, especially over here in Bahrain, she'd proven to him in ten short minutes that she was being as safe as possible. She wasn't making waves, not pissing people off. Even if he wished she'd stand up for herself a bit more and had more self-esteem when it came to her own charms, he was confident that she was in no danger.

Unfortunately, the same couldn't be said for himself.

Two hours later, Rocco, Ace, and Gumby lay on a damp dirt floor beneath a general goods store in Block 424, one of the most dangerous places in Manama.

The store should've been closed and unoccupied, as Jeo Bitoo and his wife were visiting relatives in Africa, and their sons were supposed to be sitting in a class-room at the conference on the American naval base.

The SEALs had been looking around the store when the back door flew open and somewhere between ten and fifteen men entered. They all had baseball bats—and while the SEALs were certainly able to hold their own in close combat, they were no match for a literal mob. No one said much, just enough for Rocco to get the impression the Bitoo brothers were among the group, and that they'd been tipped off by someone in the neighborhood that men had entered their father's business. They'd obviously gathered some help as they made their way to the store—and the result was the SEALs beaten to within an inch of their lives and unceremoniously shoved through a hole in the floor.

Rocco lay on his back, staring up through his one un-swollen eye as the hatch in the floor was closed, leaving them in complete darkness. They were in a storage cellar at least fifteen feet below the store.

"Well, shit," he mumbled to himself, knowing Ace and Gumby were unconscious and wouldn't respond. It was obvious that getting out of their current predicament wasn't going to be easy...if they got out at all. "Guess I'm not going to be able to meet Caite for dinner after all." It was the last thing he managed to say before passing out himself.

CHAPTER FOUR

Caite looked at her watch for the hundredth time. Five thirty-two.

At first she just assumed Rocco was running late. Then she thought she'd been stood up...but remembering the look on his face, and how he'd so solemnly told her that nothing would keep him away, slight dread settled in her belly.

She thought something was wrong, but she had absolutely no way to check on him.

He didn't have a cell phone. Most of the employees had already gone home. And Caite had no idea if anyone even knew they were Navy SEALs. Hell, *she* wasn't even sure of that fact.

But as much as she worried about him, the niggling doubt wouldn't leave the back of her mind. It wasn't as if she really knew him. He'd promised to be there to take her out, but he could've had second thoughts.

Sighing, Caite got up from the bench she'd been sitting on and started walking toward the front gate of the base. She wasn't going to waste her time sitting around for hours waiting on someone who would probably never show up.

"His loss," she whispered...but she couldn't keep her lip from quivering.

Rocco groaned and rolled over. He opened his eyes—well, the one eye that *would* open—and still couldn't see a damn thing. It was pitch dark and it smelled like mold and dirt.

"Ace? Gumby?" he croaked.

"Yeah," Gumby replied weakly.

"I'm here," Ace said.

Rocco sighed in relief. They weren't out of the woods, but at least his buddies were conscious. He lifted his arm, gritting his teeth against the pain the action caused. He touched the button on the side of his watch and swore when he saw it was eight at night. They'd been unconscious for hours.

"Sit rep?" he asked.

"We're in some sort of cellar," Gumby told him. "While you and Ace were napping, I looked around as best I could. I didn't notice any ladder or steps, but admit that I didn't really do a thorough search yet. But do you want to hear the good news?"

Rocco had no idea what the hell could be good about the situation, but he dutifully said, "Sure."

"We won't starve to death," Gumby said. "There are boxes of food down here, and I even found a stash of water bottles too."

"Goody," Ace grumbled. "But how are we going to get out?"

"That's the tricky part," Gumby said. "I'm pretty sure my ankle is out of commission. When those assholes shoved us down here, I wasn't able to land right. You guys?"

"My wrist is fucked," Rocco said. "But my legs seem all right. One eye isn't working too well either."

"My head is bleeding, but I'm pretty sure nothing's broken," Ace added.

"Right. So we're good," Gumby said.

Rocco didn't even crack a smile. His teammate was right. Their injuries might be insurmountable for normal people, but SEALs weren't normal. As long as they weren't bleeding out or completely immobile, they could still fight. "I remember looking up at the hatch right before I passed out," Rocco told the others, "And we're about fifteen or so feet below."

"Easy-peasy," Gumby said, and Rocco could hear the smile in his voice.

"As long as they haven't blocked it or otherwise locked it," Ace said.

"Yup," Gumby agreed.

With every second that went by, Rocco was more

and more lucid. His wrist hurt, yes, and his head, but he was pissed. He'd missed his date with Caite. He'd promised he'd be there, and here he was instead. He couldn't stand the thought of her waiting outside her building in vain. He didn't want to even contemplate what she might be thinking about him. Probably that he was a player. With her self-esteem, she probably thought him not showing up was all about her.

Clenching his teeth, Rocco forced himself to his feet. They had to get out of this hole in the ground. It wasn't good that the brothers had caught them red-handed in their parents' shop.

"Gumby, did you find a flashlight when you were looking around earlier?"

"No. But I found a box of candles and I've got my flint on me."

Rocco smiled. "Those clay tablets could be stashed somewhere down here. The commander's intel could be faulty as well, in thinking the father was the only one in on the smuggling deal. I'm guessing the sons might know a lot more than the commander thinks. And if those tablets *are* down here, they'll eventually have to come back and open that hatch."

"Which means we're screwed," Ace said. "It won't be hard to take us out from up there." He motioned to the hatch above their heads.

Rocco completely agreed. If they found the tablets, they had confirmation that the brothers would be back sooner rather than later—and they'd most likely have more than just baseball bats this time.

"Looks like it's hide-and-seek time," Rocco said. "We don't know how much time we've got, so let's look through all this shit then figure out a plan. I don't know about you guys, but I'd like to make it as difficult as possible for those assholes to kill us."

The other two men agreed, and within minutes there were several candles lit. All three got down to business searching every nook and cranny of their temporary prison.

"It's good to hear from you, honey," Caite's mom said.

Just hearing her voice made Caite homesick. She enjoyed her job most of the time and liked being able to see a different part of the world not many got to experience, but she was depressed tonight and wanted to hear a familiar voice.

"You too," she said.

"Uh-oh," her mom said. "What's wrong?"

"How do you know something's wrong?" Caite asked.

"I just do. What's up?"

Caite sighed. "I was stood up tonight…and it sucks."

"I'm so sorry. What happened?"

Caite proceeded to tell her mom everything about Rocco. How they'd met, about how competent he and his friends had been in the elevator, their chat under the trees, and how he'd promised to be there tonight to take her out. She even told her mom about the kisses, and the affect they'd had on her. "He made me feel pretty. I thought he really cared about me. I thought I was done with high school games, but I can't think of a good reason why he'd come see me this afternoon and then not show up tonight if he was serious about wanting to take me out. Doesn't have a cell phone...I can't believe I actually fell for that!"

There was silence on the other end of the phone for a beat before her mom spoke. "Honey, you *are* pretty. I never understood how you couldn't see that. But that's beside the point. You're a good judge of character. I've never known you to be attracted to a man this fast before. From what you've said, I don't think Rocco was playing you. If he's as nice as you claim, why would he go to the trouble of asking you out if he wasn't going to show up?"

"Maybe he met someone else?"

"In the few hours between when he saw you and when he was supposed to pick you up?" her mom asked skeptically.

Caite sighed. "I know, but...it's easier for me to think that than the alternatives."

"Do you think something happened to him?"

That was the thing. She did. Rocco had said nothing would keep him from meeting her tonight, and yet, he hadn't shown. His mission today was supposed to be reconnaissance, but what if something went wrong? What if he'd been hurt...or killed? She'd like to think that his friends would find her and tell her if that was the case, but she just wasn't sure.

"Caite?" her mom prodded.

"I don't know. It's possible. He didn't come out and tell me, but I think he's a Navy SEAL. Generally, the sailors that come here don't come for only a week unless they're doing something super-secret. I'm not sure who I can even ask about him without getting him into trouble."

"Sounds like you're in a sticky situation," her mom said. "My suggestion is to get a good night's sleep. Maybe things will look clearer in the morning. You have to go into work tomorrow, right?"

"Yeah. Joshua is off, and I have to check in the people who are only coming for Saturday's job fair. There's a lunch planned that I have to make sure the caterers are all set for. I'm off after that."

"And personnel have to check in with someone before they leave the country, right?"

"Yeah."

"Then check the computer and see if your young man has done that. If not, maybe you can see where he's staying and go visit him."

"Mom!" Caite exclaimed. "I can't do that!"

"Why not?"

"Because! For one, it's illegal. And two..." Her voice lowered. "What if he answers his door and has a woman in there with him? Or it's super awkward because he was trying to ghost me."

"Ghost you? What in the world is that?"

"When someone doesn't have the guts to tell someone they don't want to see them anymore. Or use their services or whatever. They just stop emailing, calling, texting, hoping the other person gets the hint. I don't want to be the chick who can't take a hint."

"Jeez," her mom said in exasperation. "I don't get people. Wouldn't you rather *know* than spend days worrying about him? And don't bother to tell me you wouldn't worry, I know you."

"Yeah."

"Then do it. It's not like you're looking into sealed military records or anything. Just peek in and see where he was assigned to stay while he's here."

Caite nodded to herself. It *was* a good idea. "Okay, Mom. I will."

"Good. And honey?"

"Yeah?"

"If this guy stood you up, fuck him."

"Mom!"

"What? I'm not allowed to swear? Seriously, if he can't see what an amazing, awesome, beautiful, wonderful person you are, then he doesn't deserve you."

"Thanks, Mom," Caite whispered. She wasn't sure she felt better about the situation with Rocco, but her mom never failed to make her feel better about herself.

"Let me know how it goes," her mom ordered.

"I will."

"I'll let you go now. Get some sleep. I love you."

"Love you too," Caite told her. "Say hi to Dad for me and send him my love."

"Of course. Be safe over there."

"Always. I never leave the base...what trouble could I get into?" Caite told her.

"Right. Good night, honey.

"Bye, Mom."

"Bye."

Caite clicked off the phone and curled up on her side in her bed once more. She shut her eyes. Sleep didn't come easily—thoughts of why Rocco hadn't shown up kept running through her head—but eventually she drifted off into an uneasy doze.

"Bingo!" Ace said.

The search wasn't easy, between the darkness of the room, the dampness, and their injuries, but it looked like their persistence finally paid off.

Ace held up something wrapped in newspaper and smirked.

"Jesus!" Gumby exclaimed. "Put that down before you drop and break it!"

"I'm not going to drop it," Ace said calmly and began to unwrap the newspaper. It was moldy and smelled funky, but none of the men noticed. They all hunched over the cuneiform tablet and stared at it in awe. It was light tan and there were etchings that they all knew was writing used in Mesopotamia. The fact that it was literally thousands of years old, and had survived, was truly a miracle.

"Holy shit," Rocco said softly.

"How many are there?" Gumby asked.

Ace carefully wrapped the tablet back up and handed it to Rocco. Then he turned to the box and rifled through it for a moment. "Six."

"Only six?" Rocco asked with a frown. He remembered Commander Horner telling him there were more.

"Yup."

"We should keep looking," Rocco said. "I think there's supposed to be ten."

Without complaint, the others nodded. It wasn't as if they had anything else to do at the moment. They had to find those tablets before they made any escape attempt. Besides, the later it got, the better their chances of slipping out of the area undetected—providing they could even get out of the cellar. They'd overestimated their ability to blend into the dangerous neighborhood. Even with their beards and tan skin, they'd obviously stuck out.

Rocco glanced at his watch. Oh-one hundred. One in the morning. He hoped Caite was asleep, that she was okay. That she wasn't too upset.

He'd never been in the middle of a mission and not been able to keep his mind from wandering to a woman.

But this wasn't just any random woman. He wondered what she was doing. What she was thinking. If she was all right.

He should be worrying about his own ass. About getting the hell out of the pit they were in. About finding the missing tablets.

But instead, all he could think about was how disappointed he was that he'd missed dinner with Caite. That he'd broken a promise. That he hadn't been able to help her experience life outside the naval base's gates.

"Help me with this box," Gumby said as he struggled to move a heavy box from the top of a large stack.

As Rocco helped his teammate, he vowed to get his head back in the game. The sooner they found the damn tablets, the sooner they might get the hell out of here...and he could get back to Caite and grovel for her forgiveness.

Caite knew she looked like hell. She'd slept a total of about two hours the night before. She had bags under her eyes and she hadn't cared much what she'd thrown on to wear that morning. She hated working on the weekends, needing them to recharge herself. Usually she read a few books and just chilled in her apartment.

But today she was back at work, dealing with men who thought they were better than everyone else and trying to find her normal calm. The morning sessions preceding the job fair had gone off without a hitch, but the caterers were late and lunch had to be pushed back thirty minutes as a result, which threw off the afternoon schedule.

One of the lieutenants hadn't been happy about it and he'd chewed her out. She didn't mind being taken to task—except when it wasn't her fault. But, as usual, she'd just stood there and nodded her head and did her best to mollify the junior officer. She got it, the man didn't want to have to tell the attendees about the change in schedule, but shit happened.

The representatives for the organizations and businesses there for the job fair weren't happy either. They'd set up interviews in advance, and now their schedules were all messed up. But again, it wasn't her fault. She'd scheduled the caterers correctly, but one of their vans had gotten a flat tire on the way. The conference had run like clockwork until that point. If the attendees couldn't deal with a delayed thirty-minute break for lunch, that wasn't her problem.

Thankfully lunch was almost over, and Caite was sitting at one of the empty lunch tables in the large space, trying not to think about how she'd done something this morning that she never would have attempted before...namely, searching the computer for Rocco's room number. It wasn't as if she were selling state secrets or anything, but she still felt guilty. She'd found out that he and his friends were still marked down as having the rooms for another few days. They hadn't left yet.

She had a pad of paper in front of her that she was doodling on, passing the time and trying to look busy so no one would interrupt her to chew her out again. She thought about what she wanted to say to Rocco. She was going to head over to the dorm after the job fair got underway and tell him what she thought of him—that he was a dick for standing her up.

Voices from behind caught her attention. She didn't move, didn't stop doodling, but she did blatantly listen in on their conversation. It was the same group of men who had been speaking in French the other day. The ones who had discussed what she'd be like in bed and wondered if she might want to take on five brothers at once. She couldn't tell who was talking since her back was to the group, and she had to concentrate hard to understand their words, as they were speaking with what was obviously a dialect of their home country, but they weren't talking about her this time.

No, they were talking about something much more terrifying.

"*Why are we here? We need to get back to Pop's place and kill those assholes!*"

"*Shhhh, keep your voice down!*"

"*We're speaking in French. No one understands.*"

"*What about that bitch right there?*"

"Her? Please. She's American. Everyone knows Americans don't bother to learn any language other than their own. Self-centered assholes."

"How do you know?"

"Because. Watch. Hey! Bitch. I want you to come over here and suck my cock."

Caite didn't respond. She continued to look down at the paper in front of her and doodled as if she didn't have a care in the world. Her heart was beating so hard she could barely hear anything over the *thump thump thump*. Every muscle in her body was tense, ready to spring to safety if she needed to. The lunch she'd recently eaten threatened to come up and she had to swallow hard several times to control the urge to barf.

There weren't many times in her life when Caite had been scared. Truly terrified. But this was one of them. These men has spoken about her so crudely earlier that week. She could hardly think, she was so frightened. The last thing she needed on top of everything else going on in her life was to be sexually assaulted.

But there were lots of people still in the room. They wouldn't just haul her out of her chair and force her to go with them...would they? She had no idea, and it didn't help that her back was to the men. She couldn't see if they were sneaking up on her. She wouldn't be able to defend herself if they decided to do something. *Shit. Shit. Shit.*

"See?"

"Fine. But keep your voice down anyway."

"Right. As I was asking. Why are we at this stupid conference instead of taking care of those soldiers at Pop's shop?"

"Relax. They can't get out."

"But they're in the cellar with the tablets! We need to get them out as soon as possible."

"And we will. But we can't do anything with those assholes down there."

"So what? We just leave them down there? They aren't magically going to disappear. We have to do something."

"Guns."

"What?"

"Guns. We need to shoot their asses. We should've offed them last night. We can go back and kill them."

Caite's heart was beating even faster now. Soldiers. In a shop. They had to be talking about Rocco, Ace, and Gumby...didn't they? The conversation was confusing because they were talking so fast, and the accents didn't help.

Thinking about the men she'd met being in trouble made the danger even more real. She'd been scared when these guys were talking about her, but knowing they were possibly talking about Rocco and the others was even scarier.

Caite thought about standing up and heading over to where a group of men were talking on the other side of the room, but she couldn't make herself move. She was sweating at the same time she shivered with cold.

"Where are we gonna get a gun?"

"I don't know. Maybe Chambers can help."

"That asshole's an American too. He doesn't care about anything but getting those tablets to his buyer."

"He'll care if his precious tablets are confiscated by the US Navy."

"Shut up, you two. Look, Henri's right. Those guys aren't going anywhere right now, but we can't get to the tablets until we deal with them."

"Are you sure they can't get out?"

"Of course. They were all unconscious when we dumped them down there, and we fucked them up bad. Even if they did somehow manage to get to the hatch, we pulled that table over it that Pop uses to display the crafts and shit from back home. It's heavy as hell."

"What about the guns?"

"Can you think about anything other than guns for one second?"

"We need to kill them! They'll come right back here and report us."

"Of course they will. It's not like they were there by accident. We'll kill them, but not tonight. We need to lay low and establish our alibi. We'll stay here and continue to pretend we're

interested in this shit. Then we need to be seen around our neighborhood to throw suspicion off of us. We'll leave those assholes down there another night and go back Sunday evening."

"And the gun?"

"I'll take care of it. I know a guy."

"Can I shoot one?"

"Not fair! I want to!"

"Shut up! God, you two are pathetic."

"But there's only three of them and five of us. I want to make sure I get in on the fun."

"Fine, you can kill one. David can have another, and Marc can kill the last."

"What are we gonna do with their bodies?"

"Leave 'em there to rot."

"But...won't they start to stink?"

"Yup. Pa will find them and call the cops. They'll arrest him, Ma'll have to go back to Gabon, and we'll get the store. It's the perfect solution. Don't look at me like that, Emirck. You don't want to go back home any more than the rest of us. It's the only way."

"I know, but—"

"No buts. You're either with us or against us."

"I'm with you."

"Good. So we're all on the same page? All right, then everyone spread out. And try to look a little interested in this shit. We'll meet up after the job fair and head home. I'll get the gun and we'll head to the store around eight tomorrow night. Got it?"

"Yup."

"Yes."

"Good plan."

"Cool."

Three soldiers.

Caite could taste the bile at the back of her throat and was two seconds away from spewing all over the table, but when she saw movement to her left, she raised her head and forced her lips into a smile as three of the Gabonese men passed the table. They leered at her, and she mentally prayed that they weren't about to attack. Seeing their intense stares, she forced herself to ask, "Everything all right?"

"Perfect," the tallest of the men replied.

"Enjoy the rest of the conference," she said as friendly as she could, and they continued walking.

They didn't say anything else as they headed for the doors that led into the ballroom, where the job fair had been set up. She hadn't even heard the announcement that the room was now open for the prospective applicants.

The second they disappeared, Caite jumped to her feet. She was shaking badly, but she forced herself to walk as quickly as possible, without running, to the door on the opposite side of the room.

She passed one of the caterers and smiled at him, but couldn't force any words past her tight throat.

Glancing at her watch, she saw it was one in the after-noon. She had to talk to someone. Get someone to listen to her. But who?

Her boss was off and he'd told her in no uncertain terms to never contact him when he wasn't at work. This was an emergency, but she didn't think he'd care. He'd probably think she was making everything up.

She'd met Joshua's boss, Commander Horner, several times. He'd even been there that morning, hobnobbing with the conference participants, but she had no idea how to get ahold of him on the weekend. It wasn't as if she had his cell number. She could see if he had an address in the system, but...would he believe her?

Shit, she was going to have to call Joshua. She didn't want to, but she had no idea who else could help. He was her direct supervisor, after all, and could at least give her the commander's phone number or pass on the information himself.

Tomorrow at eight, those men were going to kill Rocco and the others, so there wasn't a lot of time to convince someone she wasn't crazy—that there really were three navy personnel in big trouble.

She hurried down the stairs to her floor and went straight to her desk. She sat there for a second, trying to compose herself. Her hands were shaking, and she knew she was sweating like a pig.

Taking a big breath to try to get her composure before she called Joshua, Caite forced herself to calm down. It felt like she'd just sprinted a mile. Her neck and shoulder muscles hurt from being scrunched up and she had a headache from hell. It was hard to think straight, but she had to make sure she sounded calm and levelheaded when she talked to her boss. He'd never listen to her if she was shrieking like a crazy person.

Taking one last look around to make sure she was alone, she reached for the phone. She quickly dialed Joshua's home number and waited with bated breath for him to answer.

"Hello?"

"Hi Mr. Mullen, it's Caite. I have a problem and I need your help. I was at the conference today and—"

"You had better not be calling me about some stupid little detail, Ms. McCallan. Your job is to take care of things yourself. And if you can't handle something as simple as a conference, then maybe I need to see about finding someone who can."

Irritated, Caite forced herself to stay calm. "No, it's nothing like that. There was a problem with lunch but I took care of it. I'm calling because I overheard something, and I think there may be some navy personnel who need assistance and—"

"No."

Caite blinked at the harsh cutoff. "What?"

"I said no. I can't believe you're calling me about *gossip*! Did I not tell you that I was on leave until next week? You know I don't like to be bothered when I'm with my family."

"Yes, sir, but—"

"If you say one more word, I'm going to write you up," Joshua said, not letting her finish. "In fact, if I discover that you tried to bother anyone else with some nonsense you *overheard*, I'll make sure you're on your way back to the States without a job so fast, it'll make your head spin. Got it?"

Caite was so shocked at the venom in Joshua's words, she couldn't respond even if she wanted to.

"Now get back to work," Joshua said before hanging up the phone.

Caite stared at the phone in her hand before slowly reaching forward and putting it back on its base. Now what? Her boss had shut her down, effectively cutting off any means of getting help to Rocco and his friends.

She could defy him and try to find the commander's phone number some other way...but she needed this job.

Thinking hard, she considered what her next steps should be. She could forget she'd heard anything, but the thought of the men going to that store and slaughtering Rocco, Ace, and Gumby when she could have done something to prevent it wasn't acceptable.

Information. She needed information.

Everyone at the conference had been required to submit basic details about themselves before they were accepted. She unlocked her desk drawer and grabbed the folder of participants at the conference, flicking through the papers until she found what she was looking for.

Timothee, Henri, David, Marc, and Emirck Bitoo.

The pictures that were taken for their visitors' badges were attached to each of their applications. Timothee was the oldest at thirty-five, and she assumed he was the one who had done most of the talking, the one who'd said he'd be able to get a gun. The ages of the brothers were close, with Emirck being the youngest at twenty-five.

Her eyes flicked over the pages and her heart sank. The same home address was listed on all five applications. And the men had specifically said that Rocco and the others were being held at their father's store.

Panicking, she flipped back to Timothee's application and forced herself to read every word, slowly and carefully. She needed a miracle. She needed to know where that store was. What she was going to do with that information, she had no idea, but she needed it.

It wasn't until she got to Emirck's application that she finally breathed out a sigh of relief. On the question about an emergency contact, the youngest of the Bitoo family had listed his father...and included an address. He'd even made a notation that it was both his father's work and home address.

Not wanting to turn on her computer in case someone checked her log-in records, Caite pulled out her phone. She put in the address—and almost cried.

Just as she suspected, it was located smack-dab in the middle of the area she'd been warned not to go into under any circumstances on account of the high crime rate.

Biting her lip, she fretted until a noise down the hall startled her, and she jumped. Whipping her head around, she saw one of the janitors getting off the recently repaired elevator. She smiled at him and quickly put the applications back into the folder and jammed it into her desk.

"Still working, huh?" the older gentleman asked.

Caite nodded as she relocked the drawer. "Yeah, but I'm done, thank goodness. I hate working on the weekend."

"I like it. It's quiet," the janitor said with a smile.

"I bet." Caite hated the small talk, but knew she needed to act as normal as possible. "Thank goodness my part in the conference is done. I just had to come back and make one last report about the caterers being late. Now I can go home and enjoy what's left of my weekend."

"Don't do anything I wouldn't do," the man said jovially, and Caite internally winced. What she was thinking about doing was something no one should do.

"I won't," she called as she made her way toward the stairwell.

"See you later."

"Later!" she returned, and waved as she pushed open the door. Once inside the stairwell, Caite leaned against the door and took a deep breath. She brought her phone up and clicked it back on. She stared at the map with dread. She really, *really* didn't want to go there herself. But her boss had given her little choice. She had to do what she could to help Rocco, Ace, and Gumby herself. If something happened to them, and she could've done anything to help, she'd never forgive herself.

According to the Bitoo brothers, they were going to stay away from the store until tomorrow night. So she had time to get there, do what she could to help Rocco, and get the hell back to base.

Knowing she was being incredibly stupid, Caite pressed her lips together and jogged down the stairs. She had to get back to her place and change clothes. It was prohibited for US military members, their families, and DOD employees to wear the traditional Bahraini abaya, but this was an emergency. She couldn't exactly go traipsing all over the city in her American jeans or slacks. She had to blend in.

She'd bought a beautiful abaya from a street vendor last month. It was black with pink accents on the hem, down the front where the material came together, and around the wrists. She'd planned to wear it as a bathrobe, but when she'd gotten it back to her apart-ment, decided it was too pretty to wear around the house. The saleswoman had even talked her into buying a hijab. Caite hadn't been able to say no, especially when one of the vendor's young children had poked her head out from under the table. She'd bought the head covering even though she knew she'd never wear it.

But right this second, she was thanking her lucky stars she had it. The only thing she needed now was the courage to head out into Manama by herself, in the dark, to a part of the city that was known to be dangerous to foreigners.

Once dressed, she almost chickened out. Caite stared at herself in the mirror and wondered what in the hell she was doing.

But then she thought about Rocco. Being stuck in that cellar, especially when he didn't like enclosed spaces. He was probably hurt badly, as were Ace and Gumby, if the Bitoo brothers' words were anything to go by. They couldn't get out. She had to help them.

Taking a deep breath, she closed her eyes and swallowed hard. Then she turned without a second glance at herself dressed as a woman from Bahrain, and prayed no one would recognize her as she headed out of her apartment and started walking north. She'd catch a taxi as soon as she got farther away from the base, then change taxis once she made it to the city center, just to prevent anyone from knowing she was headed into the off-limits area.

"You'd better be there," she whispered to herself as she walked, head down, staring at her feet and hurrying along the sidewalk.

CHAPTER FIVE

They were going to die.

There wasn't really any way around it.

And that sucked.

The possibility of him dying on a mission was something Rocco and the others were always aware of, but this just seemed so wrong. He'd always imagined himself biting it in a much more dramatic way. Roadside bomb. Saving one of his teammates from a bullet. Or even fighting hand-to-hand with a terrorist.

Trying to take cover behind beaten-up old crates and bags of food while being shot at from above wasn't how he'd thought he'd go, even in his wildest imagination.

It *really* sucked that they wouldn't get to say goodbye to the others. They were going to be missed Bubba, Rex, and Phantom. They were more than mere teammates; they were like brothers. They'd talked about dying before, and they'd all agreed that if they had to die for their country, they'd prefer to all go together. Morbid, but for people like them, it wasn't anything unusual.

Rocco and the others had been quiet for a while, resting up and racking their brains to try to come up with a feasible way to break out of their prison before the Bitoo brothers returned. Which they would; they couldn't just leave three strange men beneath their father's store. And as far as Rocco was concerned, the chances the brothers didn't know the tablets were hidden in the cellar were slim.

They hadn't found any more of the ancient tablets though. Rocco was sure Commander Horner had told them there were ten. But they'd searched every inch of the cellar and hadn't found any others.

He glanced at his watch. Eleven at night on Saturday. It had been over twenty-four hours since they'd been stuck underground—and since he was supposed to pick up Caite. He knew he should stop thinking about her, about their missed date, but he couldn't.

There were much more pressing things to obsess over—like the fact that they couldn't get out of the deep cellar they'd been thrown into.

Since Gumby's ankle was messed up and Rocco's wrist was definitely not at one hundred percent, Ace had been elected the best person to try to open the hatch high above their heads. During their extensive search, they'd found a stepladder tucked behind some boxes, and Rocco had climbed up a few steps and braced himself. Ace climbed onto his shoulders holding a broom, to see if they could force the hatch open. Whatever the men had put on top of it wasn't budging though. No matter how hard Ace tried, he couldn't get enough force to be able to open the hatch.

They'd talked for hours about what the plan was when the men returned—and they *would* return, that was inevitable. They'd be back, most likely with reinforcements.

Basically, the SEALs were screwed. All three men knew it. They were good fighters. They could hold their own, but with all of them injured, they knew any fight would be extremely lopsided. Even if the Gabonese men didn't bring reinforcements, the fact that they were stuck in this cellar made them sitting ducks. All it would take was a rifle or pistol, and they could be picked off one by one, and there wouldn't be a damn thing Rocco and the others could do about it.

They'd discussed hiding, making it seem as if they had escaped and jumping whoever came down to search for them, but that wouldn't help them get out in one piece, as the others would most likely be waiting up top inside the store.

The bottom line: the only chance they had—a very *slim* chance—was the element of surprise. The second someone removed whatever was holding the hatch closed, they'd have to strike. Gumby was very good with his knife, could take someone out in seconds, and Ace was scarily effective at using his bare hands to kill...but they had to get out of the cellar first.

So the plan was for Rocco to basically throw Ace up and out of the hatch the second it was unsecured or opened. Even with his bad wrist, he had the most upper-body strength.

They all knew the move was most likely a suicidal one, but they had no choice. Ace would do his best to fight whoever was up there as soon as the hatch was opened, or at least try to block a few bullets until Rocco could get Gumby up to assist Ace. When they were able, they'd throw down a rope and Rocco would join the fight.

It was risky, and likely to fail, but it was the best they could do under the circumstances. They'd practiced the "throwing a teammate of a hole" move back in training in California. It came about because intel had come down the line that the Taliban had begun digging holes in the desert. They threw men in them in the hopes they'd die of thirst and their bodies would simply decompose and turn to dust, with no one the wiser. So Rocco and the rest of the team had attended a brainstorming session with Wolf, Abe, Cookie, Mozart, Dude, and Benny, and they'd come up with a way to get out of almost any hole.

They'd done a modified version to get Caite out of the elevator car...

Shit, was that days ago? It seemed so much longer.

Basically, one man would stand on another man's

shoulders. The man on the bottom would then hold the other man's feet in his hands and squat. At the appropriate time, he'd spring upwards and straighten his arms. The man standing on top would jump, and the combined height of the two men, plus the force of their momentum, could propel the man on top to a height of around twenty feet...if done right.

They'd practiced over and over in the gym at the base in California. They'd switched partners and everyone had taken both positions, getting the feel for what it was like to be the jumper and the jumpee.

With Gumby's bum ankle, he wouldn't be much good on the bottom, but he could be propelled upward. The move would hurt Rocco's wrist, but he could take it. The important thing was getting the fuck out of this hole.

But right now, they were stuck until someone came for them. Bad guy, good guy, random bystander. It didn't matter. They weren't going anywhere until whatever was holding down the hatch was moved.

"Any regrets? Ace asked quietly as they sat and waited.

Caite immediately came to mind. "She'll never know why I didn't show," he said quietly. "She'll think I stood her up."

His friends didn't say anything. There was nothing *to* say. They both knew who Rocco was referring to, and that he was right. It wasn't like anyone would tell her anything about the top-secret mission the SEALs had been on. Hell, no one even knew she existed in his life. He'd simply be the man who'd asked her out, then ghosted on her. It sucked.

"I always wanted a dog," Gumby said.

No one laughed at him and told him he was crazy for thinking about a dog right before he'd most likely be killed.

"Growing up, we moved too much and my old man refused to let us get one, saying it was too hard to get good navy housing with one. But I've always loved them. Told myself it wasn't fair to get a pet when I was gone so much. But dammit, I wish I'd done it anyway."

"What kind?" Rocco asked.

"A pit bull," Gumby said immediately. "I know they have a bad rep, but I've met so many that are the biggest smoosh faces. And these were former fighting dogs too. I'm not saying they're all well-adjusted and safe, but I've always wanted to give one a second chance. Show him or her what it's like to have an owner who's compassionate and kind."

They were quiet for a moment. Neither Ace nor Rocco had any words of encouragement for their buddy. They knew the score.

"I regret that I'll never have kids," Ace said after a while. "I always figured I'd have lots of time to settle down and have them."

"How many you want?" Rocco asked.

"As many as my wife'll let me give her," was his response. "I don't care if they're boys or girls. Growing up as an only child, I always envied my friends who had big, boisterous families. Now that my folks have both passed, I don't have much family left. I always wanted to have a ton of kids so no one ever felt as if they were alone."

Again, no one had a reply, and silence fell over the group.

The cellar was surprisingly soundproof. They couldn't hear anything other than each other's breathing and water dripping from somewhere.

While they were confident in their fighting abilities, all three knew the odds were against them this time. Maybe if Bubba, Rex, and Phantom were there as well, they'd be able to come up with a plan to get out. Hell, Phantom would probably somehow find a way to *dig* out. But among the three of them, the mood was solemn and reflective.

Rocco wasn't ready to give up. A SEAL never called it quits until the absolute end. But he was also a realist.

I'm sorry, Caite. I hope you find a man who appreciates the beauty he's got in you.

It was eleven-thirty at night and it still felt as if it was at least ninety-five degrees outside. Caite was sweating like she'd run a marathon. The hijab was itchy and the abaya kept wrapping around her legs and trying to trip her. She wasn't used to walking with all the extra material.

Caite concentrated on the temperature rather than how scared she was. There was a reason the US authorities had said this part of the city was off limits. She'd already seen things she'd thought only happened in movies. Prostitutes on every corner, men doing drugs right on the street, a huge fight outside of a bar, and even what she thought was a woman being violated in a dark alley.

The cab driver had refused to take her any farther than the outskirts of the neighborhood she needed to be in. He'd taken pity on her and had given her directions to get to the general area where the store was located, but even when she'd offered the guy a hundred bucks, he'd still refused to drive her there.

And that's how she'd ended up walking the last mile to the store. Caite kept looking behind her to see if she was being followed, even though she really couldn't see a damn thing. She was extremely paranoid. And she was definitely pushing her luck. She'd been fortunate so far, but she knew her luck would end sooner or later.

She'd gone over in her mind time and time again what she'd heard the brothers saying at the conference. Someone had to have seen Rocco, Ace, and Gumby go into the store, and had contacted the Bitoos. How else would they have known to go to their father's store and ambush Rocco and the others? And if someone saw the Navy SEALs, who were probably really good at *not* being seen, surely they'd see *her*. Women weren't supposed to be out by themselves.

They should always be accompanied by a male. She'd been lectured to about that very thing by both taxi drivers.

It didn't matter that she was pretending to be a local. In fact, it was probably worse being alone looking the way she did than if she'd flaunted the fact that she was a foreigner. It was too late now to change what she'd done.

Holding her breath, she hurried down the sidewalk, ignoring the sweat that dripped down her back. She had on a black tank top and leggings under the abaya, and it felt as if she were wearing a wool coat in the middle of summer. She knew if she stripped off the tank, she could probably literally wring it out, it was so soaked with sweat. She wanted nothing more than to strip off all her clothes and sit in front of a fan turned on high.

So focused on how hot she was, Caite almost didn't realize that she'd made it to her destination. There were several single-story buildings standing side by side. There was about two feet between each, just enough to slip through and get to the back side...or for someone to hide and ambush her.

Shivering at the thought, Caite looked around, trying to find the correct building.

There. Tucked between what looked like a barber-shop and some sort of tobacco store was a faded, broken sign that said "Bitoo's Grocery." There was a metal shutter pulled down over the front and a large padlock holding it secure. The building was just as rundown as the others around it, and looked like it would blow over with the next dust storm.

Since she couldn't get in through the front, and because she wanted to get off the street, Caite took a deep breath and plunged into the dark, narrow alley next to the store. It smelled like piss and rotting food, but she didn't stop to examine what she was stepping on. She just hoped she didn't trip over someone sleeping between the buildings.

Sighing in relief when she reached the backside, she wasn't surprised to see no streetlights illuminating the area. If possible, it was creepier than the front, but at the moment, the darkness was her friend. The last thing she wanted was someone seeing her and coming over to harass her...or have her arrested.

There was a wooden door in the back that looked promising. She turned the knob and pushed, and was disappointed when it didn't budge. Knowing the locked door wouldn't be a possibility but vowing that she hadn't come this far to fail now, she studied the single small window. She could break it and get inside, but breaking the glass would make a lot of noise, and she couldn't risk drawing attention to herself.

Caite went over to the small window and, just on a lark, pushed on it.

It opened inward so fast, Caite stumbled forward and almost bashed her head against the windowsill.

She blinked in surprise at the now open window. It was about shoulder height and wouldn't be easy for her to get through, but buoyed by how easy it was to find a way inside, Caite dragged a foul-smelling box closer to the window. She had no idea what was inside, but the stench was horrible. Holding her breath, she cautiously stepped on the closed box and prayed her foot wouldn't break through and touch whatever smelled so awful.

Moving quickly, she braced her hands on the windowsill and jumped. Her belly landed on the wood, which dug into her stomach, but she ignored the slight sting and wiggled until her upper body was inside the store.

It was dark inside and smelled of incense. The quiet was unnerving, but Caite didn't let it stop her. Not knowing how else to get inside, she simply pushed herself the rest of the way, landing on her hands and knees on the cold, hard floor. The sound her body made as it landed was loud in the silent room, and she held her breath for a long few seconds, trying to determine if someone outside had possibly heard her.

After a moment, hearing no one shouting in protest, she got to her feet and turned around to shut the window. The box underneath the window was enough of a red flag that someone had gotten inside that way; she didn't want to leave the window open as well.

At the last second before leaving her apartment, she'd grabbed a small flashlight as an afterthought. She fished it out of the waistband of her leggings now and clicked it on.

Looking around the store, she was struck by how

little food there was. There weren't any fresh vegetables on the shelves and only a few random cans of meat and soup. There were a few bags of chips and some bottles of water on a shelf, but that was about it in the food department. There were a ton of other items for sale, however. Most of which looked like junk to Caite. It was like a large garage sale back home. What looked like used pots and pans and other kitchen supplies sat on shelves alongside a rack filled with clothes that had seen better days.

Caite quickly lost interest in what Mr. Bitoo was selling in his shop. She was there for a reason. Tiptoeing across the floor—which was silly because it wasn't like there was anyone around to see her—Caite saw a large table sitting in the middle of the space. It had one wide central leg that flared slightly to four supports at the bottom, and it looked like it was made out of concrete or stone.

On top of the table were wooden carvings and some batiks. She knew from seeing the vendors who set up outside the base that they were probably the African crafts one of the Bitoo brothers had talked about.

She got down on her knees in front of the table and ran her hands along the floor. Feeling what she knew had to be a handle, she shone her flashlight on it. Yup. A small ring was almost hidden in the scuffed and dirty floor of the shop.

Relief hit Caite so hard, she almost passed out. She'd done it! She'd found Rocco, Ace, and Gumby.

She wanted to call out to them. To tell them she was there and that she'd open the hatch so they could get out, but she kept quiet. She had no idea how thin or thick the walls were, and the last thing she wanted was someone walking by to hear her yelling.

She stood so fast, she hit her head on the underside of the table. She groaned and put her hand on the back of her head and closed her eyes for a second, trying to keep down the yelp of pain that threatened to escape.

When the pain receded to a reasonable level, she slowly backed out from under the table and tried to push it off the trapdoor in the floor.

It wouldn't budge.

Swearing, she tried again, grunting with the effort to slide the table the two feet or so backward off the hatch. Because all the weight was on one central support, it was way too heavy for her, damn it.

Hoping that moving some of the wooden carvings off the table would lighten it enough, she began to move some of the odds and ends that were on top to the nearby counter.

After five minutes or so, she tried to push the table off the hatch again.

"Dang it!" she swore when the stone table was *still* too heavy for her to move. But there was no way she'd come this far, only to fail. No way in hell.

Shining her flashlight around the room, she searched for something, *anything* she could use to move the table.

She almost missed it.

There. Behind three huge pots. A coil of rope. It was brand new and still in plastic.

Caite stumbled over and snatched it up. She quickly opened it, feeling guilty all of a sudden. Poor Mr. Bitoo had no idea what his sons were doing. He was back home in Gabon at the moment, at least according to the brothers.

She reached into the pocket of her abaya—one of the very reasons she'd chosen this style over some of the more ornate ones the vendor had on display; she didn't like to wear anything that didn't have pockets—and pulled out a five-dollar bill. She'd made sure to bring plenty of cash so she could pay the taxis. She placed the bill on the shelf where she'd gotten the rope.

Feeling better now that she wasn't stealing, Caite hurried to unwind the rope. She tied one end to the center support of the table and wrapped the other around a huge wooden spool that was sitting nearby, displaying various odds and ends.

Using it the rope as a type of pulley, she tugged with all her might.

At first, she didn't think it would work—but slowly, ever so slowly, the table began to move. "Come on, come on," she muttered, straining with all her weight against the rope.

Finally, *finally*, the table moved enough so that it wasn't on top of where she thought the hatch was located.

Feeling proud of herself and accomplished, she made her way back toward the hatch.

Distracted by the sweat under her arms, soaking her tank top and dripping down the back of her neck under the hot hijab, Caite wasn't prepared for the hatch to fly open.

The sound it made as it crashed against the floor was shocking.

But it was the man who came flying out of the hatch toward her face that was the bigger issue.

Screeching in surprise, Caite took a step back and tripped over the flowing material of her abaya. She fell backward at the same time the man grabbed her around the neck, and they both fell to the floor with a crash.

"You hear that?" Gumby whispered.

"Yeah," Ace said.

At the same time, Rocco said, "Hell yeah."

"They're back," Gumby said unnecessarily.

The three men tracked the movement above their heads by the sounds of the footsteps.

"It only sounds like one person," Ace said. "Could one of them have been stupid enough to come back by himself?"

"Maybe he wants the tablets and he's going to double-cross his brothers," Rocco suggested.

"We might just get out of this in one piece after all," Ace said, the eagerness easy to hear in his voice.

"Don't get cocky," Rocco warned. "There still could be more of them."

They heard grunting above them, and the rustle of things being moved around.

"What's he doing?" Ace whispered.

"No clue. You ready?" Rocco asked.

Ace nodded, and Rocco slowly and silently stepped up onto the stepladder they'd placed under the hatch. He looked up and made sure he was positioned right under the hatch. If he screwed up when he threw Ace, he could seriously hurt his friend.

More scraping noises sounded above their heads, and they knew it was getting close to time. Whoever was up there was moving the table off the hatch. Once it was removed, Ace would have only the slightest window to take him by surprise and disarm him. Their goal wasn't to kill anyone, but they wouldn't hesitate to do so if needed.

Ace climbed up behind Rocco and confidentially stepped onto his shoulders. "Okay?" Ace asked.

"Good," Rocco returned. He felt Gumby's hand on his back, steadying him. The second Ace was thrust upward, Gumby would take his place and Rocco would get him up and out of the cellar as well. Then it was his job to step aside and wait for one of them to throw down a rope so he could climb up and join the fight.

Ace lifted one foot, and Rocco bent his arm and

put his hand under Ace's boot. Then he did the same with the other. He slowly bent his knees, ready to put as much energy as possible into throwing Ace up and out.

"Almost..." Ace said. Rocco's gaze was fixed on the step of the ladder in front of him. He trusted Ace to know when the timing was right.

"Ready?" Ace asked quietly.

"Ready," Rocco confirmed.

"On three. One. Two. *Three*."

The second the word left his mouth, Rocco grunted and lurched upward as hard as he could. He straightened his arms and felt Ace push off with his own jump. The hatch burst open with a huge crash.

Rocco didn't even look up. He squatted back down immediately and put his hands near his shoulders to get ready for Gumby. He knew his buddy's ankle hurt, but they'd wrapped it as best they could with what they'd found in the cellar. He also knew Gumby wouldn't let out one complaint. He'd do his job as well as he was able.

"Ready," Gumby said confidently.

"On three," Rocco said. "One. Two. Three!"

Then he once again sprang upward. It was a bit more awkward this time, as Gumby was taller and heavier, and Rocco didn't have the luxury of someone bracing him from behind as Gumby had done when he'd lifted Ace. But the other man made it up and out of the cellar with no issues.

Rocco quickly moved the stepladder out of the way and looked up. Waiting.

It took several moments—and Rocco didn't hear any scuffling. The only thing he'd heard was a thud after Ace had burst out of the hatch, then a slight surprised screech...then nothing.

After what seemed like an eternity, Gumby's face appeared at the edge of the hatch. He slowly lowered a rope ladder over the edge. "Don't forget the tablets," Gumby said.

"Everything okay?" Rocco asked.

"Tablets, Rocco," Gumby repeated, not answering.

"Fuck," Rocco muttered, and turned and grabbed the box of priceless artifacts. His wrist was throbbing but he ignored it, holding the box under one arm and using the other hand to climb up the swaying ladder as if it was child's play.

The sight that greeted him when he reached the top stopped him in his tracks.

Gumby put a hand on his arm and said, "She's okay, man. Don't panic."

"What the absolute fuck?" Rocco asked.

A woman lay on the floor. Ace was kneeling next to her with a hand on her shoulder. She blinked and looked up at him.

"Hi, Rocco."

"Caite?" Rocco asked, not understanding what the hell was going on. He couldn't get his brain to process the fact that the person on the ground wasn't one of the

Bitoo brothers, but instead a woman. A woman dressed in a traditional abaya and wearing a hijab.

Caite.

That it was *Caite*.

She slowly started to sit up, and groaned.

Within seconds, Rocco had put the box of tablets on the floor as if they weren't worth millions of dollars and rushed to her side. He put his arm around her back and helped ease her to a sitting position. "Are you okay?"

"Yeah. Are *you?*"

Rocco was never speechless. He always had something to say. But he couldn't for the life of him think of one thing to say at the moment. Seeing Caite there, dressed as she was, wasn't something he could ever prepare for. He was having a hard time thinking at all.

"We need to get out of here," Ace said softly. "We made enough noise to bring the entire neighborhood running, especially since the store is supposed to be empty."

Rocco knew his friend was right, but he couldn't move. "Caite? What in the hell are you doing here? How did you find us? What are you wearing?"

She winced. "It's a long story. A *very* long story."

"One that we don't have time for," Gumby warned. "We need to disappear."

"Dammit," Rocco swore, but he got to his feet. He easily hauled Caite up as well and looked her up and down. "You're okay? What happened up here?"

She wouldn't meet his eyes, so Rocco looked to Ace.

"I did as we planned. Attacked the first person I saw. Except she was already in the process of falling backward. I grabbed her by the throat, as much to try to stop her from falling as to stop my own forward movement. We both fell to the floor and she hit her head. But she's fine. We need to go."

Rocco knew his adrenaline hadn't subsided yet, could feel it coursing through his veins. "You put your hands on her throat?" he hissed at his friend.

"Rocco," Caite said, putting a palm on his cheek and trying to get him to look at her. "He didn't know it was me. And he didn't hurt me. I'm okay."

He loved the feel of her hand on his skin. Her palm tickled his beard and made him want to press against her hand. "How are you here?" he asked, still confused beyond belief.

"I overheard the brothers saying they'd thrown you guys into the cellar of their dad's store. They planned to come back tomorrow night to shoot you. I...I didn't know who to talk to about it and my boss wouldn't listen. I wasn't sure who knew you guys were here, or *why* you were here. So I found the address of the store on one of the brother's conference registration papers and...here I am."

There were so many holes to her story, Rocco didn't know where to start.

"Not now," Gumby warned once more. "We need to get the fuck out of here. I'll take the tablets. You and

Caite head out, and me and Ace'll have your back. We'll follow you until we're out of the neighborhood. We can hail a cab but since we don't have any money, we'll have to carjack it."

"Um...I have money," Caite said hesitatingly.

"Of course you do," Gumby said with a slight smile. "Right, so we'll follow you two until we can find a cab. It might be a long walk. This isn't exactly the best neighborhood for taxis to be driving around."

"I had to walk a mile to get here. My driver refused to go any farther," Caite informed them.

Rocco's head was throbbing. He couldn't fucking believe this. "You walked a mile in this neighborhood?! *Alone?*"

Caite nodded.

"Fuck! It's a miracle you made it here in one piece," he hissed.

"I know." Her response was soft and wobbled a bit.

Rocco felt like shit. He hadn't meant to scare her, especially when it was obvious she knew as well as he did how dangerous the area was.

Something else struck him then. She hadn't ventured far from the base because she was so uneasy. And yet she'd come, by herself, to one of the worst neighborhoods in the city...because *he'd* needed help.

He knew for a fact that nothing he could ever do in his life was as brave as what Caite had done tonight.

"How'd you know they were talking about us?" he asked Caite, putting his hands on her shoulders,

107

needing this one question answered before they left. "For all you knew, they were talking about a drug dealer in the neighborhood or some other asshole."

"They called you soldiers. And said something about the US Navy. I don't really remember all of it. After you didn't show up Friday night, I checked the computer and saw that the three of you hadn't checked out of housing. I thought you might've just decided you didn't want to go out after all. I mean, I wouldn't blame you if you had, but then those guys started talking about three asshole soldiers and killing them on Sunday night and I just...I had a feeling it was you guys. It was stupid."

Rocco put his finger under her chin and forced her head up so she had to meet his eyes. Her face was flushed with the heat and he could see sweat beaded on her forehead. He couldn't see any other part of her. Not her hair, as it was covered by the hijab, and not her body, as it was similarly engulfed in the miles of material of the abaya. But her eyes told him all he needed to know.

She'd been hurt when he hadn't shown, just as he knew she would be.

He hated that he'd disappointed and upset her, even if it hadn't been his fault. "It wasn't stupid," Rocco told her. "You saved our lives, *ma petite fée*. I'm not sure we can ever repay you for that."

His praise obviously flustered her. "Anyone would've done it."

"You're wrong," Rocco told her. And he wasn't lying.

Time and time again, they'd come across people who were more concerned with saving their own skins than helping others. And that included fellow navy sailors, SEALs, and civilians. He could name on one hand the number of people in his life who had surprised him as Caite had.

"Rocco..." Ace warned.

He knew his time was up. "You ready to get back to your apartment?"

"More than," she said, obviously relieved at the change in subject. "I'm never leaving again."

He smiled at her.

"We'll follow you two. We'll attract less attention if we're not all together."

"Oh!" Caite said, and she dug in her pocket and pulled out some bills, holding them out to Ace. "Here. It's a mix of Bahraini dinar and American bills. I wasn't sure which the taxi drivers would take."

Ace reached out and took the wad of cash. He thumbed through it, taking half, and gave the rest to Rocco. "Best you take this, just in case."

Rocco nodded. The last thing he needed was for Caite to be caught with money in her pocket. It would be a miracle if they were able to make it back to the base without encountering one of the city's more unsavory residents.

"We'll meet you back at the base, Rocco," Gumby said.

He nodded. They needed to get the tablets to

Commander Horner and debrief. "You okay on that ankle?" he asked his friend.

Gumby smiled. "Walk in the park."

Rocco knew he was downplaying his injury, but they couldn't do a damn thing about it right now. They'd have to wait until they were back on base. Same with his wrist and Ace's head.

"Be careful," was all he said.

"You too," both Ace and Gumby returned.

Rocco watched as Ace untied the rope from the table and the spool and shoved it under one of the shelves. Gumby pulled the rope ladder back up and out of the cellar and returned it to a hook on the wall. Ace closed the hatch and both men moved the table back into place. They carelessly placed a bunch of the African carvings back on top.

"There. It looks as normal as it's gonna. It'll buy us some time if anyone looks in here, and it'll give the brothers quite a shock when they come to off us tomorrow night," Ace joked. "They'll be wondering for days how in the hell we escaped."

"How did you get in here?" Gumby asked Caite.

She pointed to the window. "It was unlocked."

"Damn," Ace said, and shook his head. They all walked over to it and Ace went out first. It was a tight fit, but nothing they hadn't been through before. Gumby followed.

When Rocco was alone with Caite in the store, he

took her face in his hands and put his forehead against hers. "I'm pissed at you," he told her tenderly.

"I know," she replied, and held on to his forearms with a death grip.

"You could've been killed."

"I know," she repeated.

"Raped."

"Uh-huh."

"Pressed into prostitution."

She nodded wordlessly this time.

"Thank you," he told her in a whisper. Rocco had seriously thought he'd never see her, or anyone else, ever again. He'd come to terms with his death and had actually looked forward to going down fighting. But one look at Caite lying flat on her back in the last place he'd expect to see her had made him realize how much he *wasn't* ready to die.

"You're welcome," she whispered back.

"Roc?" Ace whispered from outside. "Pass her out."

"Ready to get out of here?" Rocco asked her.

"God, yes," she said with enthusiasm.

Knowing if he kissed her now, he wouldn't be able to stop with just a chaste peck on the lips, he pulled back and turned her so she was facing the window. "Put your arms over your head. Pretend you're diving out the window. Ace and Gumby will be there to grab you. Keep your body tight until you're out. Got it?"

She nodded and dutifully put her arms up. Rocco easily lifted her and she did exactly as he'd asked, and it was only a matter of seconds before she was out of the store.

Taking one last look around, and shaking his head, Rocco followed close on her heels. The sooner he got Caite out of this dangerous part of the city and back to her apartment, the better. He had a ton of questions for her, but not until they were safe. He wanted to know what the fuck was going on more than he wanted his next breath, but he'd wait. Her safety came first. Period.

CHAPTER SIX

Caite breathed a sigh of relief when the taxi turned into her apartment complex next to the base. There had been several times when she hadn't thought she was going to make it back in one piece.

But looking at Rocco, she couldn't be sorry that she'd taken the risk. He looked awful, but as she'd found was typical of a lot of soldiers and sailors, not one complaint had left his mouth. His eye was practically swollen shut and the bruises on his face were alarming.

He hadn't had any problem helping her out the window back at the grocery store, but he'd shifted in his seat several times. If his face looked as bad as it did, she assumed the rest of him was probably also bruised as well. His hair was disheveled, and if she'd run into him looking the way he did now, she'd probably have walked quickly in the other direction.

The taxi came to a stop and Caite climbed out and

waited for Rocco to do the same. They'd made it out of the area where Mr. Bitoo's store was located by the skin of their teeth. A group of men had followed them almost from the second they'd appeared back on the street. Rocco had made her walk at a fast clip for over a mile. The men behind them calling out taunts and threats the entire way.

They'd said things in Arabic, then English, and even some French. Rocco didn't react in any way. He behaved as if he couldn't even hear them. But the iron grip he had on her arm belied his relaxed outward appearance. Every muscle in his body had been tense, and at one point, he'd whispered for her to run if anything happened.

As if. She hadn't risked her life to find and save him, only for Rocco to get knifed or shot on the street. No. If the men had made a move, she'd been ready to do what she could to help.

But in the end, it hadn't been necessary to do anything. A taxi happened to drive by right when things were getting ugly. Rocco had literally stepped in front of the car, forcing it to stop or run him over. It really wasn't a surprise that the driver had done as Rocco ordered and stayed put until they could both get inside. He was big, beat all to hell, and pissed off.

Rocco had stuffed Caite inside and hadn't even needed to tell the driver to floor it. The second the door was shut, they took off, leaving the group of men yelling and shaking their fists behind them.

Caite hoped Ace and Gumby had also been able to get a taxi, but when she'd opened her mouth to ask Rocco what he thought the odds were that his friends were okay, he'd shaken his head and motioned to the driver. Understanding that he didn't want her to say anything that could be overheard, she'd bitten her lip and tried to control her breathing.

Rocco had taken her hand in both of his and held it tightly the entire trip back south toward the base.

The second they exited the taxi, it took off, heading back toward the center of Manama.

He walked her to a lighted area near the doors that led into the apartment complex then turned to face her. "I don't have a lot of time, Caite, but I need to know how you found us."

Taking a deep breath, she told him the CliffsNotes version.

When she was done, Rocco frowned. "I can't believe you found us with so little information."

Caite rubbed her temple wearily. "I can't remember absolutely everything they said now. I was freaked out and scared that they'd realize I could understand what they were saying. It's all kind of a blur, if I'm being honest. I just remember the bits and pieces I told you. Then I looked up their conference paperwork and found the address of the store. It was really luck more than anything else."

"Are you sure you don't remember anything else?" Rocco asked.

Caite frowned. She was so overwhelmed after everything that had happened. It felt like it was weeks ago that she'd heard the brothers talking. She shook her head.

"Okay, don't worry. I'm sure if you remember something important later, you'll let me know, right?"

"Absolutely." Caite wasn't sure there was anything more to remember. And she really just wanted to forget about it altogether at this point. "Do you want to come up?" she asked, changing the subject.

He looked down at her with an expression she couldn't interpret. On the one hand, she knew he had stuff he needed to do...but she didn't want him to go yet.

"I wish I could."

Caite grimaced. "Right." She tried to take a step back but he tightened his hold on the hand he hadn't let go of for the last twenty minutes.

"Stop," he ordered.

She froze.

"There's nothing I want more than to come up to your apartment and spend time with you. If I could get away with it, I'd let you make me a huge sandwich, because I'm starving after eating the shit that was down in that cellar. I'd sit on your couch and you'd tell me every second of every *minute* that passed since I didn't show up for our date. After I wrung a promise from you that you'd never, ever, *ever* do something that foolhardy and dangerous again, I'd follow you into your bathroom, strip you naked, and make sure you're clean from head to toe. Then I'd take you to bed and show you exactly how proud and in awe of you I am, by making love to you for the rest of the night."

Caite stared up at him with huge eyes. Her heart was beating out of control and she shifted on her feet.

She wanted that. Every single thing he'd said.

She'd never had a one-night stand before, and instead of his words being creepy and too forward, after what they'd been through and what she'd done for him, they sounded exactly right. She wanted to feel him inside her, to know in the most carnal way possible that he was alive and well.

Tonight had been too close. She knew as well as anyone that they'd been lucky. If she didn't know French, or if she hadn't been paying attention, or if someone had stopped her, or if she didn't have an abaya to wear...so many things could've gone wrong. But they hadn't. And she wanted to reaffirm that they were both alive and well in the most basic way possible. Sex.

"But I can't."

His words jolted her out of the erotic fantasy she'd already begun to weave in her head of the two of them rolling around naked on her bed. Caite wanted to protest. To tell him that he could. That she needed him. But instead, she licked her lips and waited for him to continue.

"Ace and Gumby are expecting me. We need to get those tablets to the authorities and talk to our commander and tell him what happened. We'll have to be involved in meetings with the local authorities and give them our statements. There are still four tablets missing, the brothers will have to be rounded up and questioned. There's a million and one things that have to be done... and not one of those feels like it's more important than you right now. I want you to know that. But I don't have a choice. I have to do what I came here to do."

"Will I have to testify or talk to someone?" she asked.

Rocco shook his head. "No. You're done. You're out of this. I don't want *anyone* knowing you had anything to do with this. Not because I'm not proud as fuck, but because I want you safe. You'll be here for another eight months, at least. The last thing I want is someone targeting you for retribution."

Caite hadn't even thought about that. It was extremely frightening. She nodded and asked, "How will you say you got out of the cellar?"

"We'll just say it took us a while to overcome our injuries enough to figure out a plan to reach the hatch, and that it opened easily when we finally managed it."

Caite wasn't sure Commander Horner would believe that, but she didn't contradict Rocco.

"Are you okay?" he asked softly.

"Yeah. You?"

"I'm alive, and that's more than I thought would happen when that hatch opened," he said dryly. "It's hard to surprise a Navy SEAL, Caite, and tonight, you surprised the hell out of all three of us."

"I'm sorry." It was the first time he'd admitted to being a SEAL.

"Don't be," he told her immediately. He brought her hand up to his lips. "I'll never forget what you did for us. For *me*."

It sounded like he was saying goodbye, and that sucked.

"So this is it?" she couldn't help but ask.

"It?"

"Goodbye?"

"For now," he said sadly. "We'll be busy with meetings and briefings, and then we'll be heading back home to the States and the rest of our team."

"Oh."

"But that doesn't mean that when you get home, I wouldn't like to meet up. Have a drink. Take you out for that dinner we didn't get to last night." His words were hesitant, as if he wasn't sure she'd agree.

"I'd like that," Caite said immediately.

"I'll give you my number," Rocco said. "But only if you promise to use it. Don't make me use my connections to hunt you down," he teased.

"You think you'd be able to find me?" she asked.

"Absolutely. If you give me the slightest bit of encouragement, *ma petite fée*, you won't be able to get rid of me."

"You don't even know me," she protested, even though she loved hearing that.

"The hell I don't," he retorted. "I know all I need to know in order to be absolutely certain I want to see you again. That I want to take you out. That I want to see where things between us might go...and I'm not just talking sexually. I have no doubt that in *that* area, we'll be combustible."

She blushed. "You can't know that."

"*Ma petite fée*, every time I get near you, I get more excited simply holding your hand than I can ever remember feeling with any woman in the past. And if those two short kisses were any indication, we're not going to have any problems in bed."

He was right. She'd felt the same way; it was part of the reason she'd been so disappointed and hurt when he hadn't shown up on Friday after work.

"If I give you my number, will you remember it?" he asked.

She nodded.

He recited his phone number, and made her say it back several times before he was sure she'd remember it. "Text me the second you land back in San Diego," Rocco ordered. "I'm going to be counting down the days."

"You'll..." Her voice trailed off.

"What? You can ask me anything."

"I wasn't going to ask you a question. I was just going to tell you to be careful. I guessed you were a

SEAL before you told me tonight, and I know what you guys do isn't exactly safe."

"It's usually a lot more boring than what happened here," he told her.

"Uh-huh," she said skeptically.

"I'll be careful," he said. "I've got this gal I want to take out when she gets back to San Diego," he said quietly.

She blushed harder.

"And I want you to meet the rest of my team."

"Why?"

"Why?"

"Yeah."

"Because I have no doubt they're going to love you as much as Gumby and Ace do."

She grinned. "How can they love me? I've known them for like two-point-three seconds."

Rocco chuckled. "They know all the important things about you. That when push came to shove, you overcame your fears and did what had to be done. It wasn't smart, you could've been killed, but you did it anyway. We wouldn't have thought less of you if you hadn't done anything, but the fact that you *did* solidified your place in our hearts and minds. In case you somehow managed to hit your head and get a concussion on the way home that I didn't notice, and I forgot...you saved all three of our lives tonight. We were stuck down in that cellar with no way out. Like you said, the Bitoos were going to come back and kill us.

Bubba, Rex, and Phantom are gonna bend over backward to make sure you understand how much you're appreciated."

"Hmmm, well, I'm kind of a one-guy-at-a-time girl," she teased, uncomfortable with his praise. She'd been terrified tonight. But she wouldn't have been able to live with herself if she'd done nothing.

Rocco grinned. "Damn straight you are." He looked at his watch. "I really need to go."

"Right." Caite tried to take another step back, but once again he wouldn't release her hand.

"A kiss for the road?" he asked.

It should've sounded corny, but it didn't. Her mouth suddenly dry, Caite nodded.

Rocco took a step toward her and wrapped one arm around her waist and pulled her into him so they were plastered together. The other hand went to the back of her head. She wished her hair was free so she could feel his fingers tangled in the strands, but she forgot all about the hijab she was still wearing when his head lowered.

The hair of his beard tickled her skin for a moment, just like it had the last two times he'd kissed her, making her shiver in anticipation.

His lips were warm against her own, and she immediately opened for him. His tongue swept inside her mouth, and she closed her eyes and gave herself over.

Rocco didn't disappoint; he took control of the kiss, and Caite swore she saw stars.

How long they kissed, she had no idea, but eventually he pulled back. He didn't move far though. "Damn, I hate my job sometimes."

His words made Caite inhale sharply. He didn't hate his job when it almost killed him, but he hated it when he had to stop kissing her? Holy shit. She didn't know what to say to that. It was the most amazing compliment she'd ever received. Not that she'd received a ton of them, but this one still took the cake.

"Be safe, Caite," he ordered. "Bahrain is a fairly safe city, unless you get yourself mixed up in the middle of a smuggling ring and start sneaking around in the dark of night in the worst areas of Manama."

She gave him a small smile. "I think my days of trying to be a superhero are over."

"Damn straight," he agreed, then leaned down and kissed her once more. It wasn't as deep or intense as their previous kiss, but it wasn't a mere peck on the lips either.

"You feel warm," he observed when he finally pulled away.

"*You* try wearing this getup and running around in this heat and see how you feel," Caite told him.

Instead of smiling, he frowned. "Don't get heat-stroke," he said. "Make sure you drink a ton of water when you go upstairs and take a long cool shower. If you feel lightheaded or dizzy, go to the clinic."

"I will," she reassured him.

Taking a deep breath, Rocco nodded, then backed

away from her. They held hands until the last possible second.

"Be safe," Caite told him again.

"You too."

"See you in a few months."

"Absolutely."

They stood outside her apartment staring at each other for a long moment before he finally said, "You need to turn around and go inside."

"I know."

"Please, *ma petite fée*. I can't leave until you do." Rocco's tone sounded tortured.

She'd never forget how his nickname for her sounded on his lips. She nodded, and turned her back on him, and headed for the front door of her apartment complex. She opened the door and stepped inside, turning to look back one more time.

He was gone.

CHAPTER SEVEN

The next few days at work were uneventful. Caite kept her eyes peeled for any sighting of Rocco, Ace, or Gumby, but never saw them. Even Commander Horner had been absent for the last couple days. She'd finally succumbed to her curiosity and checked the computer to see if the SEALs were still on base.

To her disappointment, they weren't. They'd checked out on Tuesday.

Sighing, she turned her attention back to the final report on the Archaeology and Museums Conference. She was responsible for typing up the report for Joshua to present to his superiors. Of course, work held no appeal for her at the moment. But neither did sitting in her apartment, wishing she was hanging out with Rocco.

"Ms. McCallan, can I see you in my office please?"

her boss asked, scaring the crap out Caite because she'd been daydreaming.

"Of course," she said and pushed back her chair.

She followed Joshua into his office and sat on the edge of the chair in front of his desk.

He didn't leave her wondering what was going on. He immediately began speaking. "It's come to my attention that you went off base this past weekend wearing an abaya and a hijab. Is that true?"

Caite's mouth opened and closed and she had no idea what to say.

"And don't lie," Joshua said darkly, with a hint of glee.

She clenched her teeth and pressed her lips together as she tried to figure out what to say that wouldn't get her in trouble and would keep the details about the SEALs under wraps.

"On second thought," Joshua said, holding up his hand, "I don't want to hear your excuses. You know the rules. You know wearing the traditional Bahraini garb is against the navy's regulations. You signed an acknowledgement when you took this job."

"I know, but—"

"No buts," Joshua interrupted. "Either you did or you didn't. Which is it?"

Feeling sick inside, but knowing she couldn't lie, Caite said, "I did. But—"

"You're fired," her boss said with a small smirk. "I knew you couldn't handle this job. The only thing keeping me from calling security and having them escort you from the premises is the fact that you didn't lie about it. I have security video from your apartment showing you leaving wearing the clothing, and then coming back in the middle of the night and making out with someone right outside the building. Conduct unbecoming," he said smugly.

Caite wanted to protest. Wanted to say that since she wasn't actually *in* the navy, it wasn't conduct unbecoming because that only pertained to officers. Besides, she wasn't even on the base when she'd kissed Rocco. But it was obvious Joshua had been looking for any reason to fire her.

And she *had* worn the abaya and hijab when she'd known it was prohibited. Though it had been for a good reason. A reason there was no way she was giving to Joshua. He'd wanted to hire his friend since the minute she'd stepped foot in the building, and now he'd get his chance.

"I've talked to the commander, and because you've been a satisfactory employee, your expenses to get home will be paid for. You have a flight the day after tomorrow. I suggest you pack up your stuff from your desk—and leave all of the electronics you've been issued."

Caite stared at Joshua in disbelief. The day after tomorrow? He wasn't messing around.

She stood up without a word and turned for the door. She should fight for her job, but she was sick of doing all the work and having Joshua take credit for it. She was sick of the heat. She missed her mom and, frankly, she was homesick.

"Oh, and Caite?" Joshua said when she'd reached the door.

She turned back to look at him.

"Make sure the conference report has been sent to me before you leave."

Caite didn't bother responding, leaving his office without a word.

Fuck him. She wasn't sending him shit. Maybe he should've actually stuck around and attended the damn conference he'd been responsible for.

She went back to her desk, not making eye contact with anyone, and sat. She woke her computer and promptly deleted the Word file she'd just saved. Then she went into her trash folder and deleted it from there too. It wouldn't keep a computer expert from finding it in the depths of the machine, but it would at least make Joshua sweat for a while.

She packed up the few personal odds and ends she'd brought with her and left, leaving her work cell behind.

The security officer stopped her before she left the building. "I'm sorry, Caite, but I have to take your badge."

It was the last straw. Tears filled her eyes as she unclipped the DOD employee badge from her shirt and handed it over.

"If it's any consolation, everyone knows Joshua's a douche," he said sympathetically.

"Thanks. Take care of yourself."

"You too, Caite."

She nodded and left the building without looking back.

Two days later, Caite sat in a middle seat on a crowded plane headed back to California. She hadn't had time to think about much of anything other than packing and figuring out who to call to get what little amount of stuff she'd brought to Bahrain shipped back home. She'd called her mom and cried, then took a deep breath and got on with figuring out the rest of her life. She needed a place to live, a car, a job, and to get her stuff out of storage.

But now, settled on the plane, she finally had time to think about what happened.

Joshua had said there was surveillance footage from outside her apartment. Was he telling the truth? It made sense, security cameras were a normal part of life now...but how had he gotten ahold of the tapes? And why? It made no sense.

But in all honesty, he'd done her a favor. Her jaunt into the bowels of Manama had done what the four months before hadn't been able to. It had made her more than ready to go home. The only thing she wasn't happy about was the fact that any chance of getting another government contractor job was probably shot to hell. She knew Joshua wouldn't give her a good recommendation, and why would anyone else hire someone who had been fired?

She sighed.

Now she'd have to start all over after years with the military. Luckily, she'd saved everything she'd made while overseas beyond a portion to pay off some debt, so she had a pretty good number in her savings account. But soon, she'd be right back in the same position that had forced her to take the job in the first place.

Deciding that there was absolutely nothing she could do about it, Caite, put her head back and tried to ignore the cranky child kicking the back of her seat and the large, somewhat smelly man snoring next to her.

"Fired?" Rocco said incredulously. "What the hell for?"

"For wearing an abaya and hijab out in public," Tex said.

Rocco had been sitting at home watching television when his phone rang. He'd been surprised to hear the former SEAL on the other end of the line—and now he was furious.

"That's bullshit!" he exclaimed.

"Yup. But I'm wondering if there wasn't another reason," Tex said calmly.

Rocco stilled. "Like?"

"Like it was a pretty big coincidence that she was fired right after you and the others left the country. It's almost as if someone knew she had something to do with those tablets being found and that big smuggling bust."

"Shit," Rocco swore. "Have the Bitoo brothers said who their contact was?"

"No, because they're still in the wind," Tex said. "The authorities, both naval and Bahraini, haven't been able to find them."

"Well shit. It would make things a whole lot easier if someone got off their ass and found them...and *made them* give up their contact," Rocco said.

"Yes, it would," Tex said. "Anyway, rumor has it that four tablets arrived safe and sound here in the States," Tex said.

Rocco shook his head. It was scary the shit Tex knew. "Do you know who has them?"

"I know where they entered the country and I know who they were *supposed* to go to, but I guarantee that any raids on the man's property would turn up nothing. He isn't an idiot. His lawyer has already gotten involved. They'll never find those tablets. They're gone. Poof. Disappeared."

"What aren't you telling me?" Rocco asked. As far as he was concerned, he didn't care about the damn tablets. Yes, they were a part of history, but he'd done his job by getting some of them back. Now it was up to the Iraqi government to protect the six they'd recovered.

"Someone lost a lot of money in that deal," Tex said. "I'm sure they aren't happy. And shit rolls downhill, if you know what I mean. If the boss isn't happy, neither is the man under him, or under him, or under *him*."

"You think someone found out about Caite's involvement in getting the tablets back and had her fired."

"I think that you need to watch your six," Tex said. "Someone with some serious money was behind this. I doubt he'll get his own hands dirty, but he might take out his loss on someone else, who might want revenge on the person under him, and so on. I don't know how far down you might fall in that revenge list, but it's possible it could happen."

"And Caite?"

"Maybe her being fired *was* the revenge on her. But maybe it wasn't. All I'm saying is that whatever's going on over there in Bahrain stinks. Commander Horner is trying to shut this shit down, but in the meantime, there are an awful lot of people with their hands in the pie."

As Tex said, it *was* a bit too much of a coincidence that Caite was fired right after the tablets were returned to the Iraqi officials. Yes, she'd broken protocol, but she either hadn't told anyone why or, as Tex suggested, someone wanted her out of the way regardless.

Rocco had no doubt that Caite had kept her mouth

shut. There was no way she'd tell anyone about what had happened. It simply wasn't her way.

"I'll keep my eye on her," Rocco told Tex.

"I had a feeling you would," the other man said. "Now, have you seen Wolf or the others lately?"

"Saw the entire team when we got back. I wanted to let them know that the training we did on how to get out of deep places was invaluable on this mission."

"Good. My wife has been bugging me to get back out there. Maybe I'll pack up the fam and take a visit."

"I'm sure everyone would like that," Rocco told Tex. "Hey, one more question before you go."

"Anything."

"Do you have any contact information for Caite yet? I gave her my number but with everything that happened, I have a feeling she'll feel weird about using it."

"I looked her up before I called you, and there's nothing yet. The only thing I have is the address of the storage unit she's been using. She hasn't signed a lease yet or gotten a cell phone."

"Okay. Will you let me know when you get either?"

"Already made a note," Tex reassured him.

"'Preciate it."

"Anytime. Later."

"Later."

Rocco hung up and stared blankly at the television. He wasn't happy that Caite had gotten fired because of him. Oh, she probably wouldn't look at it that way, but he knew that was the case.

He wanted to talk to her. To make sure she was all right. To touch base. He also couldn't stop thinking about what Tex had said. Yes, they'd recovered the tablets, and the remaining ones that had been smuggled out of Bahrain technically weren't his issue anymore. It was up to Customs to investigate and catch those responsible.

But the fact that Commander Horner thought he had a mole in his department, and now Caite had been fired, wouldn't leave his mind. Maybe they weren't related. But what if they were? A top-level smuggler wouldn't give a shit about a DOD secretary. But, like Tex inferred, someone down the line might, especially if he or she had gotten in deep shit for the ruined operation.

He hoped Caite would call, but even if she didn't, she'd still be hearing from him. He'd give her a bit of time to get settled, but if she didn't reach out to him, he'd get her information from Tex and "happen" to run into her. He'd make sure she knew that he still wanted to go on that date he'd promised.

———————

"I told you to take care of her," the man bit out the second his contact in Bahrain answered.

"I did!"

"Then why is she currently in San Diego looking for an apartment and a job?"

There was silence on the other end of the secure line for a beat before the younger man said, "You wanted me to *kill* her?"

Controlling his ire, the man sitting in his office on the naval base in San Diego said, "That's what 'take care of her' means."

"How was I supposed to know that? Dude, I'm a computer geek. I wouldn't know the first thing about offing someone! I hacked into the security cameras around her apartment and got that video of her wearing those Arabic clothes. I sent the footage to her boss with an anonymous note. He fired her the next day. Problem solved."

"The problem is *not* solved!" the man said impatiently. "She overheard those idiots say my name. She knows who I am!"

"Wouldn't she have said something by now if she did?"

"Maybe, maybe not, but I can't take that chance. I've spent my life working to get to where I am and no twenty-something bimbo is going to take that away from me. I've got at least five more shipments in the works and they'll set me up for life. If you were confused about what my instructions meant, you should've asked for clarification," the man said.

"But I wasn't confused," the guy retorted. "I thought you wanted her fired."

"Goddamn incompetent fools," the older man mumbled under his breath. Then louder, he said, "You know nothing. If you so much as fart in my direction, you'll regret it."

Clearly understanding he could be in big trouble, the twenty-four-year-old kid, just out of college, almost fell over himself reassuring the man on the other end of the line. "Yes, Sir. I mean, of course not, Sir. I'd never say a word. I need this job. My girlfriend is expecting a ring and I need the money. I'll keep my mouth shut. Yes, Sir."

"See that you do—or your girlfriend will be mourning the death of her almost-fiancé." He hung up before the punk could say anything else. He tucked the untraceable throwaway phone deep into his bag and made a mental note to get rid of it on his way home that evening.

The naval officer leaned back in his chair and linked his hands behind his head. His uniform was perfectly pressed. Not one medal on his chest was out of place. He looked as aboveboard as a career officer could. He enjoyed his work; it was too bad the pay was so shitty.

And now he had to deal with Caite McCallan. He'd had another connection in Bahrain interrogate the idiot brothers before the authorities could get to them. They'd admitted to talking about the plan to get rid of the SEALs at a conference they'd attended, but had sworn no one could understand them.

Of course, they hadn't realized the damn secretary

had majored in French in college. She'd heard every word, and had obviously used her own connections to get the SEALs rescued—along with six of the ten tablets he'd promised to a collector in Washington, D.C. He was going to be paying for that fuckup for a long time.

The secretary had heard his name. She had to die. It was that simple.

Things would've been easier if the punk kid had done what he'd asked while she was still in Bahrain. It would've been easy to have her snatched off the street and killed. Everyone would've thought it was a random attack. But now she was back in the States and things were trickier.

But that didn't change the fact that she had to die. She knew too much. Even if he suspected she didn't yet realize it.

The man sat up and rested his elbows on the desk in front of him. He steepled his fingers as he thought about what his next steps should be.

"Sir?" his secretary said through the intercom on his phone.

He pushed a button and replied, "Yes?"

"You said to let you know when your two o'clock appointment arrived. He's here."

"Thank you. Send him in."

He didn't have time at the moment to solve the problem of Caite McCallan, but he would. The bitch had to go. Permanently. It was the only way he'd be safe.

CHAPTER EIGHT

"Seriously, Caite?" her mom asked with a hint of irritation in her voice.

"Yeah, Mom. I need a job, and for the moment, this is what I can get."

"But a convenience store? That's about the most dangerous job you could've gotten! I watch the ID Channel. People who work in those places die in shootouts and robberies every day!"

Caite wanted to laugh, but couldn't. "Mom, you need to stop watching those shows. Pretty soon you aren't going to want to leave the house. It's okay. The store is in a good part of San Diego and it's close to my new apartment. It'll be fine."

"I don't like it."

To be honest, Caite didn't like it much either. But she was desperate. She needed a job, and being a cashier would bring in some much-needed cash while she looked for something more appropriate for her education and background. She'd already given herself a week and a half to find a secretarial position after getting back from overseas and finding an apartment, and when she hadn't, she'd made the decision to take any job she could get in the meantime.

"It's only temporary," she tried to reassure her mom. "Once I find another admin job, I'll quit."

Her mother sighed. "You know if you need money, all you have to do is ask your father and me. We're happy to help out."

Caite knew as much, but the last thing she wanted was to be *that* daughter. The one who sponged off her folks. "Thanks, Mom. I appreciate it. For now, I'm okay."

"I just worry about you."

"I know. I love you. I gotta get going, I'm almost home."

"You shouldn't talk on the phone while you're walking," her mom scolded. "You should be paying attention to your surroundings."

"I am."

"Fine. I'm only letting you go so you can be more aware of what's going on around you."

"Okay."

"I love you, sweetie."

"I love you too, Mom. Say hi to Dad and tell him not to work so hard."

The older woman chuckled. "Yeah, right. Bye."

"Bye."

Caite clicked off the cheap cell phone she'd picked up at the store the night before and stuck it in her purse. She continued walking down the street toward her apartment. She'd lucked out and gotten a studio not too far from where her old apartment had been. She already knew the bus routes and, on a whim, she'd stopped into the twenty-four-hour convenience store and inquired about a job.

She'd been hired on the spot. She'd told the manager that she couldn't work the night shift, making up a story about a nonexistent kid she had to be home for, and he'd agreed. Caite felt bad about lying, but she wasn't an idiot. She watched many of the same shows her mom did. She knew the statistics, and knew that nothing good happened in convenience stores in the middle of the night.

She was putting off buying a car for the time being, wanting to stretch the money in her savings account as far as possible. While she might've paid off most of her credit cards, she still had student loans, and now rent and other living expenses.

The sidewalk was cracked and broken and Caite was looking down, making sure not to trip over any of the worst spots. She passed the bus stop outside her apartment and made her way toward her building. The doors to the individual apartments in this complex were on the outside, which she wasn't thrilled about, but she couldn't afford to be picky.

"When you find a real job, you can move," she said to herself as she headed toward the stairway that led up to the second floor, where apartment three was located.

"You didn't text me," a deep voice said, and Caite jerked in surprise.

She looked up and saw Rocco leaning against a royal-blue four-door car.

At first she was excited to see him—but then she remembered why she hadn't gotten ahold of him.

Embarrassment.

Rocco pushed off the car and walked toward her. When he got close, his eyes went from her face down to her feet, then back up again. "Are you okay?" he asked softly.

Caite nodded. Then her brows furrowed and she asked, "How did you find me?"

"I knew you'd been canned, and when you didn't get in touch with me, I used my connections to track you down." He looked up at the apartment then back down at her. "You need help getting your stuff from the storage unit?"

Caite should've been pissed at how much he knew, especially after being fired because someone had been super nosy, but this was Rocco. She couldn't be pissed.

"I wasn't going to bother," she told him honestly. "I've got an air mattress and my stuff from my apartment in Bahrain. I'll be okay until I can find a new place to live. I didn't want to go through the hassle of moving everything in and having to move it all out again."

Rocco shook his head. "No way are you gonna be sleeping on the fucking floor," he said, more to himself than her. Then he pulled out a phone and clicked on something and brought it up to his ear.

"What are you—"

"Hey, Bubba, it's Rocco. I need some help this afternoon...Caite's stuff is still in a storage locker over on One Hundred and Third Street. She hasn't gotten around to moving it to her new place... Awesome. I'd appreciate it. An hour sounds great. See you then."

"Rocco, no. I'm fine, I don't need—"

"It's already done, *ma petite fée*. The team is headed over to your storage unit right now to get your stuff. Can you call and tell the place it's okay to cut off your lock, and that the guys are authorized to remove your things?"

Caite crossed her arms over her chest and glared at Rocco.

He grinned, but quickly got serious. He raised a hand and tucked a piece of hair behind her ear. "Caite, you need your stuff. It's not a big deal for us to help you. We can get all your shit moved in before it gets dark. Besides, it would save you the monthly payment at the storage place."

He was right, but it still felt weird. "I just..." Her voice trailed off. She didn't know what she wanted to say.

"I'm sorry you were fired," Rocco said softly. "You

didn't deserve that. You could've fought it. Told them why you were wearing the abaya and what happened."

She immediately shook her head. "No. I didn't want to get you guys in trouble."

"Hon, we wouldn't have gotten in trouble. We were in the country on an official mission."

"I know, but you said you didn't want me involved."

"For your *own* safety," he rebutted. "If I knew you were going to get fired, I would've made sure you were in the clear. I would've at least told Commander Horner who you were. He knows there was a woman involved who saved our lives, we made that clear, but he respected my wish to keep it off the record. I'm so sorry, *ma petite fée*."

Caite shrugged. "It's okay. I hated my boss, and honestly, after that night, I didn't feel safe at all. I feel safer walking on the street here than I did there."

"Let us help," he implored.

Out of arguments, Caite finally nodded.

"Thank you. Now, invite me up."

That was the last thing she wanted. She wasn't quite embarrassed about her apartment, but she wasn't exactly ready to entertain anyone either. "We could go to lunch or something while we wait for your friends."

Rocco shook his head. "Nope. I want to hear about what you've been doing since you've been back. Have you found a job? Can I help in any way?"

"We can talk at lunch," Caite said hopefully.

Rocco eyed her critically. "Why don't you want me

in your apartment? Have you changed your mind about going out with me?"

He took a step away from her, and Caite immediately felt bad that he'd thought that even for a moment. "No!" she blurted.

"Then what is it?"

"I'm embarrassed, okay?" she said softly. "I don't really have furniture and there's nothing on the walls. I haven't had time to unpack much of anything yet, and I just...it's *embarrassing*."

"Caite, you just got back into the country. And I'd never think badly of you because of the way your apartment looks. Unless it's buried in trash or something." He grinned.

She shook her head. "No, it's clean. It's just...sparse."

"I can deal with sparse. Come on." Rocco reached out and took her hand in his, and Caite was immediately thrown back to Bahrain, when he'd done the same thing. It felt good...and right.

He led the way up the stairs, straight to her apartment, and she realized that he really *had* gotten information from someone about her. That should've worried her, but it didn't. She felt safe with Rocco. She'd saved his life, and somehow that bound them together closer than anything else could've.

He waited while she pulled the key out of her pocket and unlocked the apartment door. He held it open for her and followed her in. Caite let him step past her and watched his reaction to her place while he looked around.

His facial expression didn't change as his head swiveled from the kitchen to the living area. The only piece of furniture she had was one of those low patio chairs. It had a crack in the seat, but it was better than sitting on the floor.

"Do you want something to drink?" she asked. She'd been to the grocery store and stocked up, at least.

Rocco turned back to her and didn't say anything for a long moment before shaking his head. "I'm good."

Several uncomfortable seconds went by. "Well? Go ahead, say something. I know you're dying to."

"About your apartment?" he asked.

She nodded.

He moved then. Came toward her so fast, she took a couple involuntary steps back, which put her up against the wall just inside the apartment. Rocco leaned his forearms on the wall near her head and hovered over her. She raised her hands and put them on his chest, not pushing him away, exactly, just resting them there.

"You want to know what I think about your apartment?"

Caite swallowed hard and nodded.

"I hate it."

She didn't have a comeback for that. She'd asked. But he didn't give her a chance to say anything, anyway.

"I hate that all you've got in here is a fucking chair that someone threw away. The place lacks any kind of personality, and that's just wrong, because you've got personality oozing from your every pore. I imagine you living in a place surrounded by ordered chaos. Pictures, flowers, TV on with some home-renovation show, fluffy pillows on the couch. But I'm gonna do my best to give that back to you, *ma petite fée*. We'll move your stuff in then see what else you need. We'll ask our friends for help. Wolf and his team and their women will set you up. We'll fix this."

Caite's throat closed with unshed tears. He was exactly right. Empty, the apartment was depressing and even scary. She'd slept there for the last week and a half, scared out of her mind. Every little noise made her jump, and she'd even placed the crappy plastic chair in front of her door, hoping it would slow someone down if they managed to break in.

"I'm gonna add a deadbolt to your door as well. This isn't the worst area, but it's not the best either. I don't like the fact that your door opens to the outside, but I get this is what you can afford right now. I'll help make you feel safe. Whatever you need, I'll make sure you have it. Okay?"

Caite nodded. She would appreciate an extra lock on the door more than a television or dining room table.

"So...have you found a job?" he asked, not moving away from her.

Caite wanted to tell him to step back, but another part of her liked having him this close. "Yeah. Just today, as a matter of fact."

"That's great news. Where?"

She knew that question was coming. "The convenience store down the street." He frowned, and she hurried on. "I know, I know, but it was what I could get at the moment. I'm still looking for something in my field, but there aren't too many positions for French language majors, and I'm pretty sure me getting a job on the naval base is out, considering I was fired and kicked out of Bahrain. But administrative assistants are a dime a dozen. I'll find something soon, I'm sure."

Rocco didn't say anything, but Caite watched the muscle in his jaw flex. "At least tell me you aren't working nights."

"I'm not working nights," she said immediately. "I lied and told the manager I had a kid and had to be home every afternoon to get him off the bus."

Rocco's lips quirked up at that. "At least that's somethin'," he said after a beat. Then he stood up straight and Caite let her arms fall to her sides. He gently grasped her elbow. "Come on, let's see what you've got to eat in this place," he said. "The guys'll be here before too long."

He pulled her over to her kitchen and gestured for her to hop up on the counter. She did, and then watched as he opened her refrigerator and bent over. Caite couldn't help but look at his ass. Rocco was wearing a pair of worn blue jeans that molded to every inch of his amazing form. She'd thought he looked good in his khakis, and the black pants he'd been wearing that night in Bahrain, but there was nothing like a man in a tight-fitting pair of jeans.

"Are you checking out my ass?" he asked, looking over his shoulder, the humor easy to hear in his tone.

"Yup," Caite told him even as she blushed.

"Right. Then carry on," Rocco quipped and turned back to investigate the fridge.

It had taken everything in Rocco to not demand that Caite quit her new job right then and there. A convenience store? For fuck's sake, that was the least safe job he could imagine anyone having, let alone *Caite*.

But he was trying not to be a douchebag. They technically weren't even dating, as he hadn't managed to take her on a single date yet.

And her apartment made him incredibly sad. He knew she was embarrassed by her lack of things, but he didn't give a shit about that. She deserved everything. He also knew offering her money wouldn't go over well, and he wouldn't know where to start when it came to shopping for a woman. But...Caroline, Alabama, and the other wives of Wolf's SEAL team would. The second they heard about her circumstances, they'd bend over backward to make sure she was set up.

At least her refrigerator and cabinets were full of food. He was thankful for that. He made them each a sandwich, and then learned more about her meeting with her boss, when she'd been fired, and about how she'd basically been whisked out of the country faster than anyone he'd ever heard of before. He listened as she talked about her parents and how great they were. Her mom had offered to drive down from the San Francisco area to help her get settled, but Caite had refused.

She had no brothers or sisters, and ironically, both her parents were only children as well, so she had no aunts or uncles to rely on either. No cousins.

Rocco was anxious for the rest of his teammates to meet her. He knew without a doubt that they'd all take to her as well as he had. Well, maybe not *quite* as well as he had.

A knock sounded on the door and Rocco said, "Stay put. I'll get it." They were both sitting on the counter because there'd been no other place to eat their lunch. Caite nodded, and he felt her eyes on him as he hopped down and headed for the front door.

He liked the way she watched him.

Rocco wasn't an idiot. He knew he was good-looking. But it had been a long time since he'd cared. His life had been too busy with training and missions. And that was it. He'd long since gotten tired of the bar scene and the dating game. He was too old for that shit anyway. Thirty-five wasn't exactly ancient, but hanging around the twenty-something newbies at the bar made him feel like an old man. Besides, getting to know Wolf and the others, with their growing families, had made him yearn for something he couldn't even put into words.

It was more than simply having a wife and kids. Hell, he could go out and marry the first woman who'd have him, if that's all he wanted. No, he wanted the *connection* the others had. He wanted to know down to the marrow of his bones that he was loved. Wanted to give that same love to someone else.

He didn't know if Caite was that person or not, but he felt a hell of a lot more for her than any other woman he'd met in the last five years or so. It didn't hurt that she was selfless, brave, and that she'd literally put her career on the line for him, Ace, and Gumby.

Taking a look through the peephole, and seeing his teammates on the other side of the door, Rocco opened it. "Hey."

"Hey."

"Yo."

"Howdy."

The other two men just gave him chin lifts.

"Everything go okay at the storage facility?" Rocco asked.

"Yeah. No issues," Rex said as he entered the apartment.

The others filed in, and Rocco headed straight for Caite, who was now standing next to the counter in the kitchen, looking uncertain. He reached for her hand, and something inside him settled when she immediately grabbed it.

He pulled her out into the living room where his team waited. "Caite, I want you to meet the best set of friends and teammates a man could have. You know Gumby and Ace." He nodded to the two men.

"Yeah. Hi," Caite said softly. The men looked a hell of a lot better than the last time she'd seen them. Like Rocco, they no longer had any bruises on their faces, and they'd even trimmed their beards.

Gumby stepped forward and pulled her into a tight embrace. She had to let go of Rocco's hand or have her arm twisted behind her.

"Move over, my turn," Ace insisted. The second Gumby let go of her, Ace pulled her close.

Gumby kept his hand on her upper arm, even as Ace hugged her, and said, "Thank you, Caite. Seriously."

"It wasn't a big deal," she mumbled.

"Not a big deal?" Bubba said, then pulled Ace back and put his hands on Caite's shoulders. "You kept my friends from being murdered. It's *definitely* a big deal."

"Guys," Rocco warned, but they ignored him.

He didn't like Bubba's hands on Caite. He was the youngest of their crew at thirty-one—and the guy most women seemed to gravitate toward. He was the only one of their group who didn't have a beard, and Rocco had seen women literally throw themselves at him when they'd had too much to drink. The last thing he wanted was his buddy turning Caite's head with his clean-cut good looks.

But he needn't have worried. Caite didn't have time

to be dazzled by Bubba, because Phantom stepped up to their little huddle and threw in his two cents. "They might be assholes sometimes, but we've been a team since we graduated from BUD/s. I don't know about the others, but I'm not sure I could continue being a SEAL if they weren't around to have my back."

Then Rex, arguably the scariest-looking man on their team, pushed Bubba out of the way and stood in front of Caite.

Her eyes widened as she stared up at him. He wasn't the tallest of the group, but with one arm covered in tattoos and his hair long and a bit wild around his head —and with the scowl currently on Rex's face—Caite looked ready to bolt. Even Rocco had to admit that if he put the man in a plaid flannel shirt and threw an ax over his shoulder, he'd look like a stereotypical lumberjack. The only thing saving him from that fate was his longer hair.

Rex didn't touch Caite, just leaned close and stared at her. "You don't look like you could hurt a fly," he said baldly. "What made you think you could do one damn thing to rescue my buddies?"

"Um...nothing?" she croaked.

"Rex," Rocco said in a low, hard tone, but he ignored him.

"Right. So *you*, a woman in a country known to be somewhat hostile toward women, trotted off into the bowels of a city you knew nothing about to track down three Navy SEALs?"

Caite didn't say anything, but she swallowed hard.

"And not only did you find them, you managed to free them from their prison and help them sneak out of the neighborhood, without one shot being fired and without anyone being hurt. How the fuck could you think for *one second* that isn't a big deal?"

Caite bit her lip and shrugged slightly. "Because you guys do it all the time? Because I couldn't just sit around and do nothing? How would I have felt if I'd read in the base paper that three of our navy guys had been found murdered if I had information and didn't do anything about it? Was I supposed to just go home and forget what I'd heard? Forget that Rocco asked me out? Do you have any idea how long it's been since I've been asked out on a date? It might've been years before I had the opportunity again."

By the end of her little speech, Rocco knew she was relaxing a bit, and it made him feel better about her state of mind. But he wasn't prepared for Rex's response.

"I'll take you out. Name the time and place."

"Me too," Bubba echoed.

"No fair, we knew her first," Gumby grumbled. "If she's going out with *anyone*, it should be me or Ace."

Rocco was done. "Shut the fuck up," he told his friends and reached for Caite. He snagged her around the waist and pulled her backward until she was against his chest. He wrapped his other arm diagonally across her chest for good measure—and to further stake his claim. "She's not going out with *any* of you yahoos. She's already going out with me."

Rex was grinning, but his smile died when he looked back down at Caite. "It *was* a big deal, sweetheart. Maybe not smart, but a big deal. And like it or not, you've now got six big brothers at your disposal. You need anything, you call one of us. We'll move your shit from a storage unit to your apartment twenty times over and it won't faze us one bit. You need someone to carry your groceries back from the store, call us. Need a hundred bucks to pay the electric bill? We've got your back. You need a date for your second cousin once removed's wedding? Call one of us and we're there. What I'm sayin' is, what you did in Bahrain was above and beyond, and as a result, we'll have your back no matter what. Got me?"

"Five brothers," Rocco corrected into Caite's ear. He felt her shiver against him, but she didn't take her eyes from Rex.

"Got you."

"Good."

"Although I'm drawing the line at borrowing money. Nothing good ever comes from borrowing money from family members."

Ace swore under his breath.

"Way to go, asshole," Gumby muttered.

Rex simply smiled but didn't respond. Rocco wondered if they'd already hidden a few bills amongst her belongings. He wouldn't put it past them.

"How about we get started on moving her stuff in?" Bubba asked. "This place needs furniture more than any place I've ever seen."

"Right," Rex said, then leaned close and brushed his lips against Caite's cheek, forcing Rocco to let her go. "Thank you." Then, without waiting for her to respond, he headed for the front door.

The others followed behind him, but not before stopping and kissing her cheek just like Rex had.

When all five men had left, Rocco turned Caite to face him. "You okay?"

"Your friends are intense," she said.

"You think?" he asked.

"You don't?" Caite retorted.

Rocco shook his head. "I guess I've seen them in too many precarious situations to think *that* was intense."

"Right. We should go help."

"Nah. They've got it."

Caite pulled his arm. "Seriously, Rocco, we should go help. It looks like Gumby's ankle is okay though."

"Seriously, Caite. They're fine. Gumby's ankle is good. We're all fine. Healed up without any issues. You need to stay up here and tell them where to put your shit when they bring it in."

She nodded as if that made sense. "Then why are *you* not going to help?"

"I have to stay here and make sure my friends don't put their lips on you again."

Caite rolled her eyes, but she smiled. "You're crazy. They were just thanking me."

Rocco didn't want to tell her they'd been completely serious about taking her out. If she gave any of them the slightest hint that she was interested, he'd have a fight on his hands. And kissing her? Yeah, it was to thank her, but they were also giving him shit. They knew he'd hate it. And he had. The only person who should be touching her with his lips was *him*.

The next hour and a half went by quickly, with lots of laughter and teasing between the men and Caite. Rocco was happy to note that, once she got more comfortable with the team, she held her own when it came to bantering.

The guys helped her unpack the boxes, and when they were done, the apartment wasn't exactly full, but at least she had a small couch, a few chairs and, most importantly, a bed to sleep in.

"We gotta get going," Bubba said. Then he turned to Rocco. "You need any more help, let us know."

"I will."

"See you at PT in the morning," Gumby told Rocco as he left.

The other four men followed suit, and soon it was just Rocco and Caite.

"Can I have your number?" he asked.

Caite nodded. "Of course. Although it's only a temporary disposable phone until I can get to the store and get a new one."

"Will you let me take care of that for you?" Rocco asked, knowing the answer but asking anyway.

"Thanks, but no. I'll take in my old phone and get them to transfer the SIM card, so I'll have all my contacts and pictures and stuff. I just haven't gotten around to it yet and it was easier to just grab one of these cheapies from the store in the meantime. I need to upgrade my old phone anyway, and now is about a good a time as any."

"Is that going to be a hit for you?" he asked.

"You mean the price?" When Rocco nodded, she shook her head. "No. I budgeted for it. I'm going to hold off on getting a car for the time being, until I find a better-paying and more permanent job. But I can afford a phone."

"You sure?"

"I'm sure. But thank you."

"Is there *anything* I can do to help you?" Rocco asked in frustration.

Caite smiled up at him. "You can call me. And text me. I've found over the years that my friends from work are only 'work friends.' We get along when I'm there, but the second I leave, *poof*, they never call or email anymore. I could use someone to talk to other than my mom."

"That's easy, *ma petite fée*. I was going to do that anyway. I meant, is there anything *else* I can do for you?"

She nibbled on her lower lip. "You said something about adding another deadbolt to my door?"

"Yup. I'll pick up the stuff and come back tomorrow, if that works for you."

Caite nodded. I'm working from eight to four tomorrow, so it'll have to be after that."

"Done. Want me to bring dinner?"

"How are you even real?" Caite asked.

"I'm real," Rocco reassured her. "What do you want me to bring tomorrow?"

"I'm not picky. Just grab something easy. I'll pay you back."

Rocco rolled his eyes. "As if."

She giggled. "You sound like a teenager."

He didn't smile. "You're not paying me back, Caite. When a man brings a woman dinner, she doesn't pay. Are you working this weekend?"

She nodded.

"But not at night, right?"

"Right."

"Then how about Saturday evening for our date?"

"You bringing dinner over tomorrow isn't our date?" she asked.

It annoyed him that she was dead serious. Stepping into her space, he wrapped his arm around her waist and loved how her hands immediately landed on his chest. "No, *ma petite fée*, that's *not* the date that's making up for the one we missed in Bahrain. It *is* a date though."

"Okay," she said with a small smile.

158

"Okay," he echoed. Then after a beat, said, "I'm having a hard time leaving."

She chuckled. "Want me to say something bitchy to make it easier?"

Rocco shook his head. "I don't think you have a bitchy bone in your body."

"Oh, I do," she countered. "I'm sure I'll say something sooner or later that will have you wondering what the hell you're doing."

"Same here. I'm not perfect," he warned her.

The smile on her face didn't wane. "I'm not either. Rocco, I'm not expecting a movie-version boyfriend from anyone. I'm ridiculously easy to please. Be nice to me, and don't be rude to other people we come into contact with when we're together, and I'm good."

"I'm nice," Rocco confirmed, although he wasn't sure that was always the case.

As if she could read his mind, she clarified, "I mean, be nice to people who *deserve* it. You don't have to play the good guy to anyone who cuts you off in traffic, who flips you the bird when you're simply minding your own business, or who refuses to respect you or what you do for a living."

"You're a bloodthirsty little thing, aren't you?"

"You have no idea," Caite said with a smirk. "Now... do I need to say something mean to get you to leave?"

"No. I'm going. But first..." Rocco leaned down and gently kissed one of her cheeks, then the other. "I need to replace the feel of their lips on your skin."

Caite relaxed against him, and Rocco had never felt so masculine as he did holding her in his arms. She was a curvy handful, and he struggled to keep his hands where they were and not grope her ass like he wanted.

"I think Rex's lips touched mine," she teased. "Although I can't be sure because of that beard of his. It's a little weird that you all have beards, isn't it?"

Not bothering to answer her question and explain how the beards helped them blend in when they went overseas, Rocco lowered his mouth to hers without hesitation.

How long they stood in the middle of her apartment kissing, he had no idea. He couldn't remember the last time he'd kissed a woman with absolutely no expectation of going further. He wanted to do more, but not right at the moment. He was completely satisfied learning what she liked and feeling her hands on his chest.

When she began to suck gently on his lower lip, Rocco finally pulled back.

"You didn't like that?" she asked. Her cheeks were flushed and her blue eyes were slightly dilated.

"I liked it *too* much. And I'm trying to be nice."

"Screw being nice," Caite mumbled.

Rocco chuckled. "We'll have plenty of time, Caite," he reassured her.

"That's what you said in Bahrain and look what happened. I had to track your ass down," she quipped.

Barking out a laugh, Rocco said, "Point taken. But

this time, I'm serious. I'll be back tomorrow with dinner and to install your lock. I'll call, you'll text, and we'll get to know each other better. Saturday, we'll go on that date and we'll see where things go from there."

Caite smiled and nodded.

Rocco kissed her once more then stepped away. "The second you get your new phone, I want to be the first person you text. Don't make me track you down again," he mock warned.

"You never did tell me how you found me," Caite said, brows furrowed.

"Nope. That's for me to know and you to never find out," he teased. "I have a feeling I'll need an ace in the hole to keep one step ahead of you."

Caite rolled her eyes again. "Whatever. I'm perfectly harmless."

"Whatever," Rocco echoed, but smiled as he said it.

"Thanks for helping me out today," Caite told him.

"Any time. And I mean it."

She nodded.

"Tomorrow," Rocco said, then backed toward her front door.

"Drive safe."

"I will. Be careful at that new job of yours."

"Of course. Bye, Rocco."

"Bye, *ma petite fée*."

Rocco reluctantly closed her door and heard her locking it behind him. He headed down the stairs toward his car. He hated to leave her, but it wasn't as if he could stay. They hadn't even been on a date yet.

But after Saturday, all bets were off. Yes, he was moving fast, but it was easy to see that Caite was on the same page he was. He didn't know her thoughts on how soon was appropriate to have sex after she started dating someone, but in the end, it didn't matter. Whether he had to wait a week or a year, he had a feeling she'd be worth it.

As he drove away from her apartment toward his own, Rocco had the sudden thought that he couldn't wait to introduce Caite to Wolf and Caroline. He respected the man more than he could ever say, and the fact that he wanted the retired SEAL to know Caite spoke volumes.

He had no idea he was smiling the entire drive home.

"She just got a job at that shitty convenience store down the street from her apartment," the man on the other end of the line said.

The naval officer nodded. "Fine. Does she have a car?"

"No."

"So she's walking to work?"

"Yes."

"Perfect. Arrange a nice and tidy hit and run. I'm

sure you'll steal a car to do the deed. Don't let anyone see your face, and make sure you hit her hard enough to kill her. I don't want her waking up in the hospital banged up but still alive." He'd learned the hard way that he had to be clear when giving directions. No more "take her out" shit.

"I want her dead," he reiterated.

"Yeah, yeah, I got that," the man said. "I'll get it done. When will I be paid?"

"Half now and half when she's lying in the morgue," the harried man said from his corner office on the naval base.

"I'll be at the gas station where we met for the first half of the money. Tonight at five," the gang member responded. "Don't be late."

Hanging up without a reply, the officer shifted impatiently in his seat. With every day that passed, Caite McCallan had more and more time to recall his name. He had to prevent that at all costs.

Looking toward his office door, he quickly picked up the throwaway phone and dialed once more. He had another shipment of priceless artifacts that was about to be on its way to the States, and this time it couldn't be fucked up. The buyer was suspicious and antsy—and a mean motherfucker. Everything had to go off without a hitch if he wanted to get his money and live to see another day.

CHAPTER NINE

On Saturday morning, Caite smiled as she made her way to work. She walked on the sidewalk that ran along a major street. She was looking down at her phone, occasionally glancing up to make sure she didn't run into anyone.

Rocco: Good morning, beautiful.

Caite: Morning. Are you sure you can't tell me where we're going tonight?

Rocco: I'm sure. You really don't do surprises well, huh?

Caite: No. They drive me crazy. How do I know what to wear? What kind of shoes?

Rocco: Maybe you don't need clothes. Maybe I'm taking you swimming.

Caite: Well, that would be disastrous, as I

can't swim.

Rocco: What? Seriously?

Caite: Yup.

Rocco: Well, now I really need to take you so you can learn.

Caite: I can float, but not very well.

Rocco: We'll start out in the ocean, the saltwater makes you more buoyant.

Rocco: Caite? You still there?

Caite: I'm not sure that's a great idea. I want to make a good impression, not have you exasperated because I can't swim.

Rocco: Can you talk?

Caite: We are talking.

Rocco: I'm calling.

Caite was typing a response when the phone rang in her hand. She stopped at an intersection and waited for the light to turn green as she answered. "Hey."

"I'm not going to be exasperated because you can't swim," he said in lieu of greeting.

She sighed. "I know. It's just weird that I can't swim. Growing up in San Francisco, we went to the beach a lot but I always played in the sand. When I got old enough, my mom put me in lessons, but I screamed in fear and refused to try anything the instructor said. So my parents took me out and decided they'd try again when I got older. Something about being in water over my head freaks me out."

"So you really can't swim at all?" Rocco asked.

Caite didn't hear any censure in his voice, just curiosity. "I can float. Barely," she told him. "As long as I don't have to put my face in the water I'm okay, but the ocean makes me really uncomfortable."

"Why?"

"Why? Rocco, it's full of *animals*! Big ones with teeth! And if it's not sharks or crabs with pinchers, it's jellyfish. Those things might not have teeth, but they can still sting." She shuddered. "Nope. If I have to be in the water, it's shallow, chlorinated, and clean water for me, thank you very much."

"You know pools aren't really that clean, right?" Rocco asked.

"Oh lord, please. Don't tell me," Caite said as she walked across the street when the light changed.

"You trust me, right?" Rocco asked.

"Yes." Caite didn't even have to think about her response. She trusted him more than just about anyone in her life. He'd come over and installed the extra dead-bolt on her door, and then they'd stayed up late talking about their lives and getting to know each other. He'd told her how hard it had been, trying out to be a SEAL, and how close he and his friends had gotten during that time. She knew him a lot better already. Not to mention, he'd easily gotten her through the streets of Bahrain. Yeah, she trusted him.

For her part, she'd told him how she'd had some close friends in high school, but when they all split up and went to different colleges, they'd drifted apart. She'd also had a lot of friends while she was studying at the university, but they'd all had different career paths and hadn't really kept in touch.

Caite admitted that she was close with her mom, but she didn't get to see her as much as she wanted. She told him more about how scared she'd been in Bahrain when she'd been by herself, trying to find where he and the others had been stashed.

But from the second she'd met Rocco, she'd felt safe with him. She never would've agreed to go out with him if she didn't. And nothing that had happened since they'd met had changed that.

"Right, you trust me, so do you really think I'd do anything that would embarrass you or put you in danger?" he asked.

Caite swerved around a family and smiled at them as she continued down the sidewalk toward the convenience store. "No."

"Damn straight I wouldn't. If I promised to make sure no sharks ate you, would you be willing to come to the beach and let me teach you more water safety?"

Caite bit her lip. Her first reaction was to say no. That she didn't need to know how to swim. That she was too scared.

But this was Rocco. She didn't want to disappoint him almost as badly as she didn't want to embarrass herself. "And you *promise* nothing will eat me?"

"No sea creature, for sure," Rocco responded.

It took a minute for his words to sink in, but when they did, Caite blushed.

"Sorry," Rocco said, not sounding sorry in the least. "That slipped out. You'd be able to see me in a swimsuit if you agreed…"

"You don't play fair," Caite said with a laugh.

"Nope. Not when it comes to something I want."

"I'm not sure, Rocco. I'm not confident about doing new things like you are."

"Caite, I swear I'll make it fun for you. I'm not going to force you to swim a mile in choppy seas. I'll make sure we go on a day that's calm and the water's smooth. I swear you'll float so easily, you'll wonder why you were ever unsure about it. The saltwater tastes like shit, but it's the best way to learn how to swim and float and to get more sure of yourself in the water."

"Okay. But only if you promise to let me ogle you in your suit as much as I want."

"Deal. But I get to do the same."

Caite barked out a laugh. "I'm not sure I'm ogling material," she said honestly.

"Wrong," Rocco said immediately. "I've ogled you plenty when you were fully dressed, and I've already been turned on by what I've seen. You in a suit? I have no doubt I'll embarrass *myself* by getting hard, and a swimsuit can't actually hide that shit for a man."

Caite was blushing now, but she chuckled anyway. "Thank you."

"For what?"

"For being so down-to-earth. For making me excited to go out with someone again."

"I think that's my line," Rocco said.

"I'm getting close to work," Caite told him. "I gotta go."

"Okay. I'll be at your apartment at five-thirty. Is that enough time for you to get home and get ready?"

"Yeah. I should be off at four."

"Be safe, and I'll see you later."

"Hey, wait," Caite said suddenly.

"Yeah?"

"Where are we going? You never said."

"Nope. I never did."

"Rocco...I still have no idea what to wear," Caite complained.

"We aren't going mudding and we aren't going to the opera," Rocco told her. "Dress like you would to impress a first date."

Caite nodded. He was right. She was overthinking this. Even though Rocco was extremely fit, it wasn't as if he was going to take her rock climbing or something. At least not on their first official date.

"Okay. I can do that."

"Later, *ma petite fée.*"

"Bye." Caite clicked off her phone and carefully tucked it into her purse. More than once, she'd dropped and cracked her screen, and since this phone was brand new, and money was tight, that was the last thing she needed.

Smiling, she crossed the last street and headed across the parking lot to the convenience store. Now that she had a few days under her belt, she was more comfortable with the job and what to expect. It wasn't hard, but it was tiring being on her feet all day.

Making a mental note to take the time that weekend to look for another administrative assistant position, Caite opened the door and headed for the back room to store her purse before starting her day.

By the time the end of her work shift came around, Caite was exhausted. She'd been on her feet all day and her face hurt from smiling. She was used to dealing with the general public from her job as an admin, but working at the store was completely different. She had to be on the lookout for shoplifters, be helpful and courteous, even when the customers weren't. She stocked shelves, poured ice into the soft-drink machine, cleaned up spills and generally tidied the store.

Not only that, but the night-shift employee who was supposed to relieve her was late. So Caite didn't get out of the store until four-twenty, which meant by the time she got home, she wouldn't have that much time to shower and figure out what the heck to wear for her date with Rocco.

She debated calling him and asking for an additional fifteen minutes to get ready, but ultimately decided she could make it. And she honestly didn't think Rocco would have a problem waiting if she wasn't quite ready when he got there. She didn't know if he'd made reservations anywhere, which he probably had, but she had confidence she could get ready in time.

Pulling out her phone, Caite scrolled through her emails as she power-walked toward her apartment building. She wanted to see if she'd heard back from any of the inquiries she'd made about jobs so far. She'd taken some time on her lunch break to apply online for a few secretarial positions. She was disappointed when she didn't see any return emails, but then remembered it was Saturday. Most offices would be closed on the weekends.

Caite smiled at seeing she'd received an email from her dad. Her father was eccentric. He was also one of the smartest men she'd ever met. He liked to do the *New York Times* crossword puzzles and almost always finished them in one sitting.

He also sent random emails about conservation of the earth, and little ditties about what he'd been up to. But the emails she liked the most were the ones that included his hand-drawn cartoons. They ranged from political to nonsensical. Sometimes she didn't even understand them, as whatever he was parodying went over her head. But she loved receiving them regardless.

She'd just opened the email and was waiting on the picture of his latest cartoon to load when Caite heard a noise behind her. She glanced back at the same time a man running toward her shouted, "Look out!"

Caite was frozen for a heartbeat when she realized what was happening.

A large black pickup truck was headed straight for her.

The right tires were up on the small strip of grass next to the road and all she could see was the giant front grill.

Acting instinctively, Caite threw herself to the side and grunted when her shoulder hit the brick building next to her. Her hair blew across her face as she slammed against the bricks, and she could literally feel the air rush by her from the truck careening past.

Somehow, Caite managed to stay upright and keep hold of her phone.

The truck bounced down the sidewalk toward the man who had yelled out the warning, then abruptly turned back onto the road. Once all four wheels were back on the pavement, it took off down the street as if the hounds of hell were after it.

Caite stood plastered against the brick building for a moment, stunned.

"Holy shit! You almost got run over. Are you all right?" the man exclaimed as he reached her.

Caite nodded, slightly dazed. "Yeah. I'm fine."

The man turned around and glared in the direction the truck had gone. "I didn't get the plate number. It happened too quickly," he said, then looked back at her. "Are you sure you're okay? You hit the wall pretty hard."

Caite gave him a shaky smile. "I'm a lot better than I would've been if that truck had smashed me against the building."

"True that. Shit! That was crazy. Asshole was probably on his phone. Glad you're okay." And with that, the man, still muttering to himself and shaking his head, continued on his way past Caite and down the sidewalk.

Caite took a deep breath and automatically looked down at the screen of her phone. The cartoon from her dad had finished loading. It was drawn using his typical stick figures, and Caite couldn't help but shake her own head.

In the first frame, one person was saying to the other, "You know what the problem is with being smart? You pretty much know what's going to happen next."

The next frame had the other person asking, "So, what's going to happen next?"

And in the last frame, the first person said, "I don't know."

It made her chuckle. "I wish *I* had known what was about to happen so I could've gotten out of the way faster," she muttered. Caite saved the picture to her phone and took a deep breath. She glanced at her watch and swore. She was even later now.

Putting the harrowing incident to the back of her mind, she hurried down the sidewalk, thinking about what she was going to wear. She wavered between a skirt and a nice pair of black slacks. She wasn't really a skirt or dress person, but this *was* a first date. She wanted to make as good an impression as possible. She wanted to look nice for Rocco.

By the time she got back to her apartment, she'd almost forgotten about the truck, telling herself it was probably just as the stranger had said, someone texting while driving or simply not paying attention. People were idiots.

She rushed inside her apartment and threw her purse onto the kitchen counter and was stripping off her shirt before she'd even gotten to her room. She was cutting it too close, and knew she probably wouldn't be ready by the time Rocco arrived.

Twenty minutes later, Caite had decided on a flirty royal-blue skirt instead of pants. Because of Bahrain's extremely conservative society, she'd worn nothing but slacks while there. Deciding to wear something outside her norm, she put on the skirt and a pair of two-inch heels. A white blouse with cut-out shoulders completed her look. She still needed to dry her hair and put on a bit of makeup when Rocco knocked.

She pulled open the door and immediately turned back around and headed for her room. "Make yourself at home," she called out as she went. "I'm not ready yet!"

She was almost back to her room when a strong arm curved around her waist and pulled her backward. She giggled and allowed herself to be turned around in his arms.

"I know I'm late, I'm so sorry," she babbled. "I got off work late and was going to call you, but I still thought I'd be finished before you got here."

"You smell delicious," Rocco said, right before he buried his nose in the side of her neck.

Caite tilted her head, giving him room. "Rocco, I need to go dry my hair."

"Mmmmm."

He wasn't helping. "Rocco," she insisted. "I'm assuming you have reservations somewhere, since it's Saturday night. If you don't let me go, we won't make them and we'll have to eat at McDonald's or something...not that I mind that...I love me some Mickey-D fries, but I just figured you probably had something else planned."

"We're not going to McDonald's," he said as he ran his nose up and down her neck.

Caite shivered at the sensation. His beard tickled her skin where it touched her, and she had the urge to tell him that she didn't want to go anywhere. To pull him into her bedroom and throw him down on her bed and straddle him.

But the second she had the thought, he straightened. He looked from her hair down to her toes. "I love the skirt," he said after a beat.

"Thanks," Caite said shyly.

"You look perfect just the way you are," he told her as he tucked a piece of damp hair behind her ear.

"I need to finish getting ready," she said in a near whisper.

Rocco nodded and took a step back.

"Help yourself to a drink if you want. Or anything else."

"I'm good."

"Okay, then...I'll hurry."

"You're fine, *ma petite fée*, take your time. Our reservation isn't until seven."

"Oh. Okay." Then she smiled at him, turned and fled into her bedroom.

Fifteen minutes later, she came out of the small hallway and smiled at the vision that greeted her.

Rocco was sitting on her couch, one of her romance books in his hand, seemingly oblivious to the fact that she was standing there.

"I'm ready," she said.

He didn't flinch, and Caite realized he'd known she was there all along. He placed the book back on the table next to the couch where she'd left it and stood.

"You don't seem like the romance-book type," she said a bit nervously.

Rocco strode forward until he was right in front of

her, and she had to crane her neck back to hold eye contact with him.

"I'm not usually, but what I read of that one...it's good," he told her.

"It's a romantic suspense. I like it when there's an external conflict at the end, rather than a fight or something between the hero and heroine. I also like it when the heroine kicks some ass and isn't afraid to stand up to the bad guy."

"Hmmm. You look beautiful," Rocco said.

Caite knew she'd been babbling about the book because she was nervous, and she pressed her lips together to keep herself from saying anything else stupid.

Rocco leaned down and brushed his lips against her cheek.

Caite hadn't taken the time to drink him in earlier, but did so now. He was wearing a pair of khakis and a white polo shirt. His brown hair was brushed and didn't stick up anywhere, as she'd seen it do in the past. His beard even looked as if it'd been trimmed. In short, he looked yummy.

Then something else occurred to her.

"Our shirts match," she blurted.

He smiled. "So they do."

"I can go change," she said, her mind racing as to what else she could wear that would match her skirt.

"Why?" he asked, and reached for her hand. Twining his fingers with hers, he said, "I like it."

"Is there anything you *don't* like?" she asked, tilting her head.

He chuckled. "Lots. Assholes who prey on those weaker than them. Peas. Climate change. But us wearing the same color doesn't even come close to fazing me."

Caite smiled. "Okay."

Rocco swiftly pulled her closer, and Caite stumbled and threw out her arm. Her fingers landed on the middle of his chest, but he caught her easily, steadying her. "Easy."

"Sorry," she apologized. "I'm so clumsy."

He shook his head. "I shouldn't have surprised you. Although I definitely don't mind your hands on me. Ready to go?"

Caite's head spun with the change of subject, but she nodded.

They headed for the door, and she took a moment to grab a smaller purse and transfer her wallet and phone to it before they left. He waited and didn't rush her and stood patiently at her back as she locked her door. She put her keys inside the purse and turned to Rocco with a smile.

He returned it and they walked down the stairs to his car. He held open the door for her and, once she was inside, shut it carefully.

Caite took a deep breath and watched Rocco stride around the car to the driver's side. He was one hell of a man, and she couldn't believe *she* was on a date with him. She wasn't anyone special, and had no idea what he saw in her. But that didn't mean she wouldn't do everything she could to keep his interest. Because he was definitely the best thing to happen to her in a very long time.

He was brave, and honorable, and trustworthy...not to mention good-looking. Caite was a big believer in "things happen for a reason" and, at the moment, she couldn't have been happier that she'd been fired. If she hadn't, she'd still be in Bahrain working for her asshole boss, dreaming about the Navy SEAL she'd probably never see again.

Rocco couldn't take his eyes off of Caite. She looked so fucking pretty, he was having a hard time not ravishing her. When he'd first gotten to her apartment and she'd opened the door, he'd immediately gotten hard. With her hair wet and down around her shoulders, all he could think about was seeing her that way after they'd showered together. It was a good thing she rushed back to her bedroom to finish getting ready, because otherwise she would've gotten an eyeful.

But after she'd dried her hair and put on a bit of makeup, he was completely blown away. She was so beautiful, he had no idea how she wasn't already snatched up. But whatever the reason, she was with *him* now.

He'd taken her to a small family-owned seafood restaurant on the beach by the naval base. It wasn't super fancy, but it wasn't a shit hole either. He knew the owners, and they'd given him a table right by the beach.

They'd spent the last three hours laughing and getting to know each other.

"Thank you for bringing me here," she said.

They'd watched the sun set and had been talking and sipping wine for the last hour. Rocco didn't want the night to end, but unfortunately the place was closing soon. "My pleasure. You ready to go?"

She looked down at her empty glass for a moment, then back up at him. "Yes...and no."

"Explain," Rocco said.

"Yes, because we're done eating and I'm exhausted from working all day and my feet hurt. But no, because I don't really want the night to end."

Her response totally summed up what he was thinking...other than his feet hurting. The waiter had returned his credit card an hour earlier, so Rocco just stood and held out his hand. "Come on, *ma petite fée*, let's get you home before you turn into a pumpkin."

Sighing, she took his hand and he helped her to her feet. He wrapped an arm around her lower back and led her out of the restaurant. He made sure to walk on the outside of the sidewalk as they made their way to the parking lot. Neither said anything as they walked, enjoying simply being with each other.

He stopped next to his car, Caite's back to the door.

She looked up at him, and he could see the anticipation and eagerness on her face. He supposed he probably looked the same way.

Putting a finger under her chin, he asked, "May I?"

Caite nodded. "Please." Then she licked her lips.

Leaning down, Rocco covered her mouth with his own.

They made out for what could've been minutes or seconds. Not caring they were in standing in public going at it like they were teenagers. It had been a long time since Rocco had kissed a woman for as long and as creatively as he did every time with Caite. Generally, kisses for him were a precursor to getting to the good stuff. But with Caite, they *were* the good stuff. He could taste the wine she'd been drinking and the combination with her natural taste was delicious.

Her hands roamed up and down his back, even dipping to his ass now and then. His did the same. Touching her generous curves did nothing to help control his hard-on. He pressed against her belly and groaned when she wiggled.

Eventually, Rocco pulled back. He had to stop things now or risk embarrassing himself. Besides, the last thing he wanted was to treat Caite as if she was easy, or make her think he didn't treasure what she was giving him.

"We need to stop," he said, his voice husky with desire.

"I know," she said just as quietly.

Rocco drew her close, putting his arms around her and simply holding her to him. She lay her head on his shoulder and held on just as tightly. How long they stood there, Rocco wasn't sure, but eventually a shout from the beach made it clear it was time to go. He didn't want to put Caite in danger by being down here in the dark.

The voices seemed to break the spell for her too, as she pulled back and smiled up at him ruefully. Without a word, he opened the door and helped her in, then jogged around to the driver's side. The second he pulled out of the parking lot, he reached over and took her hand in his.

They held hands all the way back to her apartment. Rocco helped her out of the car and walked her up to her door. After she'd unlocked it, he waited for her to turn around.

"Do you want to come in?" Caite asked shyly.

"You know I want to, but you're tired," he said gently. "I'm not saying anything would happen if I came in, but I think with how tonight went, we both know that's where we're headed. And I couldn't be more thrilled about that. But I'm not some asshole who only took you out because he wanted to get in your pants. I like you, Caite. A hell of a lot. And I can see us being together for the long haul. But the first time we make love, I want you to be completely ready...and awake." He smiled. "I don't want you falling asleep in the middle of my seduction."

He could see her blushing again, and loved that about her. "I wouldn't fall asleep," she protested.

Rocco reached out and palmed the back of her neck gently. "Sometimes anticipation makes everything more intense. Better."

She frowned and dropped her gaze from his. He wasn't sure what she was thinking until she said, "If you're putting me off because you're trying to be a nice guy and don't want to tell me that you're not interested, I'd rather you just say it."

"Caite," Rocco scolded gently, "have I given you *any* indication that I want to end things between us?"

She shook her head as best she could with him holding her neck.

"That's because I don't. I *am* trying to be a good guy here. I can tell how tired you are, and I'd rather you go inside and get a good night's sleep than letting me come in and make you even more tired. Got it?"

"Yeah. I just...I like you, and I really want to see where things go between us too. I just panicked. Sorry."

He relaxed. He knew her words were a knee-jerk reaction to try to protect herself. That alone pissed him off. Not because of what she'd said, but because someone had to have treated her like shit for her to even think he was playing her. "You have to work tomorrow, right?" he asked gently.

She nodded.

"Right. I'm flattered that you don't want me to go, *ma petite fée*, I am. And believe me, I want to see you naked under me more than I want my next breath, but there's no rush. We're gonna get there, I know it."

"How'd I get so lucky?" Caite asked.

Rocco shook his head. "Nope. That's my line," he said with another smile. "How about a kiss for the road?"

Without words, Caite stepped toward him and went up on her tiptoes. Her arms went around his neck and she tipped her chin upward. Rocco held her steady with his hand on her neck, the other going to her ass and pressing her against him. The kiss they shared was hot and wet and full of anticipation.

Rocco nibbled on her lower lip before reluctantly releasing her.

"If anyone else put their hand on my neck, I'd be annoyed and probably accuse him of trying to control me. But when you do it, it makes me melt. Don't hurt me, Rocco," Caite said with a hint of desperation. "I've had a hard couple of weeks and it would kill me if you were playing me."

"I'm not playing you," Rocco told her. He couldn't even be pissed that she'd had the thought. He understood trying to protect your heart. "I want everything from you, Caite. All your fears and hopes and dreams. I want to be the man you lean on when life gives you shit. I want to be the first person you think of talking to when you need to vent or to celebrate something. And I'd never hurt you. I might put my hands on you in a way you haven't experienced before, but I will *not* do so in anger or in order to control you. Got it?"

"Got it," she confirmed. Then she reached out and brushed her hand over his beard. "It's really soft."

"It's gotten too long. I need to trim it down even more than I did tonight before our date."

She brought shy eyes up to his. "Maybe not right now. I've never been with a man with a beard before."

Her words brought more carnal images to mind, and Rocco forced them back. "I can't wait," he told her. He kissed her on the forehead then made himself let go of her and step back. "I'll text you tomorrow," he said. "Be safe at work."

"I will."

"I had a good time tonight. Thank you."

"Thank *you*," she returned. "I'll talk to you later."

"Yes, you will," Rocco said. "Go inside and lock the door, Caite."

She nodded, bit her lip, then backed up. She kept eye contact with him until the very last second when the door closed between them.

Rocco heard the locks engaging and nodded in satisfaction. Looking at his watch as he made his way back to his car, he realized that it really wasn't that late. He had the momentary idea that he could go back up to Caite's apartment, but nixed the thought. No. She needed her sleep. The first time he made love with her, he didn't want to have to worry about either of them getting up early for work. He wanted to take his time and love her the way he was craving.

Driving back to his place, Rocco shook his head. He never imagined he'd be as crazy about a woman as he was for Caite. There was still a chance things between them wouldn't work out. That she'd do something crazy, or she wouldn't be able to handle the fact he was a SEAL. And there was an equal chance that *he'd* fuck up and say or do something she couldn't forgive.

But for the first time in his life, he was excited about the prospect of getting into a long-term relationship with a woman. He didn't dread it or worry that she'd have deeper feelings than him. If anything, he worried that he'd care a hell of a lot more for her than she did him.

Taking a deep breath, Rocco decided to take things one day at a time. As he'd told her, they had all the time in the world.

"Are you shitting me?" Captain Isaac Chambers bit out. He was standing in his underwear on the back patio of the house he shared with his wife and their three children. He'd told her that he needed to make a quick phone call, digging out the disposable phone and going outside so she wouldn't overhear.

"Unfortunately, no. I tried, but there were witnesses. I had her in my sights. She was as good as roadkill under my tires, but some asshole went and warned her and she jumped out of the way at the last second."

"Damn it! How could you fucking miss? It's not like I gave you a hard job or something!"

"I was trying to make it look like an accident, man."

"Why? Shit, you were leaving the scene anyway. Why didn't you just fucking back up and go after her again?"

"Because there were *people* around," the man on the other end of the phone bit out. "Look, five grand isn't enough money for me to risk going to jail."

"Then you should've fucking told me that before you took half the money for the job. Get your ass back out there and make sure she's fucking dead this time!"

"I'm out," the man said without any emotion in his voice.

"Oh no, you are *not*. You took twenty-five hundred bucks and you'll finish this!" Chambers ordered.

"Fuck off. I'm not one of your pansy navy boys you can order around. I'm *out*. You're gonna have to find someone else to do your dirty work."

Chambers ground his teeth together. "Then give me back my money."

"No. Sue me, asshole," the man said, then hung up.

The second the line was cut, Isaac Chambers threw the disposable phone as hard as he could against the side of his house. The phone smashed into a hundred pieces, and a chunk of plastic careened toward him and cut his face before he could move out of the way.

Swearing, he leaned over and braced his hands on his thighs and tried to control his temper. He was bleeding money faster than he was making it. His wife was constantly whining about needing cash to go fucking shopping, and he was always paying for some camp or something for his kids.

But that wasn't the main problem. His reputation was taking a hit in the smuggling circles, and he needed to make sure these last few jobs were completed without any complications. He needed the finder's fee he'd receive for getting the ancient artifacts out of Iraq and into the hands of serious collectors here in the States.

And if Caite McCallan remembered his name, his reputation would be fucked.

He'd already arranged for the Bitoo family to have a very unfortunate accident. He couldn't take the chance that the cops would find them first. One of the brothers —he didn't know which one, and he didn't care—had been dumb enough to contact him, telling him everything that had happened in Bahrain, including the SEALs' capture and escape. He'd called his contact on the naval base over there and had gotten copies of the report the SEALs had given Commander Horner.

They'd left out Caite McCallan's role in everything, but when he'd read her resume, it hadn't taken much to figure it out. The bitch spoke French. Fluently. The Bitoo brothers had already admitted they'd discussed at the conference where the SEALs were and what they were going to do to them, so it wasn't a stretch to figure out she'd overheard them.

Chambers had to shell out way more cash than he'd wanted to make sure the Bitoos kept their mouths shut —permanently. He didn't know where the bodies were or how they'd been killed. All he cared about was that his name was in the clear.

But now he needed Caite McCallan to die. Dead men—or women, in this case—told no tales. And he needed her to keep her mouth shut. It was simply a matter of time before she remembered his name. He had to act before she could.

Leaving the pieces of the phone where they lay, Isaac Chambers made his way back inside the house. He'd have to arrange for someone else to kill her. It shouldn't be hard. There were always people lurking around who needed money. He just needed to find someone more desperate than the last person he'd hired...and pay them less.

He was out twenty-five hundred bucks, and he couldn't afford to make a mistake like that again. He'd find some drug addict and get them to knock her off for half the price.

CHAPTER TEN

"Good morning, *ma petite fée*," Rocco said when Caite picked up the phone. It had been a few days since their date, and they'd spoken every day since. He'd been looking forward to seeing her again, but unfortunately, that was going to have to wait.

"Morning," Caite replied huskily.

Rocco loved hearing her voice. "Sleep well?" he asked.

"Mmmm. How could I not after talking to you right before I went to bed?"

Rocco adjusted his hard cock and forced himself to concentrate on what he needed to tell her. "That's sweet."

"I've got this weekend off," she said. "The schedule was in my email when I got up this morning."

Rocco mentally swore. "That's great. But unfortunately, I have bad news."

"What?"

He hated what he was about to say. "Me and the guys are headed out of town this afternoon."

There was silence on the other end of the line for a beat. Suddenly, Rocco wished he'd broken the news to her in person, especially this first time he had to head out on a mission with very little warning. "Caite?"

"I'm here. I'm assuming you can't tell me anything about where you're going or how long you'll be gone?"

"I wish I could."

"Okay. Please be safe."

Shit. He *totally* should've told her in person. "I will. This is who I am," he said gently. "It's what I do. It sucks for others. I get it. And if you called me up and said you had to go out of town and couldn't tell me where you were going or when you'd be back, I'd probably lose my mind. It's not fair for me to do the same to you and expect you to be okay with it."

"It's not that I'm *not* okay with what you do," Caite protested immediately. "I'm proud of you, Rocco. I admire you and your friends, and I know that we're living the lives we are here in America because of you. It's just different, now that I've gotten to know you."

"I know. Being the girlfriend or wife of a SEAL isn't easy."

"Is that what we are? Boyfriend and girlfriend?" she asked hesitatingly.

"Caite, we've talked every day since I tracked you down. I can't go even a few hours without thinking about you and wondering what you're doing. I swear I can still taste you on my lips and I dream about kissing you. I fantasize about what it'll be like when we finally make love. Yeah...I'd say you're definitely my girlfriend."

"Oh."

"Oh? That's all you have to say?" he teased. "Do you consider me to be your boyfriend?"

"Yes."

Her answer was immediate and heartfelt, and it went a long way toward soothing any doubts Rocco may have had.

"Good."

"When do you leave?" Caite asked.

Rocco frowned. "In about four hours."

"Damn."

"Yeah. I wish I could get away to see you before we head out, but we're going to be in meetings and getting our gear set up and ready to go."

"I understand."

Rocco's voice dropped. "I'm going to miss you, *ma petite fée*. You have no idea how much."

"Uh...yeah, I think I do, because I'm going to miss you the same way. I've gotten kinda used to you."

"Yeah?"

"Uh-huh. You'll call when you get back?"

"Of course. If it's okay, I'll come see you as soon as I can."

"Please." Then she sighed.

"What is it?"

"I just realized how much I've been talking to you lately. You're the first person I call when I get off work, and we've been talking in the mornings before I head off to the store. I'm going to miss having someone to talk to."

Kicking himself for not introducing her to Caroline and some of the other SEAL wives before now, Rocco said, "I'm sorry that I've been keeping you all to myself."

"Don't be. I'm not."

"Still. When I get back, I'll make sure to introduce you to some of the women who are married to my other SEAL friends. Well, they're retired SEALs now, but they still help with training. They're amazing women, and I know they'll have a lot of insight for you on how to make it through the times when I head off to missions."

She didn't say anything for almost a full minute, and Rocco asked, "Caite?"

"I'm here."

"What's wrong?"

"Introducing me to them seems serious."

Rocco sighed in exasperation. "What did I just say, *ma petite fée*? We're together. Dating. An item. Boyfriend-girlfriend. Going out. Anything I can do to make my missions easier on you, I'll do. I hate the thought of you being alone when I'm gone. Have you had any leads on admin positions?"

He knew it was an abrupt change of topic, but he just remembered that he'd wanted to ask.

"Not yet."

"Damn."

"I'm fine at the convenience store for now."

"You'll be safe?" Rocco asked.

"Of course."

"I mean it, Caite. The statistics on violent crimes are through the roof in places like that."

"I *know*. Rocco, just because you're leaving doesn't mean it gets more or less dangerous. It is what it is. I'm looking for another job, but it's not that easy."

He could hear the irritation in her voice. "I know. But I can't get to you if something happens and I'm out of the country."

His words seemed to calm her. "I'll be fine. I went through the training on what to do if someone holds up the place. I'm not working the night shift. I'm not going to do anything stupid...and that's *if* anything even happens."

Rocco wanted to tell her that the mission they were going on should be a short one. That he should be home in a week or less. But he couldn't tell her anything. He'd never been as frustrated with the secrecy that came with his job as he was at this moment.

"I'd like to give you a few phone numbers of men I trust...just in case."

Caite sighed, then asked, "You're really worried, aren't you?"

"Yes."

"You know, *I* should be the one worrying. If something happens to you, I'll probably never find out. I know how the military works; you forget that I worked as a DOD contractor for years. We aren't married. If you get hurt or, God forbid, killed, I'll never know. I should be the one lecturing *you* on being safe and watching your six. Not the other way around."

She had a point. "I'll make sure to tell my buddy Wolf to contact you immediately if something happens."

"That doesn't make me feel better," she said in a whisper.

Shit. He was definitely fucking this up. "When I get back, I'm gonna take you out...and when I bring you home, I'm not going to leave you at your door. I'm going to spend all night exploring this electric connection we have. I can't wait to see and touch every inch of your luscious body."

"That was just mean," Caite protested with a little huff. "Now I'm sad *and* turned on, and I don't have time to do anything about it before I have to go to work."

"*Now* who's being mean?" Rocco asked, a vision of her lying on her bed naked, a hand between her legs, taunting him.

"Thank you for telling me you're leaving," she said quietly.

"There will be times when we don't have as much time as we have today to prepare," he told her honestly.

"But I will never, *ever* leave without letting you know. I wouldn't do that to you."

"Okay."

"And now I really do have to go. The guys are waiting for me."

"Please be careful," Caite said.

"Always," Rocco told her. "I'll text you a few numbers later. *Please* use them if you need anything."

"I'll be fine."

It wasn't what he wanted to hear, and it wasn't a promise, but he didn't have time to press her right now. Later, he'd introduce her to Wolf and Cutter. Maybe if she knew them personally, she'd feel more comfortable calling them when he was gone. Not only that, but he'd see if Caroline and Dakota and the other women would take Caite under their wing. He remembered Wolf telling him about how alone Caroline had felt when she'd first begun dating him, when the other men on his team didn't have girlfriends yet. It was probably exactly how Caite felt.

The words "I love you" were on the tip of his tongue, but he couldn't say them yet. It was too soon. She'd think him crazy. "Be safe," he said instead.

"You too."

"I'll call when I get back."

"Okay."

"Bye, *ma petite fée.*"

"Bye, Rocco."

He clicked off the phone feeling unsettled and antsy.

He definitely wished he could've told her in person that he was leaving.

Sighing, he pocketed his phone and turned to head into the conference room. Commander Storm North and the rest of his team were waiting for him before starting the debrief. All Rocco knew was that they were headed to Africa. They were following up on a tip about more smuggled artifacts out of the Middle East.

Three days after Rocco had called to tell her he was leaving, Caite was feeling depressed. It was silly, really. She was used to living a solitary life. When she'd been working as a contractor, she went days without talking to anyone outside of work.

But Rocco had given her something to look forward to. She usually called him when she got off work, while she was walking back to her apartment, and then spoke to him again before she went to sleep.

Then he'd call in the morning to make sure she was up. Since he got up at the butt crack of dawn to work out, he was always up before her. She was usually awake already, but she loved being able to talk to him before she headed off to the convenience store.

They rarely talked about anything super interesting, but somehow over the last couple of weeks, she'd gotten to know Rocco better than just about any man she'd dated in the past. She knew both his parents were alive and well and living in Florida. He didn't have any siblings, but considered the men he worked with to be his brothers in every way that mattered.

He hated bright colors and couldn't stand tomatoes. He loved seafood and apples, but hated sushi and apple pie. He loved working out, and even though most of his friends had tattoos, he hadn't had the urge to mark up his body in that way.

And all the time he'd taken to talk and text and get to know her on an intellectual level had done what no other man had accomplished. It made Caite impatient to move their relationship to the next level.

She wanted Rocco. Ached for him. Even thinking about him made her nipples pucker in anticipation.

In the past, she'd succumbed to sleeping with the few men she'd dated because it was eventually expected. But she hadn't really needed anyone. Not like she did Rocco.

She missed talking to him. Missed telling him about her day and missed hearing him talk about his own. It was fascinating to hear him talk about his job. She'd had no idea SEALs worked out as much as Rocco and his team did. And they trained nonstop. Things like getting out of that hole in the ground. Ways to outsmart the enemy. She'd worked for the military, but she'd had no clue.

Caite wondered where he was at that moment. What he was doing. She prayed he was safe. She wasn't an idiot. She knew wherever he was and whatever mission they were on was probably dangerous. He could be shot. Captured. Tortured.

Groaning, she wiped a hand over her face and stood up straight. It was quiet in the store at the moment. She'd stocked the shelves and straightened the cigarettes behind the counter. No one was getting gas and her coworker was in the back, supposedly doing inventory but more likely smoking pot. Caite didn't care. It was hard to care about anything when Rocco was gone.

The bell over the front door rang and Caite looked up. Straightening in surprise, she stared at the man wearing a ski mask over his face.

He lifted a gun and pointed it at her. Caite immediately lifted her arms, showing him that she was unarmed.

"Give me all the money," the man growled in a deep, husky voice.

Nodding, she immediately pushed the button on the cash register that would unlock the drawer. A little bell jingled as it opened. Quickly, Caite grabbed the bills and shoved them across the counter at the man.

She couldn't see his face, except for his eyes, which glittered in the light. She knew the security camera was filming everything, and she prayed the man would say or do something that would help identify him to detectives.

He grabbed the money without even looking at it.

Caite read the intent in his eyes before he moved.

She was already throwing herself to the side when the gun went off.

A searing pain went through her arm as she fell. Her head hit a shelf behind the counter, and she had the fleeting thought of how pissed Rocco would be when he came home and found out she'd been killed in a fucking robbery.

Vision fuzzy, she could just make out the man taking a step toward the counter and peering behind it, staring at Caite on the floor, at the blood she could see in her periphery, pooling around her head. Then he spun on his heels and ran from the store. The sound of the bell over the door faded along with her consciousness.

Eight hours later, Caite was in her apartment, lying on her couch. She had her cell phone in hand and was staring at the last text Rocco had sent before leaving. It had the names and numbers of the men he'd said she should call if anything happened.

She knew she could call...but really, what was she going to say? "Hi, I'm Caite, you don't know me but I was shot today."

What were they going to do? They had their own families to worry about. They didn't know her from Adam. Besides, she was home. Alive. In one piece.

Caite thought about calling her parents, but decided to give that a few days as well. If she called her mom, she had no doubt she'd immediately start driving south. As much as she loved her mom and dad, she wasn't up to dealing with them at the moment.

The entire incident at the store had been so surreal. She'd woken up on the floor behind the counter with paramedics asking her questions and poking and prodding her.

The bullet had merely grazed her upper arm. She'd been lucky. Caite knew that better than all the doctors, paramedics, and cops who had told her so over and over.

Her head had bled like a stuck pig, but once cleaned, the doctors had discovered it was only a superficial cut. She'd gotten three stitches on her head and four more on her arm. The MRI showed no concussion and she wasn't nauseous or dizzy. The emergency room doctor had wanted to keep her overnight for observation, but Caite refused. She knew the bill for the ER visit alone was going to be way more than she could afford on her meager salary.

But now she was home and her arm was throbbing. She had a headache and was feeling very sorry for herself. The manager at the store had "generously" given her the next three days off, but Caite was seriously considering quitting.

Everything was overwhelming right now. It felt as if her life was crashing in on her. Money, missing Rocco, the pain from her injuries, almost fucking dying. She wasn't one to cry when life got hard, but she'd been strong all day. The tears started before she could force them back.

Curling into a ball, careful not to move her arm the wrong way or put pressure on her head wound, Caite gave in to the tears. She'd been able to hold them back all day. Not even breaking down when she'd overheard the cops talking about how if she hadn't thrown herself to the side, the bullet probably would've gone into her heart instead of her arm.

She was used to being strong. Used to taking care of herself. But at the moment, she didn't want to be alone. She wanted Rocco.

Rocco was glad to be back in California. It had only been three days since they'd left, but it seemed so much longer. He hadn't realized just how much he enjoyed talking to Caite. How much light she brought into his life. No longer was his entire focus on the SEALs. He constantly thought about her. Wondered what she was doing, if she'd been able to take time to eat lunch. Wanted to hear her voice and talk about his day, and hers.

After going through the debrief with Commander North and the rest of his team, he was anxious to call Caite and let her know he was home. It was late, but he didn't think she'd mind being woken up.

"She's it for you, isn't she?" Gumby asked when the team was headed out of the debriefing room.

He looked at his friend and nodded. It didn't surprise him that Gumby had asked about Caite. Rocco had talked about her a lot over the last four days. "Yeah. I'm pretty sure she is. I mean, I have no idea what the future holds for us, but she's pretty damn important."

"That's awesome," Gumby said.

"Don't you worry that you'll lose your edge?" Phantom asked.

Rocco turned to stare at him. He knew Phantom'd had a horrible childhood and had basically joined the navy to escape his abusive family, but he wasn't sure where the shitty attitude was coming from.

"You have a problem with me dating Caite?" he asked, stopping in the hall to confront him.

The entire team stopped as well.

"Yes. If it means you're going to have your mind on pussy instead of having our backs on a mission."

Now Rocco was pissed. "Would you say that shit to Wolf? Or Dude? Or even Cookie? Those men would die for their wives and kids, and they're some of the most hardcore SEALs I've ever met."

"It's different with them," Phantom insisted.

"Why?" Rocco demanded.

The muscle in other man's jaw ticked as he thought about his response. "Because they're not you."

"What does *that* mean?" Rocco asked.

Phantom ran a hand through his already mussed

hair. "It means that I love you like a brother. We've been through the worst shit anyone can ever go through together. The last thing I want is a chick fucking things up."

Rocco forced his muscles to relax. He stepped toward Phantom and put a hand on his shoulder. "Caite isn't going to come between us. Ever. This team is my family. Just because Bubba has a twin brother doesn't mean he cares about *us* any less. I care about Caite, I'll readily admit that. I can also admit that I want to see where things between us can go long term, and that there were times I was thinking about her while on this op. But that *doesn't* mean when the shit hits the fan, I can't get my job done. That I won't do whatever it takes to have *your* back and everyone else's on this team."

No one said a word as Phantom and Rocco stared at each other.

Finally, Phantom nodded. "I just...change is hard for me."

"I know. But Caite isn't like the women we've fucked around with in the past. I wish you could've been in Bahrain and seen her, Phantom. She was fucking phenomenal. Scared out of her mind, but still doing what she felt in her gut was right. Give her a chance."

"I don't have to," the other man said. "I already like her. I'm just worried about you. You were a lot quieter than usual on this op, and she's the only thing I could think of that had changed for you."

Rocco nodded. "If Wolf and his team can have families and still be able to do their jobs, so can we."

All of the men around them nodded in agreement.

"Now that we've got that settled...I need to make a phone call."

Everyone grinned, and they all headed back down the hall, making small talk about what they were going to do on their next two days off. Commander North was really good about giving them downtime when they got back from missions. Sometimes they had to come in and give statements about things that might've happened while they were overseas, but they always tried to get the meetings done as soon as they got back so they could be free for a couple of days.

When they reached the parking lot, everyone said their goodbyes and Rocco climbed into his Acura. He quickly turned on his phone...and frowned when he didn't have any messages or texts waiting. He'd thought for sure Caite would've contacted him at least once, even if she knew he wouldn't be able to respond.

He clicked on her name and waited.

Surprisingly, the call went to voicemail.

He shot off a text and tapped impatiently on his steering wheel. Rocco had been so excited to talk to her, to hear her voice. Now that he couldn't, he was disappointed. Not only that, but he was slightly worried.

Caite would be the first to admit that she didn't have much of a life outside of work, so the fact that she wasn't answering her phone at—Rocco looked at his watch—ten-thirty at night was worrisome.

He clicked on her name once more and when that call also went to voicemail, made a decision. Starting the engine, Rocco told himself he was just going to check on her. To make sure she wasn't lying hurt or worse in her apartment, not able to get to her phone.

It was irrational, but Rocco knew he wouldn't be able to sleep if he didn't see with his own two eyes that she was okay.

The drive to her apartment went by without incident and soon he was pulling into her parking lot. Looking up at her place, he saw no lights on, but that didn't necessarily mean anything. For a moment, he second-guessed himself. Maybe she was sleeping, and him knocking on the door would scare her. But he shook off the thought. He might frighten her, but he hoped once she saw it was him, she'd be happy.

Taking the steps up to the second floor two at a time, Rocco strode toward her door and didn't hesitate to knock loudly.

He waited and shifted on his feet, looking around. Everything seemed quiet. There weren't any late-night parties going on and if her neighbors were home, they were keeping to themselves.

After a moment, he knocked again.

If she didn't answer, he'd call Rex. The man could pick locks better than anyone he'd ever met. He'd have Caite's door open within seconds. He could go to the manager, but he didn't want to have to explain why and listen to the man whine about laws and shit.

When it came to Caite, Rocco didn't give a damn about laws.

That thought should've scared him, but it didn't. If Caite was in trouble, he needed to get to her.

The second he lifted his cell to call Rex, Rocco heard scrapes behind the door.

She was awake, and unlocking the door for him.

He plastered a huge smile on his face and waited with baited breath to see her again.

But the smile faded the second the door cracked open and he saw Caite.

She looked like shit. Her hair was in disarray and she had deep frown lines on her forehead. Her eyes were red and bloodshot, and he could see tracks of tears on her cheeks.

"What the hell?" he said under his breath as he took a step forward. He gently pushed the door open, forcing Caite to take a step back. He entered the apartment and quickly relocked the door. He put his hands on her shoulders, leaned in and asked urgently, "What happened?"

Instead of answering, Caite burst into tears.

Alarmed, Rocco immediately took her into his arms. She didn't protest, simply wrapped one arm around his neck and turned her face into his chest.

He could feel the wetness from her tears soaking into his shirt, but it barely registered. He guided them to the couch and sat, putting her onto his lap. He saw the multitude of used tissues strewn about on the floor, and then his eyes immediately spied the medicine bottle on the table next to the couch.

"Caite? Talk to me," he ordered, more panicked now.

In response, she only gripped him harder.

Taking a deep breath, Rocco forced himself to calm down. Caite was in his arms. She was alive. Everything else, he would figure out sooner or later.

It took a few minutes, but eventually her tears stopped and she simply sniffed. Rocco leaned over and snagged a tissue from the box on the side table and handed it to her. Without a word, Caite took it and wiped her eyes before blowing her nose.

"Are you okay?" Rocco asked after a moment.

She nodded. "I'm okay. I just had a really bad day."

"I'm sorry, *ma petite fée*."

She sat up straighter on his lap and gave him a weak smile. "You're back."

"Yeah. Got back tonight. Went to the office for the debrief then when you didn't answer your phone, I came straight here. I was worried."

She looked confused, and then glanced around her. "You called? I didn't hear it ring. Where *is* my phone?"

They found it between the cushions of the couch. And it had somehow been turned off. No wonder she hadn't heard it ring.

"I'm glad you're back," she said.

"Tell me what happened," Rocco asked. Then his gaze caught sight of something he'd missed earlier. "What the fuck...?" he asked as he brought his fingers up to her temple. The stitches had been hidden by her hair. He gently brushed the strands away from her head so he could examine the wound more closely.

"The store was held up today," she said in a toneless voice that worried Rocco. "I gave the guy the money like I was supposed to, but I could tell he wasn't going to just turn around and flee. I threw myself to the side just as he shot. I hit my head on the shelf behind the counter. It knocked me out, and I guess he thought he'd hit me when he saw the blood pooling under my head. He left, and I woke up when the paramedics arrived."

There was so much information there that Rocco's head was spinning. "He *shot* at you?"

Caite nodded.

"You were unconscious?"

She nodded again.

"Did they catch him?"

She shook her head that time.

"Fuck, fuck, *fuck*!" Rocco swore.

"I'm okay," she said. "The bullet only grazed me. I'm fine."

"*You were hit?*" Rocco exclaimed. "Where? Why aren't you in the hospital? Damn it!"

She put her hand on his chest and tried to calm him. "It was only a graze. I'm okay. I went to the hospital, they put a few stitches in and let me go. I didn't have a concussion or anything else, and I didn't want to spend the night."

Without a word, Rocco stood once more, ignoring the way Caite stiffened and let out a small screech when he picked her up. He carried her down the hall to her bedroom and sat her gently on the side of her bed. "Let me see," he demanded.

"Rocco, it's nothing."

"You were fucking shot! It's like my worst nightmare come true! You were hurt, and I wasn't here to help you. Let me see, Caite. I need to see for myself that you're okay."

She stared up at him for a beat, then shifted on the bed and pulled her arm through the long sleeve of the shirt she was wearing. Keeping herself covered—not that Rocco was thinking about anything other than her wound at the moment—she bared her arm for him.

A large white bandage was wrapped around her biceps, and Rocco felt his stomach roll just looking at it. He sank to the bed beside her.

He'd seen a lot of horrible things in his life. Limbs blown off soldiers and bad guys alike, burns so horrific he couldn't even recognize the face of one of the soldiers who had been fighting with him, and children blown to pieces by homemade bombs—but nothing had made him feel as physically sick as seeing that white bandage on Caite's creamy skin.

With shaking fingers, he reached for her and slowly unwound the bandage. He just as carefully peeled back the gauze packed around her arm, and then stared at the wound. There were only a few stitches, just as she'd claimed, but he still shuddered when he saw them. The black stitches looking like bug antennas coming out of her skin. The wound was red and puffy and looked painful, even if it was small.

He'd seen wounds like hers before, had received one himself, as a matter of fact. He knew just by looking at the gouge in her skin just how close of a call she'd had, and it made the world tilt under him.

Leaning forward, he gently kissed the skin to the right of the wound, then to the left. He closed his eyes and sat there a moment, trying to get his emotions in check.

"Rocco?"

He opened his eyes and looked at Caite. She had tears in her eyes once more, and he hated the look of vulnerability on her face. "Yeah, *ma petite fée?*"

"Can you...would you stay? Just for tonight?"

"Yeah, I can do that," he told her.

What he *didn't* say was that there was no way in hell he was leaving. Even if she would have asked him to, he couldn't.

He carefully rebandaged her arm and asked, "Have you taken anything for pain?"

She shook her head. "I haven't eaten anything, and the doctor said not to take them on an empty stomach. I was too tired to get up and make something."

Rocco hated that too. "Okay. Stay here and doze. I'll make you some soup. You *have* soup, don't you?"

"Yes, but you don't have to do that. I'll just get up and—"

Rocco put his hands on her shoulders and eased her to the mattress when she tried to stand up. "I've got this, baby. Just relax and let me take care of you."

Her lip quivered and, just like that, the tears were back in her eyes. She shut them, but not before Rocco had seen.

"Caite?"

"I'm okay," she said after a moment. "I...I was feeling sorry for myself earlier for being so alone. And now you're here. Helping me. Being nice. I should be asking if *you're* okay, but I just...I've had such a bad day!" The last words were practically wailed.

Lifting Caite gently, Rocco hugged her to him and let her sniffle some more against his chest. He wanted to do more. Wanted to track down the asshole who'd dared to hurt her, but at the moment, all he could do was hold her and try to make her feel better.

After a while, she pulled back and he lowered her back to the bed. "Better?" he asked.

She nodded.

"Okay. I'm going to go make you that soup and get your pain pills."

"Thank you."

He ran his fingertips down her cheek. "You don't have to thank me."

"You really don't have to stay. I was just having a weak moment. I'm sure you have to go into work tomorrow, and you'll need your stuff."

"I have a bag in my car," he told her. "It's got some clean clothes and some basic toiletry stuff. I never know when we'll get called out, so I always have a go-bag just in case. And I'm off for the next two days. Our commander always makes sure we have downtime when we get back from a mission. So there's nowhere I need to be other than right here."

Caite licked her lips. "Awesome."

He smiled. "Yup." Then he leaned forward and kissed her forehead. "Take a nap. I'll be back in a jiffy."

Waiting until her eyes closed and her breathing evened out, Rocco soundlessly got up and went back into the living area. First, he cleaned up the tissues and folded the blanket that had fallen to the floor. He grabbed her pills and brought them into the kitchen with him, reading the instructions. They were essentially super-strength acetaminophen, which he was glad to see. Not that he'd let Caite get addicted to any hard-core drugs, but he was glad the doctors didn't think she needed the more potent stuff.

He made a bowl of chicken noodle soup and carried it into the bedroom. He gently woke Caite and simply watched as she ate every bite of the soup. She was quiet and, he could tell, still sleepy. He gave her a pill and she swallowed it without protest. Rocco got her snuggled back down under the covers and sat by her side, watching her sleep.

After what had to be an hour or more, he finally took the dirty dishes back to the kitchen and headed out to his car to grab his bag. When he returned, he put on a pair of sweats and climbed into her bed. He stayed on top of the covers and turned on his side, continuing to watch her sleep.

It took a while, but eventually he fell asleep himself, although unlike hers, his sleep was fitful. He kept dreaming about Caite being shot to death, while he joked and laughed with his friends in a bar across town.

"You're sure she's dead?" Isaac Chambers asked the man he'd hired to kill Caite McCallan.

"Absolutely. Last I saw of her, she was lying in a pool of blood behind the counter."

Chambers paced back and forth in his kitchen. It was late, two in the morning, and he'd climbed out of bed to call and make sure the pain in his ass was finally no longer a threat. "I didn't see anything on the news," he said.

"Look, I fucking shot her, just like you wanted," the man said. "When do I get my money?"

The officer clenched his teeth. He'd hired this guy for the rock-bottom price of a thousand bucks. He didn't trust him as far as he could throw him. Knew his desire for drugs was far and away greater than making sure he did a good job.

"When I get proof that she's really dead."

"Fuck. Did you want me to stop and take the time to snap pictures?" the druggie complained.

"Where's the gun?"

"Threw it into the ocean like you told me to," the man said impatiently.

Relieved that at least the pistol couldn't be traced back to him, Chambers said, "Fine. Meet me at the same motel as before at lunchtime tomorrow. I'll have your money then."

"Man, I thought I'd get it tonight," the guy whined.

"It's the middle of the night," Chambers growled. "I'm not going to leave my family to drive all the way out there right now. You're just going to have to find another way to get a hit until I can get you the money."

"Fine. But you better be here tomorrow."

"Or what?"

"Trust me. You'll regret it."

"Don't. Threaten. Me," Chambers enunciated, quietly and deadly.

"Then make sure you're there tomorrow with my money," the druggie told him.

Chambers clicked off the phone without responding. "That bitch better be dead," he muttered. If not, she was either the luckiest person alive, or *he* was the *un*luckiest.

CHAPTER ELEVEN

A week later, Caite rolled over in bed and smiled at seeing the impression in the pillow next to hers. Since he'd returned from his mission, Rocco had spent every night in her bed. They didn't do anything other than sleep, but she had to admit that having him there, being able to talk to him until she fell asleep, was like a dream come true.

He was a perfect roommate. He helped cook. Did his own laundry. Made the bed. And most importantly, made her laugh and feel better about the fact she was now unemployed...again.

She'd made the decision the morning after she'd been shot. After having a nightmare about looking down the barrel of a gun, she'd known she couldn't go back.

Rocco had, of course, supported her decision one hundred percent.

"Take your time getting better," he'd said. "If you need money, I can help you out."

"That's not necessary," she'd said immediately. "My parents can help if I need it."

"Where do you think this is going between us?" he'd asked.

"Um...I don't know?"

"This is more than just dating, Caite," he'd said. "If you need something, I want to know so I can help you get it."

She'd agreed simply because she'd been so stunned and happy.

But now that it had been a full week, and Rocco still refused to touch her in any kind of sexual way, Caite was beginning to second-guessing their relationship. Oh, he kissed her, but was very careful not to take things any further. Maybe after living with her for a week, he'd ultimately decided things wouldn't work out between them. Maybe he didn't feel the sexual tension that she did.

All Caite knew was that sleeping next to him every night was both wonderful and torture. She wanted to reach over and pull his sweats down and see what he'd been hiding from her. She wanted to taste him, to feel him deep inside her body. But he hadn't given her the slightest inclination that he wanted the same thing. And if she made the first move and was rebuffed, it would be more than embarrassing. It would be devastating.

So she sucked it up and pretended that she was

super tired every night, desperately trying to fall asleep before he came to bed.

It had worked so far, but now she feeling better...and horny as hell. And with him being around all the time, Caite didn't even have the privacy to take care of herself.

Listening carefully, she didn't hear any indication that Rocco was home.

He'd gone back to work a few days ago and always got up before she did, making sure to wake her with a chaste kiss to the forehead and a murmured "good morning" before he headed off to meet his team for PT.

Looking at the clock, Caite saw that it was only five forty-five. She still had about half an hour before he'd be back to make her breakfast before heading off to the base once more.

Turning onto her back, Caite closed her eyes and slipped a hand beneath her pajama shorts. The other she eased under her top, pinching her nipple as she imagined what being with Rocco would be like. Would he be slow and gentle? Or would he shove her legs apart and take what he wanted?

Caite didn't know, but figured she'd like it either way.

Fingering her clit faster, she fantasized about all the things she wanted to do with him.

Her orgasm rose up fast and hard, and Caite arched her back, gasping, enjoying the sensations coursing through her.

After she'd come, she continued to stroke herself slowly, loving how wet she was now and how good her finger felt on her clit. She teased herself, making sure not to press hard enough to get herself off again, just enough to make the good feelings last.

Not sure what made her open her eyes, Caite turned her head toward the doorway—and froze.

Rocco was standing there, light from the living room highlighting his tall, taut body.

He wasn't wearing a shirt, and his sweats were sitting low on his hips. His cock was hard and long under the material...and she couldn't help but lick her lips.

Without a word, Rocco pushed off the edge of the door and stalked toward her.

Caite whipped her hand out from under her shirt, but didn't dare move the other one. Maybe he didn't know what she'd been doing. Maybe he hadn't been there that long.

Rocco sat on the side of the bed, clicked on the light, then reached over to pull the sheet down her body.

Shit. He knew.

She started to pull her hand out of her shorts, but he stopped her by grabbing her wrist. Caite could feel her nipples beading under her shirt, but didn't dare glance down to see what they looked like. She was caught in Rocco's intense dark gaze.

"May I?" he asked in a voice she hardly recognized. He gestured to her lap with his head, and she nodded.

God yes. She wanted his hands on her. Needed it.

Shifting to sit beside her with his back to the headboard, he arranged her between his legs so she rested against his chest. Then he snaked his right hand under the elastic band of her sleep shorts, and she felt his fingers tangle with hers.

He growled low in his throat when he felt how slick she was, and Caite felt it rumble against her back. "Keep touching yourself," he ordered.

Helpless to do anything other than what he ordered, and horny enough to ignore the embarrassment coursing through her body, Caite started moving her fingers over her clit once more.

She wished her shorts were gone, wanted to spread her legs apart—but she forgot everything but his touch when his thick fingers probed at her entrance. Now *she* was the one to groan, pressing her head back hard against his pectoral muscle.

Without words, they worked in tandem to bring her to another orgasm. When she was close, Rocco pushed her fingers out of the way and took over fingering her clit. He'd obviously paid attention, because he used the perfect amount of pressure and knew exactly how to stroke to make her come.

But unlike Caite, he didn't back off the second she started to orgasm. Instead, he pressed harder, forcing her orgasm higher and longer.

When it felt as if her heart was going to beat out of her chest, he finally eased his fingers off her super-sensitive clit and ran them down to her slit, smearing the wetness there, gently pressing in and out of her body.

Caite could feel his cock hard and thick against the small of her back, and she squirmed, wanting to see him. To feel him.

Rocco took his fingers out from between her legs and brought them to his face. Caite knew she was blushing furiously when she heard him suck them between this lips. She swore she also felt his dick twitch against her back as he licked every drop of her essence from his fingers.

She wanted to say something profound. Wanted for once in her life not to be a dork. But of course that was a big failure. "I thought you were gone," was what came out of her mouth.

He chuckled under her. "I figured."

"I'm sorry," she whispered, not sure what else to say.

"Do *not* say that," he ordered, then moved so quickly, Caite didn't have time to respond. He had her flat on her back under him and his arms braced on either side of her head. She could only blink up at him. "Seeing you get yourself off was the most erotic thing I've ever witnessed in my life. It was a gift. Don't be sorry, Caite. Please, God, don't be sorry."

"Okay. I won't." When he continued to just stare down at her, she said, "Do you...um...you can..." At a loss for words, she pressed her hips up until they bumped against his hard length.

"I'm good."

"You're good?" she echoed, confused. "But you're still hard."

"I am. But I'll take care of that in the shower."

She was still confused. "But...you don't want to...?" Once again, she was at a loss for words. Caite didn't understand him. She'd just been more intimate with him than she'd ever been with another man. She'd never masturbated in front of someone before, and she'd definitely not had someone else masturbate her like Rocco had.

"I want to, but I told you before, I want to take my time. I want all night. We don't have the time right now to do what I want to do *to* you and *with* you. Once I get my dick inside your hot, wet pussy, I'm not going to want to leave for a very long time. And I have plans for us today that can't wait. So...yes, I want to make love to you, Caite. I want that almost more than I want to breathe, especially after watching and hearing you come apart in my arms. But I can wait."

She blinked up at him. He could wait? Was he even real? She reached up and poked him in the chest, right over where his heart was.

He grinned. "What are you doing?"

"I just wanted to make sure I wasn't dreaming. You sure *feel* real."

"I'm real," he reassured her, then lowered his hips

until they were settled against hers. "Every inch of me is real."

Caite's breathing sped up once more. "I can feel."

"Thank you, *ma petite fée*. That was a gift that I'll treasure for the rest of my life. I know you didn't realize I was there the first time, but trusting me to give that to you a second time is something I won't ever take for granted."

All Caite could do was nod.

"And to answer the question I can see lurking in your eyes, I didn't go to PT today because I've planned something else for us. Something I hope you'll enjoy. It's part physical therapy for that arm, to help you get it moving more than you have been, and part selfishness on my part."

Caite was intrigued. "Yeah?"

"Yeah. I'm going to get up and shower...and no peeking, otherwise we'll never get out of this apartment," he warned when the word "shower" made her smile. "Then you can get up, do what you need to do in the bathroom, we'll eat breakfast and head out."

"Where?"

"It's a surprise."

Sighing, but not really upset, she tried to look stern when she glared at him.

Chuckling, he kissed her on the forehead and slowly eased his way off her. Then he blew her mind by bringing his hand up to his face and inhaling deeply as he ran his fingers under his nose. "If I could get away with never showering again, I would," he said, more to himself than her.

He stood, winked, and walked toward the small en suite bathroom.

Caite threw her head back on the pillow and let out a huge sigh. "That man is lethal," she mumbled, feeling more replete and relaxed than she'd felt in a long, long time.

An hour later, Caite was more stressed than she'd been in a long, long time.

"I'm not ready," she said.

"You're ready," Rocco replied calmly.

Caite looked away from Rocco's calm face toward the ocean. He'd brought her to a small, hidden-away beach and informed her that he was going to teach her to swim today...or at least work on her floating ability.

"I don't have a suit."

"You don't need one. The shorts and tank top you have on will be fine."

"I don't have anything to wear home."

Rocco turned her to face him and lifted her chin when a finger. "I'm not going to let anything happen to you. I packed a bag with towels and a dry set of clothes for us both. This cove is sheltered, so there aren't any waves. I'm not going to leave your side. You can do this."

Caite closed her eyes and sighed. In theory, Rocco teaching her how to swim was good. But in reality, it was a lot scarier than she figured it would be. While she went through everything that could go wrong in her mind, Rocco stood in front of her silently. She felt his hands on her shoulders, kneading gently.

She opened her eyes. "Okay."

"Okay?" he asked.

"But if I swallow half the ocean and get a brain-eating amoeba, I'm blaming you."

"Brain-eating amoebas are only found in fresh water. You're good."

Caite rolled her eyes.

"Come on. Kick off your sandals and we'll get this done."

"You're not going to give me any tips or instructions before we get in?" she squeaked out. She'd assumed she'd have a few more minutes to gather up her courage before she had to wade into the ocean.

"Nope. If I give you time to think much harder about this, you'll freak."

He wasn't wrong.

Rocco pulled off his T-shirt with one hand at the back of his neck. Caite had no idea how guys did that. She'd tried it one night at home, alone in her bedroom, and had ended up stretching the neck of her T-shirt and getting all tangled up in the material.

Staring at the beautiful chest he'd exposed, Caite could only blink at him for a moment. He had a spattering of chest hair that pointed downward to his groin, and an honest-to-God six-pack. His shorts clung to his powerful thighs, and she brought her gaze back up to his face quickly, before she embarrassed herself by staring between his legs.

He was grinning at her when she met his gaze. "Like what you see?" he asked with a smirk.

Caite once again rolled her eyes. "As if you were worried about that."

He moved quicker than even she thought he could. He grabbed her behind the waist and legs and hauled her up in his arms. Caite screeched and threw her arms around his neck even as she laughed. Rocco spun them around in circles before stopping and dropping the arm that was under her knees.

Her feet fell to the sand and she gripped his biceps tightly. She could see the veins in his forearms, and briefly had the thought that she'd never found a man's arms sexy before...until right this moment.

"Men have hang-ups about their bodies too, *ma petite fée.*"

"You have nothing to worry about," Caite reassured him. "Nothing at all."

He gave her a look that was so carnal, she knew she was blushing.

"Swim lesson," Rocco said, more to himself than her, as if he had to remind himself why they were there. He ran his fingers down her arm and twined them with hers when he reached her hand. Then he turned and tugged her gently toward the water.

Taking a deep breath, Caite reluctantly followed.

The water was surprisingly warm. Caite thought it would be cold for some reason. Rocco waded in up to his knees, which ended up being at Caite's thighs by the time he stopped. Then he turned to her. "All you have to do here at first is relax. Pretend you're lying in bed. Put your arms out to your sides and spread your legs a bit. I'm going to be right here by your side." His hand rested on her lower back, and even through her shirt, Caite could feel the heat seeping into her skin from his light touch.

"You won't let go, will you?" she asked.

He didn't roll his eyes or laugh at her. Instead, he said, "Never."

Nodding, Caite took a deep breath. She'd wandered off into the city of Manama in Bahrain all by herself and had found Rocco and his friends and saved their lives. She could do this.

She ducked down in the water until it was lapping at her neck, then she slowly lay back. Every muscle in her body was tense, and she held on to Rocco's arm with a death grip. She made sure to keep her eyes on his face the entire time. Wanted to make sure he wasn't going anywhere.

The gentle pressure of his hand on her back was constant and reassuring. He smiled down at her. "Relax,

Caite. The saltwater is going to do most of the work. It's harder to float when you're as tense as you are."

Forcing the muscles in her body to unclench, Caite tried to do as he asked. Rocco's voice was muted since her ears were underwater, but she could still hear him. He leaned down and brushed his lips against her forehead. "You're doing great, *ma petite fée*. I'm so proud of you."

It wasn't as if she was actually *doing* anything, but she'd take his praise. Rocco started moving her body, but she didn't look around, just kept watching his lips as he continued to talk to her while walking one way, then turning her body around and walking back.

Eventually, her fingers lost their death grip on his arm and she let go of him with one hand. She let her arm relax and was surprised to find that it floated next to her body almost without her even thinking about it.

"See? The saltwater makes your body more buoyant. Let go of me with your other hand and put that arm out to the side too."

Caite forced her fingers to let go and cautiously put her other arm out to her side as well.

Rocco beamed down at her. "Beautiful," he told her.

Caite saw his eyes go from hers, to the hair that was floating around her head, then down to her chest. She hadn't thought about what she was wearing until right that moment, when she saw his pupils dilate. He licked his lips and, even as he moved them around in the water, didn't take his eyes from her chest.

The thought of his gaze on her made her nipples tighten. Caite felt them pucker under the bra she'd thrown on that morning.

Without warning, Rocco's head dipped. Caite felt his hand press harder on her spine as his mouth closed around one of her nipples. She moaned.

His mouth felt scorching hot compared to the water and air around them. His fingers dug into the flesh of her back as he feasted on her.

She began to sit up, and Rocco immediately straightened and looked her in the eye once more. "Stay," he ordered.

Caite nodded and tried to relax. It wasn't until she was once again floating on her own that Rocco leaned back down. He took the other nipple in his mouth this time, nibbling and sucking through her clothes as if he had all the time in the world.

Caite didn't think about the fact they were on a public beach, that anyone could arrive and see them. She didn't think about the fact that she was floating or that Rocco was supposed to be teaching her how to swim. Every ounce of her attention was on the way he was making her feel. Sexy and beautiful.

Her eyes drifted shut and her legs opened a little more. The rush of cool water between her thighs was both torturous and erotic at the same time. She imagined Rocco's fingers dipping down and sliding under the elastic of her shorts, as they had hours before.

Realizing that she couldn't feel Rocco touching her

anymore, Caite opened her eyes to see him standing right next to her, both hands up in the air where she could see them.

"You're doing it," he told her. "All by yourself. I knew you could."

Instead of panicking about the fact that Rocco wasn't holding her anymore, she concentrated on how it felt to be floating. He was right; it was a lot easier to float in the ocean than in the pool the last time she'd tried. Her muscles were loose and she wasn't even really *doing* anything. But she was floating anyway.

"Try moving your hands back and forth a little bit," Rocco instructed. "In a scooping motion." He demonstrated above her.

She did—and was amazed when she actually moved forward. "I'm swimming!" she exclaimed in awe.

Rocco laughed above her—and just like that, Caite's attention was pulled from what she was doing back to the man standing at her side. She instinctively tried to sit up and her head immediately went under.

Before she could panic, Rocco's arms were around her, lifting her up and out of the water.

Caite coughed a little and clung to Rocco.

"You all right, *ma petite fée?*"

She nodded. "I was swimming," she said in an awed whisper.

"That you were."

She tilted her head and said, "I'm afraid to ask what I look like now that my shirt is wet."

"Beautiful," Rocco said reverently.

"Did you plan this?"

"If you mean the swimming lesson, yes. If you mean you in that white tank top? No. But I'm a guy, Caite. And you turn me on more than anyone I've ever met. I'd have to be dead not to look."

"You did more than look," she said with a smile.

He returned it. "You complaining?"

"Only that you stopped." The words came out without hesitation, and Caite had the momentary thought that she should be embarrassed, but she was finding that around Rocco, she felt anything but.

He groaned. "I brought you here so you could get more comfortable being in the water," he said, "not to seduce you."

"Can't you do both?" Caite asked, rubbing her leg up and down the outside of his thigh. The course leg hair rubbed against her sensitive inner thigh, and it made her think about how his beard would feel down there.

"Fuck, you're going to kill me," Rocco breathed. But he smiled as he said it. "Swimming first, then we'll see about the other."

Surprisingly, his words made her relax. She really did want to learn how to swim, and hearing him say that they'd be moving their physical relationship forward was a relief. Especially since this morning.

Caite wanted Rocco. Wanted him deep inside her and filling her up. She hadn't realized just how much until he'd refused to rush her this morning. She was ready for him. More than ready.

The next thirty minutes went by quickly. Rocco was an excellent swimming coach. He made her feel confident in her abilities and by the time they walked out of the ocean, Caite had mastered the art of kicking and using her arms at the same time while floating on her back to propel herself forward. All without his assistance, which felt amazing.

Caite shivered and put her arms around her waist to warm herself. Within seconds, Rocco was there. "How's your arm feel?"

"It's fine," Caite told him with some surprise. "I forgot all about it, actually."

"Good. The saltwater will also help it heal a bit faster. Don't ask why, I have no idea, but it does. Hey, what's this?" Rocco asked, pulling her to a stop and turning her to look at her back. He traced something on her shoulder blade.

Caite turned her head to try to see what he was talking about, but couldn't see anything. "What?"

"It looks like you have a bad bruise right here," Rocco said, his brows furrowed in concern.

"I had no idea. But I bruise easily." She shivered again.

"Come on," Rocco said, putting his arm around her shoulders and pulling her into his side once more. "Let's get you warm and dry."

Just as they got to the duffle where Rocco had

dropped it on the sand, a group of men in their early twenties arrived, laughing and joking and throwing a volleyball back and forth. They headed over to the court and began to talk smack to each other.

"Here," Rocco said, holding a towel out to her. "Cover up, baby."

Caite looked down at herself and winced. She may as well not have been wearing a shirt for how see-through the material was now. She grasped the towel to her chest and tried not to blush.

Rocco pulled her toward him and kissed the top of her head. "There's a bathroom over there. We can go change before we head back to your place."

Caite was all for that. The last thing she wanted to do was sit in his car in wet, clammy clothes. She nodded and reached for the bag. Rocco grabbed it before she could.

"I got it."

"I can carry it," she protested.

"I know you can," Rocco said. "But I've got it."

She shook her head in exasperation and walked next to him as they headed for the bathrooms. He reached in and grabbed his clothes then handed her the duffle. "I grabbed some things for you when I got up this morning. I hope they're okay."

"I'm sure it's fine," Caite mumbled, trying not to think about him going through her underwear drawer.

As if he could read her mind, Rocco leaned in and

said next to her ear, "It was a tough choice, but I can't wait to see you in what I picked out."

Caite giggled and backed away from him.

"I'll be waiting out here," Rocco told her unnecessarily. Where else was he going to meet her?

But she simply nodded and headed for the bathroom. Changing in a public restroom wasn't ideal, but Caite went into a stall and peeled off her wet clothes and quickly pulled on the clean, dry ones Rocco had packed. He'd chosen a pair of black lacy panties that she normally only wore when she dressed up. The bra he'd thrown in was also black and lacy, and her nipples beaded thinking about him seeing her in the ensemble.

She had a feeling that would be happening sooner rather than later, and she was okay with that. She quickly put on the jean shorts and the V-neck T-shirt he'd picked out as well. When she exited the women's restroom, Rocco was leaning against the wall. She couldn't help but sigh in appreciation upon seeing him. He was wearing a pair of jeans now with his flip-flops. He had on a black T-shirt, and once again her eyes were drawn to the veins in his forearms.

His hair was wet, as was hers, and she could see it was a bit too long, hanging in his eyes. When he saw her, he flicked his head impatiently to clear his vision. Caite had been working around military men for a while now, and she'd thought she was immune to a handsome soldier or sailor. But she had a sudden wish to see Rocco in his dress white uniform. She knew he'd look stunning.

"Hi," she said stupidly.

He grinned. "Hey. Ready to go?"

"Yeah."

He grabbed her hand and they walked toward the parking lot, which was now half-filled with cars, most likely from the young men playing volleyball or people exercising nearby.

"Thanks for forcing me to do this today," Caite told him.

"Force you? I'd never force you to do anything you didn't want to do," Rocco said, frowning.

"I didn't mean that the way it sounded," Caite reassured him. "I just mean, thank you for pushing me to try something I wasn't sure about. You should know, in general, if it's up to me, I'm perfectly happy sitting at home rather than going out and doing...just about anything. I will if you want to, but if left to my own devices, I'm a homebody and hermit. Just like in Bahrain, it's easier to just stay in my apartment than to take a risk and explore."

"I don't mind that about you," Rocco said. "Believe it or not, I'm happy to sit at home as well."

"But you're a SEAL," Caite said.

"I am. And as much as I enjoy what I do, I don't want to do it 24/7. And having someone to stay home with sounds absolutely appealing. If you were always on the go and always wanted to go out and do stuff, things between us probably wouldn't work. But, Caite, if I ever set up something for us to do that you really don't want to, all you have to do is tell me and I'll back off. I mean that."

"I know. And I appreciate it. I've wanted to learn to swim for a while now. At least to be more comfortable in the water, but I felt weird about signing up for swim lessons since they're usually for kids. And trusting a stranger to make sure I don't drown isn't high on my list either."

"You do know that you're not exactly ready to try out for the Olympics, right?" Rocco asked as they neared his car.

Caite chuckled. "I'm not? You mean I can't give Katie Ledecky a run for her money?"

"Who?"

"Never mind. I understand, Rocco. But I already feel more confident. If you're willing to continue to help me, I know I can get even better. Maybe even float in a pool as opposed to the ocean."

"Once you get the hang of it, you'll wonder how in the world you ever *couldn't* swim," he reassured her with a small squeeze of her hand in his. Then he moved his hand to the small of her back and his fingertips dipped to brush against the crack of her ass. "I don't think there's anything you can't do when you put your mind to it."

"Hand me the car keys and no one'll get hurt!" a low, angry voice said from nearby.

Caite had been lost in the teasing feel of his finger-tips against her sensitive backside but at hearing the threat, she turned to see who had spoken—and gasped in surprise and fear.

A man with a baseball cap pulled low over his fore-head, wearing all black, was standing between them and the beach.

He had a pistol in one hand that shook as he aimed it at them.

CHAPTER TWELVE

Rocco pulled Caite behind him with one hand even as he raised the other, showing he was unarmed. "Easy, man," he said, not wanting to spook the kid any more than he already was.

"Give me your keys," the punk repeated.

"They're in my pocket," Rocco said. "I'm going to have to reach for them," he told the kid.

"No. Let her do it," he ordered, waving the gun in Caite's direction.

Without a word, Rocco felt Caite's small hand reach into his pocket to search for the keys. In any other situation he'd make some sexually charged comment about being careful what she was grabbing down there, but now wasn't the time or place.

There was something about the carjacking that bothered Rocco. The kid hardly seemed like a hardened criminal. He looked scared out of his mind. Scared but determined. Rocco knew he could bum rush him and take him down within seconds, but the last thing he wanted was to leave Caite vulnerable. If the kid got off a lucky shot, he'd never forgive himself. Better to just give him what he wanted. Caite's life was worth much more than his car.

Caite's hand retreated from his pocket with the key to the Acura in her hand. She went to give it to Rocco, but the kid barked, "Bring them here!"

Rocco shook his head. "No. Take the keys and go."

"No. She has to bring them to me. Better yet, she needs to get in the car and drive."

"Fuck no!" Rocco exclaimed. "She's not going anywhere."

"Yes she is! If you want to live, that is."

Rocco clenched his teeth. There was no way in hell Caite was getting in the car with his jackhole. "Look. She's my girlfriend. I'm not letting her get in the car with you, man. Just take the car and go."

At Rocco's words, the kid's lips pressed together in frustration. "She has to come with me."

"Why?" Rocco barked.

"Why?" the kid echoed.

"You don't need her. Just take the car," Rocco repeated.

The carjacker shook his head and glanced around before meeting Caite's eyes. "You need to get in the car. Just get in! You have to."

Rocco felt Caite's hand on his back and could feel

her shaking. He was pissed off that the punk was scaring her. Enough was enough. He'd have to incapacitate him after all.

Just when he was readying himself to jump the kid in a way that would minimize the danger to Caite, he saw someone running toward them out of the corner of his eye.

Before he could do anything, shots rang out.

Rocco acted on instinct, turning and grabbing Caite while flinging them both to the ground. Grunting when he landed on his back, Rocco barely felt the pain. He was immediately rolling, covering Caite with his body as he physically hauled her around the back a car and away from the kid with the gun and whoever else was shooting.

Rocco heard shouting, but all his attention was on Caite. "Are you all right? Are you hurt?" he asked, running his eyes over her face and down her body.

"I'm o-okay," she said with only a small stutter. "You?"

"Fine," he told her, not worrying about the pain in his shoulder blades from landing on the ground. "How's your arm?"

"It's good. What's going on?"

"Stay here," Rocco ordered. "Just stay down and I'll see."

Caite grabbed his forearm when he started to straighten. "You can't!" she exclaimed.

Rocco didn't have time to reassure her, but he took

it anyway. "Caite, I'm a SEAL. I've got this. I could've taken that kid down within seconds, but I didn't want to do anything that would leave you vulnerable. I can take care of this, but I need to know you're safe. Can you please stay here? Better yet, roll under this car just in case. I'll be right back. Promise."

She studied him for a beat, before nodding and scooting under the car on her belly. "Be careful," she whispered.

Rocco nodded, thanking his lucky stars she was so levelheaded. The second she was under the car, he stayed crouched and made his way to the front and peered around the bumper.

What he saw made his breath catch in his throat.

Moving as quick as lightning, he ran toward the potential carjacker. The kid was lying on his back, gasping for air, blood trickling out of his mouth. A red circle was slowly growing on his shirt right over his heart.

Swearing, Rocco tossed the pistol out of reach of the kid and immediately pressed his hand down on the hole in his shirt. "Hang on," he told him. Then turning his head, he yelled, "Caite?"

"Yeah?" she replied immediately.

"Call 9-1-1. Tell them that we were almost carjacked and now the perp has been shot."

"Shit. all right!" she replied.

"Are you okay?" a male's voice said above him.

Rocco looked up to see a man about his age standing

nearby. In his grip was a handgun. "Move away slowly and put that weapon on the ground," he bit out.

"Dude, he had you at gunpoint," the man said without complying. "I saved your life!"

Rocco held on to his temper by sheer force of will. "Thank you. Now, please, put the gun down."

"Okay, okay, chill," the man said, and placed his gun on the trunk of the car next to him.

The kid under him coughed, and Rocco could hear gurgling in his chest. This was not good. "Hang in there," he told him. "Paramedics are on their way."

"It's not loaded," the kid gasped out.

"What?"

"My gun. It's not loaded. The guy said all I had to do was bring the girl. That's all!"

"What guy?" Rocco asked, leaning down and getting in the kid's face.

"I needed the promotion," the kid continued, ignoring the question. "He said if I did what he wanted, he'd make sure I got promoted..." He paused to cough again and blood sprayed out of his mouth. Rocco leaned back just in time to avoid it.

"*Who* said you'd get promoted?" he asked urgently.

But it was too late. The kid's eyes rolled back in his head and his body went limp.

"*Fuck*. Shit!" Rocco put his free hand against the kid's neck and felt for a pulse.

Nothing.

"Starting CPR," Rocco announced.

Within seconds, Caite was there. "What can I do to help?"

"Back up," Rocco said immediately. "I mean it, Caite. I don't want you anywhere near his blood."

"But you aren't even wearing gloves!" she protested.

"Please," Rocco begged between chest compressions. "You don't need to see this. Please, just step around that car."

"Okay."

"But don't go far," he yelled, looking up at her for the first time. "I don't want you out of my sight."

She walked around the car next to them and stood on the other side of the hood, turning her back. "Is this okay?" she asked.

"Perfect." And it was. She wasn't watching the guy who'd wanted to kidnap her die, and she was safe from any bodily fluids. He was also between her and the guy who thought he was on the set of *Live PD* or something.

It took ten minutes for help to arrive, and Rocco knew there was no coming back from a gunshot to the heart, but he kept doing CPR, just in case. One second it was just him counting out chest compressions, and the next there were paramedics swarming around him. Rocco gladly stood, relinquishing control of the scene to the professionals. He looked around for Caite and smiled weakly when he saw her standing to the side, holding a towel from the bag he'd packed earlier that morning.

She held it out. "Thought you could use this."

Rocco took it and cleaned his hands as best he could. It would take a while for the bloodstains to come out. He yanked off his shirt, knowing it had some blood on it too. Then, before he was ready, Caite grabbed him around the waist and plastered herself to his chest.

Rocco held his arms out, not daring to touch her yet. He didn't want one drop of that asshole's blood on her.

She seemed to understand why he wasn't holding her, but it didn't faze her. She clung to him and eventually rested her cheek on his pectoral muscle as they watched the paramedics try to bring the young man back to life...to no avail.

By then, the police had arrived. One deputy was questioning the man who had fired the fatal round and another came over to them. "I understand you were the couple the man was holding up?"

Rocco nodded. "He wanted my car."

"How'd that guy get involved?" the deputy asked, gesturing toward the other man with his head.

"Not sure. I guess he saw what was happening and came over to lend a hand."

"Did he say anything before he discharged his weapon?"

Rocco shook his head. "No."

"Are you sure?"

"Positive. But the kid had a weapon pointed at us. He wouldn't just take the keys and go," Rocco said, somewhat defending the civilian who'd been trying to help.

"Okay. I'm going to need both of your statements."

"Of course."

"Ma'am?" the deputy asked, looking at Caite.

She shifted until her side was against Rocco's and nodded. "Whatever you need."

"Thank you. If you can just head over there where my partner is, he'll be with you in a bit."

Rocco nodded again and draped his arm over Caite's shoulder. He first walked them over to the ambulance and requested some alcohol to wash his hands, which the paramedics gladly provided. Finally having his hands clean enough that he could risk touching Caite, he pulled her to him and held on as tight as he dared.

That had been close. Too fucking close. "Jeez, *ma petite fée*, you sure know how to make an outing exciting."

She huffed out a small laugh and said, "It's not me. It's *you*. Before I met you, nothing interesting happened to me. Now I've traipsed around a foreign country, saved the lives of three Navy SEALs, been fired from my job, almost run over by a pickup truck, been shot in a robbery, and now carjacked. Sheesh. I'm like Domino from the second *Deadpool* movie. Luck must be my superpower."

Rocco froze at her words. "You were almost run over by a truck?" he asked, trying to keep his voice as even as possible.

Something about his voice must have sounded off because Caite looked up at him. "Yeah. Um...it was the night we first went out. I was late leaving work and was hurrying home because I knew I wasn't going to have enough time to get ready before you got there. The guy jumped the curb, and someone yelled at me to watch out. I jumped out of the way just in time. My guess is that he was probably texting or drunk or something."

"The bruise on your back?" Rocco asked.

Caite frowned. "Oh...I guess."

His mind was spinning, and he recalled what the kid had said. *All I had to do was bring the girl. He said if I did what he wanted, he'd make sure I got promoted.*

"Motherfucker," Rocco said under his breath.

"What?" Caite asked, the concern easy to hear in her voice. "What's wrong?"

Rocco shook his head and pressed his lips together. He needed to get through the interview with the deputies and then have a talk with his team. Once they had the name of the potential carjacker, it should be easy to figure out who he worked under. It was possible that his boss wasn't the person they were looking for, but who else would have the clout to get him promoted?

Rocco should've realized Caite might be a target after what had happened in Bahrain. Contractors like her generally didn't get fired and rushed out of the country like she'd been. That, along with all the brushes with death she'd had, meant someone wanted her gone. Pronto.

Deciding now wasn't the time to scare her, Rocco kissed the top of her head and shook his own. "We'll talk later, *ma petite fée*."

"Okay," she whispered. After a beat she said, "Bet you're sorry you decided I needed to learn how to swim today of all days, huh?"

Rocco didn't have an answer for that. He had a feeling it didn't matter when he taught her to swim. Someone was watching her. Or him. Or both of them. At the moment, it didn't matter. What mattered was figuring out why someone wanted Caite dead.

One thing was for certain. No one was going to kill his woman.

He'd already made his mind up that he wanted Caite McCallan for his own. But learning that her life was in danger made it all the more clear.

Glancing over at the kid lying dead under the white sheet, who'd just been following someone else's orders, made him realize it could've been Caite lying there.

No. Fuck no.

He'd get the team together and they'd figure out who wanted Caite dead, and why. The alternative was unacceptable.

Two hours later, Caite sat in the middle of Rocco's

apartment, looking from one of his teammates to another, waiting for someone to start talking. Without explanation, Rocco had refused to go back to her place, but instead had driven straight to his apartment complex and called Gumby, Ace, Phantom, Rex, and Bubba for an emergency meeting.

Caite had been edgy and nervous ever since she'd told Rocco about all her bad luck...or good luck, depending on how she looked at it. Something was bothering him, and she couldn't figure out if it was something she'd said, something she'd done, or something else entirely. She knew Rocco pretty well, but obviously not well enough.

"What's going on?" she asked.

Rocco pulled the coffee table closer to where she was sitting on the couch and reached for her hands. Caite swallowed hard.

"You know how you told me about your run of bad luck?" he asked.

Caite nodded.

"It's not bad luck," Rocco told her. "Someone wants you dead."

She gaped at him. "*What?* No, that's not true."

"*Ma petite fée*, you're exactly right when you say that none of that stuff happened until you met me. But I think it's more than that. Think back to when you overheard that conversation with the Bitoo brothers. I've thought about this until I can't think anymore, and I've come to the conclusion that it *has* to be what this is

248

about. I think you overheard something that someone doesn't want getting out."

Caite immediately shook her head. "I've told you what I can remember," she said, her voice shaking. "I've tried to remember more details, but I was freaking out when they started talking. I thought they were going to do something to me at first, but then when they started discussing you guys, it was even scarier."

"Easy, hon," Rocco said, squeezing her hands gently. "You're safe here."

"Seriously, Rocco, I can't think of anything else other than what I've already told you."

Ace pushed off the wall and came over to where she was sitting. He sat next to her, putting a reassuring hand on her thigh. "You might've heard something that was minor, just a part of the conversation, and it didn't even register. Can you go through what you heard for us? Maybe we'll recognize it when we hear it."

Caite knew she was breathing too fast, and it felt as if her heart was beating a million miles a minute. "That kid today was killed because of *me*?" she asked quietly, ignoring Ace's suggestion.

"No," Rocco said. "Absolutely not. He was killed because he was greedy. Because he took the easy way out. Because that other guy got a little too zealous in his desire to protect us. That kid agreed to help some asshole because of what he could get out of it. Not caring what might happen to *you* if he delivered you as promised."

Something else occurred to Caite just then. "Are *you* in danger because of me?" she asked, her voice almost shrill. "You could've been shot today because of *me*! Holy shit!" Caite looked around as if to find an escape route, but Rocco ducked into her field of vision and took hold of her head, forcing her to look at him.

"Calm down."

She shook her head as best she could in his grip, but her hands came up and wrapped around his wrists so tightly, her fingers turned white with the pressure. "No! That's it. We're broken up! You have to take me home! Forget you ever heard my name."

"We're not broken up," Rocco said calmly. "And I'm not in danger. The only one who needs to worry from here on out is the asshole who wants you dead."

"Is my family safe?" Caite asked. "Do I need to call my parents and tell them to take a vacation to Timbuktu because someone thinks I overheard something I didn't?"

"I'll make sure they're covered," Phantom said as he pulled out his phone.

Her eyes flicked from Phantom to Rocco. "You guys are kinda scary," Caite said. "Who's he calling? Superman?"

Everyone chuckled but Rocco. "Are you with me?" he asked instead.

"With you?"

"With me. Dating. My woman," he clarified.

"Um...yes?"

"Right. So from here on out, whatever you need, you'll get. Whether that's a fucking spa day, chocolate during a certain time of the month, or protection for your parents."

"That's... I don't know what that is."

"It is what it is," Bubba said from the other side of her on the couch. "It's how we operate. We take care of our own, and you're one of us."

"I barely know how to swim," Caite mumbled. "How can I be one of you when I can't even swim?"

Ignoring her comment, Rocco said, "Close your eyes, *ma petite fée*. Think back to the conference at the naval base. You were sitting there waiting for time to go by and thinking about paperwork that your asshole boss didn't bother to do and you heard the brothers speaking in French. What were they saying?"

Caite took a deep breath and concentrated on the way Rocco's hands felt on her. She could feel the warmth of his body against her knees. Even the slight weight of his friends on either side of her made her feel safer. She hated knowing that she might've heard something that was now making someone want to kill her. But she hated even more having no idea what it was.

She thought back to that day. Remembered how irritated she was that she had to be at the conference when she'd rather be wallowing in despair that Rocco had stood her up. She wasn't paying attention to the people milling around her because she was irritated with the whole delayed lunch issue and was just passing the time doodling.

"Their voices stood out because they were speaking French," Caite said after a moment. "The other people talking in the room just faded into the background, but because it had been so long since I'd heard French, I was paying attention."

"What were they saying?" Rocco asked gently, shifting his hands down to hold hers.

Caite could feel his thumbs gently rubbing over the backs of her hands. It felt good. Soothing. "I had my back to them, so I couldn't tell who was saying what, but at first they were concerned that someone would overhear them and understand what they were saying. To prove that no one could, and probably since I was closest, one of the men insulted me very loudly in French, I guess to see if I'd glare at them or tell them to buzz off. But I didn't. I sat there and pretended I didn't hear."

"I'm sorry you had to listen to that, *ma petite fée.*"

Just the sound of Rocco's smooth, low voice made her relax. She realized she'd been gripping his hands way too tightly, so she consciously tried to calm down. She wasn't there. She was here. Surrounded by Rocco and his team. She was safe.

"They weren't happy about having to be at the conference. They wanted to go and kill you guys right then," she told the group.

"Why didn't they?" Ace asked.

Caite furrowed her brow and tried to remember what they'd said. "I don't know," she said after a moment. "Some of the brothers wanted to go right away and take care of you guys, but the older one, at least I think it was him, wanted to wait. Wanted to make sure they would have an alibi. I'm pretty sure they knew you were SEALs. Or at least knew you could overpower them if they weren't ready."

"They were right," Bubba said quietly.

"Guns," Caite said, sitting up straighter. "They didn't have any and wanted to get them."

"Where were they going to get them from?" Rocco asked.

"Um...I don't know. They said something about the navy taking back the tablets if they found them, and that they needed to lie low or something. They started arguing about who would get to shoot you guys, and then said they'd leave your bodies there. They didn't care if their dad got in trouble. They figured he'd be deported and they'd get to take over the store." Caite stopped and opened her eyes. "I think one said that he didn't care if your bodies started to rot." She swallowed hard as she stared at Rocco.

"I'm fine, *ma petite fée*. You got there in time. You got us out," he said gently.

Caite nodded and willed her tears back. "Damn straight I did," she said with as much bravado as she could muster.

She was rewarded when Rocco smiled at her. "That's

my girl," he praised. "Back to the guns. They didn't have any. Are you sure they didn't say anything about where they were going to get one?"

Caite closed her eyes again and concentrated. Then her eyes popped open suddenly. "One of them said a name. Asked if he could help. One of his brothers dismissed the idea, saying the guy was all the way in America and only cared about the tablets."

"Think, Caite. Who?" Rocco urged. "What was the name?"

"I don't know! Their accents were thick and I was having a hard time understanding. I leaned Parisian French. Not African French. And I think they had a local dialect too."

"It's okay...shhhhh," Rocco soothed.

"It'll come to you when you least expect it," Rex reassured her.

"We need to call NCIS," Bubba said.

"And Commander North," Rocco said, looking up at his friend. "We don't know for sure, but all indicators are pointing to the fact that this guy is probably navy. There's a mole in Bahrain, and Commander Horner believes it's someone in his unit. I'm thinking someone has to be holding something pretty big over this mole, and a high-ranking officer would certainly be able to threaten someone to do their dirty work. So if this guy really is navy, I'm guessing he's pretty high up. There's no way a junior enlisted or even a noncommissioned officer would have the clout to orchestrate something like this. Not to mention that kid today said something about being promoted if he brought Caite in. That sounds like a senior or flag officer."

"Do we know who he is yet?" Bubba asked.

Rocco shook his head. "No. He didn't have any ID on him. But if he's in the navy, his fingerprints will definitely be in the system. Hopefully they'll come back soon and this thing will be over."

"I'm not sure it's a good idea to call Commander North," Ace said. "I mean, maybe the commander knows whoever this is, maybe they're friends."

"North is clean. I'd stake my career on it," Rocco said. "And I know him. He wouldn't cover for anyone for attempted murder. No way."

"Fine. I'll head over to the base and talk to him," Ace said.

"And I'll call NCIS as soon as I leave," Bubba said. "They're going to want to interview Caite," he warned.

Caite looked from one man to the other as they discussed their next steps. Personally, she wanted nothing more than to crawl into bed and hide under the covers, but she sat docilely as the team talked about what to do.

She tried to remember the name one of the brothers had mentioned, and she just couldn't bring it up from the recesses of her mind. It was there, she knew it. But she couldn't seem to call it forth.

"Maybe we can give her a list of all the flag and

senior officers stationed here and see if she recognizes one of them," Phantom suggested.

"Maybe," Rocco said. "But not quite yet. We just figured out that someone wants her dead, most likely because of what she overheard. I think we should let her think about the conversation a bit on her own before we overwhelm her with names. Caite?"

She blinked up at Rocco. "Yeah?"

"What do you think?"

"Oh...um. Okay. Can't the navy or whoever just go and find the Bitoo brothers and ask *them* who they were going to try to get a gun from?"

Rocco stared at her for a long moment—and Caite's stomach immediately got tight. She wasn't going to like what he said next, she just knew it.

"They're dead, Caite."

She blinked. "What?"

"The authorities in Bahrain were looking for them but weren't having any luck, until their bodies washed up in an industrial area on the west side of the country."

Caite swallowed hard. She hadn't liked the men, not in the least. They were going to kill Rocco and the others...but she hadn't wanted them to be murdered.

Her hopes came crashing down. This really was on her. If she didn't remember the name of the person they'd been talking about, he'd eventually probably succeed in killing her. She'd been extremely lucky so far. She had a feeling her luck wouldn't hold much longer.

"Stop it," Rocco scolded gently.

"Stop what?" Caite asked.

"Thinking that way."

"How do you know what I'm thinking?" she asked with a tilt of her head.

"Because I know you, *ma petite fée*. And now that we all know your life is in jeopardy, *no one* is getting near you. I'm going to call in every connection I've got to make this right."

The pesky tears threatened once more, but Caite blinked them away. "Okay."

"Right. Let NCIS know I'll bring Caite in tomorrow so they can talk to her," Rocco told Bubba.

"Will do," the other man replied.

"You want us to keep watch?" Phantom asked.

Rocco shook his head. "No. We're safe enough here."

"I'll talk to the commander," Ace said. "I'll explain what's going on."

"'Preciate that," Rocco said.

And with that, the five men stood and made for the door. Rocco followed and locked the deadbolt behind them. Within moments, Caite and Rocco were alone.

He sat next to her on the couch this time and took her in his arms. "We're going to figure this out," he said quietly into her hair. "No way I've found you only to lose you now."

Caite had no words. All she could do was cling to what seemed like the only stable thing in her life at the moment.

Captain Isaac Chambers stared down at the news app on his phone. It was an alert about an attempted carjacking down by one of the beaches in the area. His gut clenched. He took a few deep breaths and tightened his fists. How he could be so unlucky was beyond him.

All the seaman had to do was bring him the girl. That's *it*. How the fuck he'd managed to get himself killed was a mystery he didn't give one shit about discovering.

"This is fucking ridiculous," Chambers muttered. "Why is it so hard to kill one slip of a girl?"

He'd paid off the junkie for shooting her in the fake robbery, but it turned out that he hadn't even hit her, had only grazed her arm. The blood he'd seen on the floor had been from the head wound she'd gotten when she'd hit it while falling.

Knowing the FBI maintained a database with the fingerprints of military personnel, Chambers swore. Now he had to deal with that as well, because the second authorities figured out the carjacker was Carter Richards—who was under *his* command—they'd likely connect all the dots and he was done for.

He quickly pulled out one of his many disposable, untraceable phones, and shot off a text to his contact in Bahrain.

Boss: Delete Carter Richards's fingerprints from the FBI database. Immediately.

Even with the time change, he received a reply almost immediately.

Dr. Who: Seriously? That's not as easy as it seems.
   Boss: I don't care. It has to be done. Pronto. Otherwise we're all fucked.

It took several minutes for a reply to come back in.

Dr. Who: I've never hacked into the FBI before. But I'll do my best.

Fuck! Chambers ran a hand through his hair in agitation. Everything had been so perfect for so long. The petty officer third class had been extremely useful in passing along information from the base in Bahrain. Chambers had easily found out everything he needed to know in order to avoid being caught. He'd met the tech expert when he'd still been a seaman, and had taken advantage of the fact that he had two kids and a wife to support.

The situation had been ideal. But everything had begun to unravel thanks to Caite McCallan's transfer to Bahrain. Of course they'd had to hire someone who was fluent in French.

And Carter Richards screwing up a simple abduction was the last straw.

Chambers was done fucking around.

"If you want something done right, you have to do it yourself," he mumbled.

Standing, Chambers went to the locked filing cabinet in the corner of his office. He wasn't supposed to have a loaded firearm, but fuck that. He fastened the ankle holster on and tucked the pistol inside.

He strode over to the window and stared outside. His office overlooked one of the training beaches for the SEALs. Watching the recruits being put through their paces in the distance didn't distract him today, as it might have in the past. All he could think about was what would happen to him if Caite McCallan wasn't taken care of.

She'd remember his name. He'd be taken into custody. His clients would learn of his arrest and they'd be pissed and, more than that, they'd be afraid of what he'd tell the authorities. He was as good as dead if he didn't get to Caite first. Chambers knew the kinds of connections the people he worked with had. *They* wouldn't have any trouble making sure he couldn't talk. He'd be dead within twenty-four hours of that bitch spilling her guts.

Damn Caite McCallan! This was all *her* fault!

Different scenarios—from walking up to her apartment, knocking on the door and blowing her face off when she answered, to pulling up next to her at a stoplight and shooting her—ran through his mind.

He needed to get her alone. Wanted to make sure she knew dying was all on her. That he hadn't wanted to go to these extremes, and it wasn't personal. If she didn't know French, none of this would be happening. She'd been in the wrong place at the wrong time, that's all.

CHAPTER THIRTEEN

Rocco was worried about Caite. She hadn't said much since his teammates had left. He was trying to give her some space to work through things in her head, but he was beginning to think he'd taken the wrong approach.

She was trying too hard to remember. He needed to distract her. "Caite?"

"Hmmm?" she said absently from where she was sitting on the couch.

"Come here," Rocco ordered from the kitchen.

He saw her turn her head and look back over the edge of the sofa. "Is something wrong?"

"No. But I need you."

That did it. She immediately stood and walked around his couch and came to his side. "What's wrong?"

"Nothing," he told her, then put his hands around her waist and pushed her back until she bumped against the counter. "Jump up," he told her.

"What? Why?"

"On the count of three," he said. "One, two, three!"

He didn't really need her to help him, but she did as asked and gave a little hop just as he lifted her to sit on the counter in front of him.

"Rocco, What are you—"

"Where were we this morning on the beach when we were so rudely interrupted?" he asked rhetorically. "Oh yeah, right about here..." His moved his hand to the small of her back and his fingers caressed the crease of her butt.

He felt her shiver and she arched her back, giving him better access. "Rocco," she protested weakly.

"Caite," he mimicked, even as he continued his assault on her senses. "I watched you sleep for a while this morning before I got up. You were adorable...and I seriously can't imagine waking up any other way from here on out. I decided to take you to Blue Cove to help you overcome your fear of the water."

His fingers kept caressing her as he spoke, and Rocco watched her eyelids droop and felt her muscles relaxing more and more with every second that passed. He knew she was probably barely listening, but he kept going. "I picked out this outfit, and thought about not invading your privacy and letting you choose your own bra and underwear...but then I got curious. What kind of underwear would you have? Lacy and sexy? Or cotton and practical? Turns out, you had both. The second I saw this matching set, however, I knew I had to see it on you."

Caite's breathing was erratic now, and she was clutching his T-shirt at his waist. Good. She wasn't thinking about what she'd overheard in Bahrain anymore. All her concentration was on him and the way he was making her feel.

"What are you doing to me, *ma petite fée*? I can't think. I spend every minute I'm not with you wondering what you're doing. Are you safe? Are you happy? It's driving me mad."

"I feel the same way. I was so scared every second you were gone," she admitted, looking up at him with dilated eyes. "I have no idea how it happened so fast."

"What?" Rocco asked.

"Falling for you," she told him with absolutely no guile. "This isn't like me. I'm too practical. I think things through before I do them. I make lists. You should've seen the list of pros and cons I made before I accepted the job in Bahrain. It was insane."

"Was meeting the love of your life on the pro side?" Rocco asked with a quirk of his lips.

"No. Neither was becoming the target of a crazy man who wants to kill me."

Shit. He hadn't meant to remind her of *that*.

"I'm in love with you, Caite McCallan. I love your strength and your vulnerability. I love that you're willing to try new things just as much as I love that you're perfectly happy to sit at home with a good book rather than go out. I love your acceptance of what I do for a living, just as much as I love that you worry about me as I'm doing that job. I love that you like my friends, and I love that you have a close relationship with your parents. I love that you trust me, and I love that you don't freak out when I get bossy."

Her eyes were huge in her face as she stared up at him. Rocco stilled his fingers and pressed against her ass, scooting her all the way to the edge of the counter. He stepped forward until he was pressed against her. There was no way she could miss his erection. He needed her more than he needed his next breath...but it had to be her decision.

Several beats went by and she didn't say a word, simply continued to stare up at him as if she'd seen a ghost. Rocco hadn't realized how nervous he'd been, and her silence was beginning to unnerve him.

Finally, she reached up and wound her arms around his neck. Her knees came up and hooked around his hips. "You haven't shown me your bedroom yet," she said huskily.

And just like that, Rocco's libido returned full force. She hadn't said she loved him back, but he knew she cared about him. He could work with that.

Rocco put his hands under her ass and lifted her as easily as he would his loaded backpack before a mission. He could almost feel her heat against his cock and with every step he took toward his room, he felt her tits brush against his T-shirt.

She didn't take her eyes from his as he carried her to his bed. Even when he leaned over and placed her ass on the edge of the mattress, she didn't look away. He bent over her and she scooted backward as he crawled onto the bed.

"This is my room," he told her.

"It's nice," she replied, even though she hadn't even taken the briefest glance around. Her hands went to the waist of his jeans and fumbled with the button there. He stayed crouched over her and simply enjoyed the moment.

Memorizing the feel of her warm fingers against the skin of his lower belly, he braced himself with his hands by her head. Her nipples were hard under her shirt, and Rocco wanted nothing more than to rip off all her clothes and plunge his rock-hard dick inside her.

But not yet.

He wanted to savor her.

They only had one first time.

Caite couldn't look away from Rocco's face as she did her best to undo his pants. His dark brown eyes bored into her own.

He loved her. It seemed impossible, but deep down, she knew this was right.

Wanting to show him how much his words meant to her, Caite pushed gently on his hips. He stood and let her push him back. Not even thinking that he might believe she was pushing him away, Caite went to her knees at the side of the bed. She tilted her head back to keep eye contact with him even as she pulled his jeans down over his ass. They fell to his ankles, but he didn't move.

Running her hands up his thighs, Caite marveled at how strong they were. How strong *he* was. When the shot rang out that morning, he'd picked her up and thrown them both to the side without thought. He'd held her safe against him and had covered her body with his own.

She thought back to when she'd opened the hatch in the floor in that shop in Bahrain. She hadn't understood what had happened at the time, but now that she knew it had been Rocco who'd basically thrown Ace out of the cellar using brute strength, she could see exactly how he'd done it.

His thighs were nothing but muscle. The coarse hair tickled her palms as she ran them up and down. He had on a pair of boxer briefs that didn't leave much to her imagination. He was big. His cock strained against the material, begging to be set free.

Caite moved her hand to the waistband of the briefs, but he stopped her.

"Will you please take off your shirt first?" he asked. "I picked out that bra and panty set this morning hoping I'd get to see you in it later."

Blushing, Caite nodded. She lifted the shirt up and

over her head almost without thought. Knowing he wouldn't ask, she undid the buttons on her shorts and sat to slide those down her legs too. Then she leaned back against the bed. She never would've been able to be so bold without his earlier words of love.

"God. *Damn*," Rocco bit out. "The reality is so much better than my imagination."

Caite looked down at herself and mentally shrugged. All she could see were boobs that were a bit too saggy for her liking, too much of her stomach sticking out, and thighs that were a little too thick to be considered hot.

But when she looked back up into Rocco's eyes, she realized something. He didn't see any of her flaws. All he saw was *her*.

Feeling more confident, she arched her back and smiled when he inhaled.

"Give me a second," Rocco said as he tilted his head back and closed his eyes. His hands were fisted at his sides, and she'd never seen anything sexier in her life.

Even standing there with his boots on, jeans around his ankles and his dick doing its best to break free of its cotton prison, he was amazing. And he was all hers.

Sliding to her knees on the floor, Caite cupped his balls through his underwear and licked him from the waistband of his boxers to his belly button.

His stomach lurched, and she hummed in delight when his hands gripped her head. He didn't shove against her, it was more like he was using her to hold himself steady. She could deal with that.

Slowly, ever so slowly, she eased the elastic over his hips until the briefs fell to his ankles to join his jeans. But Caite only had eyes for his cock.

As she stared at it, the purple mushroom head leaked a bead of precome.

Feeling bolder than she'd ever been in her life, Caite leaned closer and licked the fluid off.

Rocco groaned, and another bead of moisture appeared where the first had been. She looked up and saw that he was staring down at her with an intensity she'd never seen before.

Feeling sexier than ever before, Caite reached for the cups of her bra and pulled the black lace down until it bunched under her boobs, pushing them upward.

Her stomach clenched at the way goose bumps broke out on Rocco's thighs. He didn't have to say a word to communicate how turned on he was.

Deciding she'd teased him enough, Caite took hold of the base of his erection with her left hand and reached around to palm his ass cheek with the other. She opened her mouth and took him inside as far as she could.

His salty essence immediately swamped her senses, and although she'd never been a fan of the taste of come, on him, at this moment, it was absolutely delicious.

She didn't ease into the blowjob; instead she sucked

hard as she bobbed up and down on his cock. He groaned long and low above her, and she smiled even as she continued to work him over.

Using the pinky of the hand that was holding him still for her, she caressed his balls as she did her best to coax an orgasm out of him. She could tell he was close; his ass had tensed up, as had his thighs. The dick in her hand and mouth seemed to grow even harder, and she doubled her efforts to push him over the edge.

One moment she was on her knees in front of him with his cock in her mouth, and the next she was flat on her back on his bed. Rocco loomed over her, and then his mouth was on hers.

There was no other word for what he was doing than devouring her. And she loved it.

Caite opened her legs and felt his dick pressing against her soaked panties. She squirmed, wanting him inside her. Rocco tore his mouth away and rested his forehead against hers. She felt the silky-soft hair of his beard brushing against her chin and cheeks.

"Give me a second," he pleaded.

Caite shook her head. "I need you," she told him, pressing her hips against his.

"Fuck. Hang on," he said, then he threw himself off her. Caite would've laughed at the way he stumbled as he struggled to untie his boots and get his jeans and briefs off, followed by his shirt, but she was too enthralled at the desperation in his movements to do anything other than stare.

Her hands went to her panties and she'd started to push them over her hips when he stopped her.

"Mine," he said in a low, strangled tone.

Caite let go and put her arms above her head, letting him have the pleasure of removing her underwear, but instead, he climbed back on the bed and hovered above her like a lion waiting to strike the killing blow. His chest heaved in and out and his cock bobbed with his movements. His eyes glittered with intensity and his hands were fisted on the bed at her sides.

"Rocco?" she asked tentatively.

"You. Are. So. Fucking. Beautiful," he ground out, staring at her body. "Seriously. I can't even... Shit. I wanted to go slow. Wanted to eat you out first. Then take my time and take you the way you deserve. But I can't go slow. I hurt so bad for you, Caite. Your mouth was fucking phenomenal and I know the second I touch you, I'm gonna blow."

He looked up at her then. "Tell me you're ready for me," he almost pleaded.

Running one of her hands down her stomach, Caite eased her fingers under the waistband of her panties and into her pussy.

Rocco's eyes followed her every movement. He licked his lips as if he could taste her in the air.

"I'm ready," Caite told him.

"You're sure? I'm big," he told her unnecessarily.

"I'm sure."

Then he moved. He ripped her panties down and off

her legs so fast, Caite would've been impressed if she could think clearly.

He shoved her legs apart with his own and inched upward. Caite eagerly spread her legs farther, giving him room. At the last second, before his cock touched her where she most wanted it to be, he swore and leaned over to the nightstand. He opened the drawer so hard it came flying out and landed on the floor. But that didn't even seem to faze Rocco. He had a condom packet in his hand one second, and the next, he was gritting his teeth while he rolled it over his cock.

Then he was there. Pressing inside her with a slow and steady thrust.

Caite threw her head back and clenched her teeth together. It had been a long time for her. She was soaked, yes, but as Rocco had said, he was big.

Belying his earlier words, he took his time inching inside her. And even once he was all the way in, his hips flush against hers, he held still, giving her time to adjust.

Caite felt one hand go under her back and push, urging her to arch against him. Then his mouth closed around one of her nipples—and this time it was she who groaned. The feel of his lips around her bare flesh was so much more intense than when he'd done the same thing through her shirt and bra when they were in the ocean.

One of her hands came up and grabbed at his back, trying to find something to hold on to. Her pussy muscles tightened around him as lust coursed through her body. She needed...more.

"More," she pleaded.

Without a word, Rocco let go of her nipple with a small pop and held himself above her. Her eyes met his, and she froze, not able to look away. His hips started moving then, pumping his dick in and out of her with quick, hard thrusts.

Caite tried to meet him, but in the end, as he moved faster and faster, all she could do was lie there and let him take her the way he needed to. She gripped his biceps with trembling fingers and held on as he pounded into her. His jaw was clenched, and he looked as intense as she'd ever seen him.

Within minutes, Rocco's breathing was erratic, and she could see a sheen of sweat on his brow. "I'm coming," he got out between thrusts—and then he pushed himself as far inside her as he could go and came.

Caite loved watching him fly over the edge, and knowing she'd done that for him. She couldn't help being a bit disappointed that she hadn't come with him, but he'd warned her that he was on the edge.

It took a few seconds for him to recover, and Caite was ready with a smile when his head came up, but she squeaked in surprise when he sat back on his heels, holding her hips to his as he did so.

They were still connected, even though Caite could feel him softening. Without saying a word, Rocco's thumb zeroed in on her clit and began to stroke with quick, heavy flicks, just as she would've done for herself.

"Rocco—"

"You didn't come," he said. "Not acceptable. It's bad enough I couldn't wait and take care of you first, but no way in *fuck* are you not coming too."

"It's okay. You don't..." Her words tapered off as he continued his assault on her body.

Her back was arched and her hips were elevated, but nothing mattered except his expert touch on her clit. Within seconds, her pleasure had ramped back up and she was hurtling headlong toward a climax.

Pumping her hips up and down, she grabbed hold of the sheets tangled around them.

"God, yes! Right there. Harder! Yessssss."

Caite hung on the precipice for a heartbeat or two before flying over the edge. She couldn't think, couldn't do anything but hang on for the ride as Rocco's thumb continued to press against her, drawing out her orgasm for longer than she'd ever experienced before.

She felt his cock slip out of her body, but he immediately filled her with two fingers from his other hand. He held her on his lap, shaking and trembling from the most intense orgasm of her life, until she finally began to come back down to Earth.

His fingers pressed slowly and gently in and out of her body as she gasped for air.

"Good lord," she exclaimed softly. "That was..." She couldn't think of anything to describe what that was.

Rocco smiled down at her and eased his fingers out of her body, bringing them up to his mouth to lick clean. She knew she was blushing, but refused to look away from the man she loved.

Then he gently eased her ass off his lap and turned to the side to remove the condom. He tied it off and wrapped it in a tissue from the nightstand, all without seemingly feeling embarrassed about what he was doing. Then he was back and gently turning her to undo her bra, throwing it on the floor along with their clothes. He gathered her in his arms and covered them up with a sheet.

His loving care made the words practically fall out of her mouth.

"I love you," Caite blurted. "I didn't say it before... well...I don't know why. But I do."

"Shhh, it's okay," Rocco said.

"I just...it's not the sex. Although that was superb. It's *you*. I've never felt like this with anyone. It scares me to death because I know you could hurt me so bad."

"I'll never hurt you, *ma petite fée*."

"You can't guarantee that," Caite protested.

"How about this then—I'll do everything in my power to treat you with care. To think before I speak and to make sure to always put you first in my life."

Tears filled Caite's eyes at that. "And I'll do the same with you," she told him.

Rocco hugged her tighter.

"What time is it?" she asked.

"Don't know. Don't care."

"It's still light out," Caite said.

"Doesn't matter. I'm not done with you yet," Rocco said drowsily. "Didn't get to eat you out. And I need to make sure you know what just happened was an anomaly."

"Making me orgasm so hard I saw stars?" Caite teased, feeling weirdly energized. Funnily enough, it seemed Rocco was the one who passed out after sex rather than her.

"No, that should happen every time we make love, otherwise I'm not doing my job and being a selfish asshole. What I meant was me coming first. I don't like doing that, and I promise I won't make a habit of it. I needed to be inside you too badly this first time."

"It's okay," Caite said, not lying.

"All the same, I'm gonna take a nap, then when I wake up, I'm gonna eat you out and take you the way I wanted to all along. Slow and sweet. Then fast and hard."

"Oh. Um... Okay."

"Sleep, Caite. It might be light outside right now, but I guarantee by the time morning comes, you're gonna wish you could sleep for a few more hours."

"You aren't going to PT tomorrow?"

"No. I'm going to get all the physical training I need right here in our bed tonight."

Caite blushed. She wasn't used to this kind of frank talk.

"I'm not sure your commander will go for that."

Rocco chuckled. "Sleep, *ma petite fée*."

Every time he called her his small fairy in his adorably bad French accent, something inside Caite rolled over and showed its belly. She liked caving to him. Not that she'd do it all the time, but here in his bed? Safe in his arms? Pressed to his naked body? She had no problem with it.

Despite feeling wide awake, Caite was asleep in minutes. She had no idea Rocco watched her sleep for at least an hour before he eventually succumbed as well.

CHAPTER FOURTEEN

A week later, Rocco was even more frustrated then he'd been when he'd found out Caite had been targeted by an unknown assailant.

They'd met with NCIS and she'd been interrogated behind a closed door for five hours. Five hours during which Rocco thought he was going to lose his mind. If it hadn't been for Bubba and Ace holding him back, he would've stormed through the interrogation room door and carried her out of there.

They'd given her a book full of names, pictures, and ranks of every naval officer stationed at the base in San Diego, and when she hadn't been able to recognize any of them, they'd pulled up records of every admiral and captain in the entire navy. It had been hundreds of names overall, which only served to stress out an already exhausted Caite, rather than help her remember.

His mood hadn't gotten any better when he'd seen how tired and haggard she looked when she'd finally emerged from the room.

But with all the investigating on NCIS's side, and Commander North keeping his ear to the ground, *and* even with Tex trying to see what he could find, they still didn't know the name of the person behind the attempts on Caite's life.

The man who'd tried to run her down was long gone. Even the guy who'd held up the convenience store was in the wind. The carjacker was dead, and for some reason no one could figure out who he was. Inexplicably, the search for fingerprints had been a dead end, which didn't make sense...unless whoever was the mastermind behind all this had some serious connections.

Tex had put pressure on Customs and they'd intercepted three shipments of ancient artifacts that had tried to enter the country. Rocco knew as well as anyone that losing those deals wasn't going to go over well with the person organizing everything. The buyers would be pissed, and that meant the man in charge was going to have a lot of pressure on him to deliver.

It meant lost money, and losing money was never a good thing when it came to criminals. Not only that, but his reputation was on the line, and men who dealt with stolen antiquities wouldn't take kindly to having their priceless artifacts intercepted.

Rocco could feel the tension in Caite. He wouldn't let her go back to her apartment by herself, and everywhere she went, either Rocco or one of his teammates was by her side. He suspected she was frustrated with the lack of progress in the case and the way he was hovering. Rocco knew they both needed a break.

The only time she seemed completely relaxed was at night when they made love. She lost all inhibitions when he touched her, and he loved being able to get her out of her head, to think about nothing but him. But in the morning, he could literally see the stress leak back into her eyes, and he hated it.

Rocco had already talked to Slade "Cutter" Cutsinger about seeing if he could pull some strings and find a contractor job for Caite. Cutter was one of the best administrative assistants he'd worked with in the navy. He worked for a different commander, but Rocco figured he probably knew enough people to help Caite.

He hadn't told Caite yet, as he didn't want her anywhere near the base until whoever wanted her dead was behind bars, but he knew she needed to work. It had only been a week since the carjacking attempt, but even so, sitting in his apartment all day was beginning to get to her. She wasn't the type of woman who would be content to just let him bring home the bacon, so to speak.

Caite was currently sitting at the table in his kitchen, absently doing a word search puzzle and drinking coffee. He hadn't planned on taking her anywhere, but was desperate to see her relaxed and happy.

"There's a thing this afternoon that I thought you might want to go to with me."

"A thing?" she asked, interest sparkling in her eyes for the first time in a week.

"Yeah. Every few months, the Navy SEAL units try to have family events at the beach. Get all the families together and have a good time without having to worry about rules and regulations."

"So it's a beach party?" she asked with a tilt of her head.

"Yes and no. It's not held on the base, so there's alcohol allowed, but since there are kids there, it never gets completely crazy. There are a few beaches we rotate around to and it's generally a laid-back good time."

"Is it safe?" Caite asked.

Rocco loathed that she even had to worry about that. But he wouldn't lie to her. "As safe as it *can* be. There will be several SEAL teams there. I know how hard the last week has been for you, and I hate it. I'd love to introduce you to another SEAL team I know, and their families. Wolf is one of the best SEALs I've ever met, as are his teammates. I know being with me isn't a walk in the park, and I thought having other SEAL women to talk to would be good. I told you about them earlier. You can ask them stuff you might not want to ask me. Get their perspective on what it's like to be married to a SEAL."

At his last words, her eyes got big.

Rocco went over to her side and got down on one knee. "I'm not asking you to marry me right this second, *ma petite fée*, but I *am* saying I want you in my life long term. Neither of us knows what the future will bring, but the last couple weeks, having you by my side, has been amazing. Even with both of us being stressed. I figure if we can be happy while all this is going on, we've got it made."

Caite nodded. "I *am* happy with you. I just wish this was all done with. I don't enjoy sitting around, and I feel as if I'm holding you back from doing your job. I hated the impatient looks the investigators were giving me when I was flipping through that damn book of names and pictures. After a while, they all started to blur together. Everyone looked the same and after reading all those names, I barely remembered my *own*."

"Things will get back to normal, I know it. Either you'll remember who the Bitoo brothers mentioned, or the investigators will figure it out on their own. You'll get a job, I'll go on missions, and we'll live happily ever after."

"You have it all planned out, huh?" she asked with a small chuckle.

"Damn straight."

She sighed. "Okay, then yes. I'd love to go. I can't promise that I'm the best in social situations, but I admit to being curious to meet other SEAL wives and getting their perspective on things."

Rocco stood and picked up her hand, kissing the back. "Thank you, *ma petite fée*."

"No, thank you," she retorted. "Thank you for not bailing at the first sign of trouble. I mean, you've put a lot on your plate. An unemployed, getting-broker-by-the-day girlfriend who just happens to have someone who wants to kill her. It's a lot, Rocco."

"Don't get used to this," he warned her. "This is not our life. It's just a blip on the radar."

She smiled. "Okay."

"Okay. Oh, and I thought maybe next week we could take a trip up to San Fran to see your folks."

"Really?" she asked excitedly.

"Really. I know they've been worried about you, and getting out of town is probably a good thing."

Her smiled dimmed a bit at the reminder of why they'd be getting away from the naval base, but she asked, "Can I call and tell them we'll be visiting soon?"

"Absolutely. I already got the approval for a few days' leave from Commander North."

Caite leaned forward and kissed him. "Thank you."

Rocco ran his thumb over her lips, remembering what she'd done with them the night before. "Anything for you, *ma petite fée*."

She blushed, and he knew she was remembering too.

Standing, he picked up his cell as he made his way back to the other room. He needed to call Wolf and Cutter to make sure they'd be at the quarterly picnic. Not only because he wanted to introduce them to

Caite, but because he wanted the extra backup, just in case.

He heard Caite talking excitedly to her mom in the kitchen and nodded to himself. He loved making her smile, and made a vow to do whatever he could throughout their lives to keep her happy and content.

Caite held on to Rocco's hand as he led them down from the parking lot toward the sand. She'd been expecting a few people hanging out on the beach. But the reality was much different.

There were at least a hundred people there. Children were running amuck and everyone seemed to be laughing and having a good time. There was a bonfire off to one side of the group and she could see kids crouched next to it, probably roasting marshmallows for s'mores.

Caite was overwhelmed with the thought of being the "new girl" and meeting more of his friends, especially the other SEAL team he was constantly talking about. The last thing she wanted to do was make a bad impression on them, or their wives.

"Relax," Rocco said, squeezing her hand.

"I am," Caite lied.

Rocco stopped and turned to face her. He put down the chairs and basket he was carrying and took her face in his hands. "You aren't," he countered, then dropped his head and covered her lips with his own.

By the time he stopped, Caite felt like mush. She didn't think she'd ever get tired of his kisses.

"I know it seems overwhelming, but we're gonna go and sit with my team. You already know them. I see Wolf and his wife Caroline are already here, as are most of his teammates. "Trust me, *ma petite fée*. You're going to enjoy this."

"If you say so," she muttered.

He smiled down at her. "I'm sure Wolf has some embarrassing stories he can tell you about me," he teased.

Caite perked up at that. "Ooooh. Now that's something I'd love to hear."

"You're so mean," Rocco told her, bending down to grab their stuff.

Caite walked next to him, her hand in his, and tried not to get worked up. It was good that she was getting this out of the way all at once. And Rocco was right. She liked his teammates, and she was glad they were here. They could act as a buffer between her and everyone else. As much as she could be an extrovert, at times, it was hard.

Rocco said hello to just about everyone as he made his way toward his teammates and the section of beach they'd claimed as their own. It seemed as if everyone knew Rocco, and he knew everyone else.

By the time they'd reached Gumby, Ace, Rex,

Bubba, and Phantom, Caite understood a bit more what being a part of the SEAL "family" meant.

Rocco put their stuff down then tugged her toward a group sitting nearby. Two men stood as they approached. He dropped her hand and gave each of the men one of those manly macho-men hugs that were more back slapping than actual hugging, then reached for her hand again.

Caite hung on as he smiled at her then turned to the men. "Caite, I'd like you to meet Wolf and Slade. They're two of the most amazing men and SEALs that I know."

The man on the left reached out his hand and Caite shook it.

"I'm not sure the rest of my team would agree with that," he said as he shook her hand. "I'm Wolf. It's nice to meet you, Caite. Rocco has said nothing but good things about you."

"It's nice to meet you," she said politely.

"And I'm Slade. I've been looking at your resume. Pretty impressive," he told her as he shook her hand. "Fluent in French is a highly marketable skill. Especially with all the smuggling going on from French-speaking African countries. I don't know what that idiot was thinking, firing you. But don't worry, I've been talking about you with a contact at NCIS, and I'm fairly certain if you want the job, it's yours."

Caite looked from Slade back to Rocco in confusion. "Job?"

"Oh shit. Was I not supposed to talk about it?" Slade asked, not looking sorry at all.

Rocco rolled his eyes at his friend before answering Caite. "I asked Slade if he would see what he could find out for you in regards to getting another job on base. He's one of the best admins we've got, and I figured he'd be the one to ask to see if it was possible for you to be rehired."

Caite knew she should probably be irritated that Rocco had gone behind her back, but she couldn't be. She'd loved working for the government and had thought being fired meant she'd never be hired by them again. Turning to Slade, she asked, "Seriously? I mean, I'd love to be considered for something. I hadn't thought about working for the investigation unit though."

"Nothing dangerous," Slade assured them, although Caite saw the look he gave Rocco, as if he was speaking more to him than her. "I know they have a lot of wire-taps that they could use help interpreting, and speaking French would also come in handy when they're inter-viewing witnesses and stuff."

"I honestly didn't think I'd ever get to use what I learned in college," Caite said, looking at Rocco excitedly.

He smiled down at her. "It's not a done deal," he warned. "I just asked Slade to look into it."

"I know," she said immediately, then turned back to

Slade. "I appreciate you even taking the time to look at my resume."

"What happened to you was bullshit," the older man said with a growl. "You never should've been fired in the first place. I also looked into your boss over there in Bahrain. He's a schmuck, and I can't believe he's made it as long as he has. He's lazy and likes to take credit for other people's work."

"I know," Caite muttered.

"Anyway, that's enough about work. I want you to meet my wife," Slade said, and turned to gesture to a woman with long dark blonde hair. She smiled at him and came up to his side. "Dakota, I'd like you to meet, Caite. She's with Rocco."

The woman smiled wider, in an open, friendly way, and reached out a hand. "It's so good to meet you. Rocco and his teammates are great. They helped me when I needed them a while back. I love how all the SEAL teams work together to get stuff done."

Caite had no idea what she was talking about, but she smiled and nodded anyway.

"And this is Caroline," Wolf said. Another woman had come up to join their little group as Caite was greeting Dakota. She was about the same height as Caite, and in fact, looked a lot like her. They had the same color hair and the same body type.

"Hi," Caroline said. "I'm so glad you could come tonight. Rocco hasn't ever brought a woman to one of these get-togethers before."

"Ice," Wolf said in an exasperated tone.

"What?" she asked without a trace of guile in her voice. "She needs to know that Rocco isn't a manwhore and that he's serious about her." Then she looked back at Caite and winked. "Rocco and his team are good men. If you were with someone else, I might not be as complimentary."

"I appreciate your honestly," Caite said, smiling. She liked Caroline.

"Of course. Us navy wives need to stick together."

"Oh, Rocco and I aren't married," Caite said with a blush.

"Figure of speech," Caroline said with a wave of her hand. "I know I had a ton of questions when I first got with Matthew, and I didn't have anyone to talk to. I'd be happy to sit and talk with you later, if you wanted." She turned to gesture to the other women sitting on the beach behind her, many who were occupied playing with children. "We'd all be willing to tell you how things really are."

"How about you don't scare her?" Wolf suggested with a grin as he pulled Caroline into his side and kissed her temple.

"I'm not going to scare her!" Caroline retorted in mock affront. "I'll tell her how to deal when Rocco leaves for missions, how not to stress, and how best to pass the time until he gets back. She also needs to know what days are best for shopping on base, and which days to avoid it at all costs. I want to explain how important the women who are with other SEALs will become to her. Oh! And she needs to know what the best beaches are, and how important the commander is when her team is on a mission."

"My team?" Caite asked, liking the other woman more and more. There were a lot of details in what she'd just said, but that comment stuck out.

"Yup. You might be with Rocco, but everyone on the team is 'yours.' They have his back, just as he has theirs. He'll spend just as much time, if not more, with them as he does with you. So they're yours as much as they're his. And who knows," Caroline said, her eyes going to Slade. "They might just save your life someday."

There was a lot more behind her words than Caite understood, but she could clearly see the respect and even love Caroline had not only for Wolf, but for the other SEAL standing with them.

"I'd like that," Caite told her.

"Good. When Rocco gets done showing you off and you need a break from all the testosterone, come sit with us. It gets crazy with all the kids, but it's a good crazy."

"Thanks. I will," Caite told her, and she relaxed for the first time. Caroline was so welcoming and genuine in her invitation to talk, Caite knew she'd be silly to turn her down.

"It was good to meet you," Wolf told her.

"Definitely," Slade chimed in.

"Talk to you later," Caroline said as Wolf led her back to the group behind them.

"I'm looking forward to getting to know you better," Dakota said with a smile, before she too was led back to the other SEALs.

"Feel better?" Rocco asked perceptively.

Caite nodded. "They were nice."

"Did you expect them not to be?" he asked.

"Well, no. But sometimes women aren't as welcoming as you'd think. And you're a guy, you probably have no idea how mean women can be to each other."

"Oh, I know," Rocco said with a smile.

"How?" she asked suspiciously.

"I just do," he said. "Come on, I want to introduce you to my commander."

Two men were walking toward them. They both had on shorts and T-shirts, but there was something about them that screamed "experience" and demanded respect.

"Sir. Sir," Rocco said as the men approached, and he nodded at each. He shook both men's hands then once more turned to introduce her. "I'd like you to meet my girlfriend. Caite McCallan. Caite, this is my commander, Storm North, and this is Commander Patrick Hurt. He was in charge of Wolf's team, and is currently still commanding other SEAL units."

Storm reached out and shook her hand, then held on as he said, "Thank you."

Caite wrinkled her brow. "For what?"

"For getting Rocco, Gumby, and Ace out of that cellar."

Caite immediately shook her head. "Oh no, they got themselves out," she protested.

"That's not what the report said," Commander North replied. "I read it, *and* had a long conversation with my men. If it wasn't for you overhearing that conversation and taking the initiative to put yourself in danger by heading to an off-limits area of Manama, they wouldn't be here today."

"I'm sure they would've figured something out," Caite mumbled. She was embarrassed about being thanked so profusely. She never would've forgiven herself if she'd done nothing.

"Maybe," Commander North said, letting it drop after seeing her discomfort. "What do you think of our little party?"

Caite smiled up at him. "Little?"

All three men chuckled. "Actually, this one is a bit smaller than the last," Commander Hurt said. Then he looked over her shoulder and said, "If you'll excuse me, I see my wife gesturing for me. Looks like it's my turn to be on kid duty. It was nice meeting you, Caite. I hope we'll see more of you around."

"You will," Rocco answered for her.

Caite turned to watch Commander Hurt head toward a slender woman holding a toddler.

Glanding around, she tuned out the conversation

Rocco was having with his commander as they discussed the upcoming schedule for training and PT. Everywhere she looked were pockets of men, women, and kids having a good time. Some were swimming, some were building sand castles, others were eating. But the thing that struck her was how...*normal* everyone looked. When she thought about Navy SEALs, a picture of buff, macho men always came to mind.

And while Rocco and his team were definitely buff, they were also decidedly normal. They liked to kick back, have a beer, and chill with their friends as much as the next guy. The fact that they could be headed to some far-off country to track down terrorists or smugglers tomorrow didn't even seem to be a thought in their heads at the moment.

She respected them even more right then than she had before.

"Any luck on the investigation?" Rocco asked quietly. It was the way his voice had lowered that made Caite pay more attention.

"Unfortunately, no, but we're getting close," Commander North said. "NCIS is following a lead, and they think they'll have tracked down the culprit in a few days. The smuggling trail definitely leads to our base, which pisses me off. I can't believe one of my fellow officers is neck deep in this shit." He turned to Caite. "I'm sorry you seem to be in the middle of it. Please believe me when I say that we're doing all we can to flush out the guilty party so you can be free to live your life without having to look over your shoulder. Stick close to this guy and you'll be fine," he said, gesturing to Rocco with his head.

"You'll let me know if you hear anything?" Rocco asked.

"Of course. Now, go and enjoy yourselves. Try not to worry about anything today. The beach is filled with Navy SEALs. You're safe here."

"Thanks," Caite said with a small smile. She felt safe, but not because of the occupations of the men gathered here. Because she was with Rocco.

As they walked toward his team, Rocco asked, "You good?"

"I'm good," she reassured him.

"Sure?"

"Positive." She loved that he wanted to make sure she was at ease around his friends. She wished she had closer friends like this who she could introduce him to, but the more she was around the people Rocco hung out with, the more comfortable she felt.

Mentally reviewing the things she wanted to ask Caroline and her friends later, Caite let Rocco lead them back to their chairs. He set them up and made sure she was settled and comfortable before sitting himself. Then he reached out and took hold of her hand as they chatted with the rest of the men on his team.

Caite closed her eyes and tilted her head back, enjoying the breeze from the ocean, the salty air, the sun on her face, and the company of good friends.

Rocco talked with his friends and watched Caite out of the corner of his eye. She seemed relaxed, which was a huge relief. He knew she'd been nervous about coming today, but from what he could see, she'd needed this. Needed to get out of the apartment and not think about job hunting or who might be after her.

More importantly, it got her to stop obsessing over trying to remember the name of the man the Bitoo brothers had mentioned in passing.

He ran his fingers over hers where her hand was resting on his thigh. She smiled, but kept her eyes shut. Their intimacy felt easy. He loved making love with her, but more than that, he enjoyed holding her hand and sitting with her like this. He enjoyed when they sat on the couch and watched the news, her feet in his lap. It felt good. Normal.

They'd been talking for about half an hour when Caite stirred.

"You okay?"

"Yeah. But I think I need to get out of the sun for a bit." She looked over to where Caroline was sitting. "Do you think she'd mind if I wandered over there and chatted for a bit?"

"Absolutely not. One thing about Caroline, she doesn't say anything she doesn't mean."

"You boys going to be all right without me for a while?" she teased.

Rocco loved seeing the casual way she bantered with his friends. Something he'd never considered when thinking about settling down was the need for his woman to be tight with his team, but now that he saw it happening right in front of his eyes, he couldn't believe he hadn't thought about it before. His friends liking his woman should've been one of his main requirements, considering how tight he was with the team. Luckily, things seemed to be working out...thank God.

"I don't know," Gumby replied. "We might need some tips on how to apply eye makeup, and who will help us if you aren't here?"

"Yeah, or maybe we'll need to ask you what romance books we should read," Ace chimed in.

Caite rolled her eyes. "Don't knock them until you try them. I mean, think about it. Most are written by women. They write their fantasies, or at least what they're looking for in a man. You might get some insights into the female brain by reading them. Yeah?"

The others looked stunned for a moment before loudly proclaiming themselves experts in the female mind already. Rocco leaned over while the rest of the guys were busy reasserting their manhood, bragging about how they didn't need to read books to know how to treat women, and whispered in Caite's ear. "We can finish reading that sex scene tonight when we get home. Then I'll do my best to relive it for you."

He smiled when she blushed. He'd been surprised by how much he'd enjoyed the first book he'd read at her urging. He'd thought it would be mostly mushy, over-the-top dialogue and sex scenes, but there was actually an intriguing story that quickly sucked him in.

He kissed her goodbye and watched as she headed toward Wolf's group.

"I like her," Gumby stated when she was out of earshot.

Rocco rolled his eyes.

"Seriously," Gumby said. "I know we give you some crap about being whipped, but she's easy to be around."

"I hate that we can't figure out who's trying to kill her for what she overheard," Bubba added.

"Whoever it is will wish he'd left it alone," Phantom promised.

"Exactly. No one threatens one of our own and lives to talk about it," Rex threw in.

Rocco's chest felt tight. These men were like his brothers. Having their approval and seeing them embrace Caite as they had was a huge relief. He didn't know what he'd do if they didn't like her.

"Thanks, guys. She's pretty amazing," Rocco told his friends, forcing himself to not stare after Caite like a lovesick cow.

"What's the plan for the next week?" Bubba asked, changing the subject.

Even as they talked about what missions might be on the horizon for them, Rocco couldn't help but think about Caite...and hope that whatever the other women were telling her wouldn't scare her away.

"Don't be afraid to ask for help," Fiona said. "It's important to rely on your friends. They're your lifelines."

"I know you don't have kids yet, but trust me, saving a few bucks on formula—or anything else—isn't worth facing the crowds at the base exchange when they have their annual sale," Jessyka informed her. "Order stuff online and have it delivered and suck up the extra expense."

"Don't speed on base either," Cheyenne warned. "Although dealing with the 'punishment' after admitting it to your man when you get home might be worth it."

All the women giggled at that.

Caite's head was spinning with all the advice she'd received over the last half hour. Every single one of the women had been welcoming and happy to hear that her relationship with Rocco was going well. They were full of advice, not only about being with a Navy SEAL, but about life in general.

"Don't let the assholes get you down," Caroline said. "Seriously. Before I met Matthew, I always felt ignored. I'm not super beautiful, or skinny, or super anything really. But meeting him, and having him really see me, made me realize that it's okay not to be 'seen' by everyone. I think famous people get really sick of constantly being in the spotlight. I'm perfectly happy being the center of Matthew's world and having other people forget to hold doors open for me and stuff."

"How does *he* feel about that?" Caite asked.

"It pisses him off," Caroline said immediately. "But that's because he can't imagine that *anyone* doesn't see how beautiful and perfect I am." She chuckled. "I'm definitely not, but there's no way I'll ever convince Matthew of that, and I'm okay with it."

"Why do you call him Matthew when everyone else calls him Wolf?" Caite asked.

Caroline shrugged. "Wolf is his nickname. The name all of his buddies use. But when we met, he introduced himself as Matthew, and I really can't think of him any other way. Do you call Rocco by his real name?"

Caite shook her head. "Should I?"

"I think if he doesn't care, you shouldn't either," Caroline told her.

Jessyka leaned forward and said quietly, "Although, if you use his real name during...um...intimate times, it can really make the moment more personal."

Everyone nodded their heads and agreed. Caite hadn't thought of Rocco as Blake since she'd met him, but she had to agree that using his given name when he was deep inside her might be special.

"So, how'd he get his nickname?" Alabama asked.

Caite had noticed the woman was quieter than the others, but she didn't like her any less as a result.

"Yeah, we've wondered about it for a while now, but I always forget to ask Hunter," Fiona chimed in.

Caite shrugged. "I've never asked."

"You haven't asked?" Summer echoed, eyes wide.

Feeling awkward now, Caite replied, "Should I have?"

"Well, it's kind of a big thing with them," Caroline explained. "I mean, you should've seen how hard we tried to get the reason behind Benny's nickname out of him."

"Benny isn't his real name?" Caite asked.

Jessyka shook her head. "Nope. It's Kason."

"Dare I ask?" Caite asked the other woman.

She grinned. "I think we'll let you stew for a bit, just as we had to," Jessyka told her with a smile.

"So I guess that means I should ask Rocco how he got his name then, huh?" Caite asked the group.

Everyone nodded and answered affirmatively.

"And then make sure you remember to tell us," Cheyenne begged. "I find it so interesting how these nicknames come about."

"I will," Caite told her new friends. It felt good to have female friends. People who were nice to her simply because they liked her, and not because they had to be or because she worked with them. "Thanks for giving me your numbers. It makes me feel better to know I have someone to talk to," she said.

"And we expect you to call anytime," Caroline told her. "Most of the others have kids, so there might be times they can't meet with you or whatever, but I can. I'll be upset if something happens while Rocco is deployed and you don't call."

Caite knew she'd still feel weird about calling the other woman, but she said, "I will."

"Like, if you get shot in a robbery and Rocco's gone, I expect you to *call*," Caroline emphasized.

Knowing she was blushing, Caite merely nodded.

Caroline moved closer and put her arm around Caite's shoulders. "I know you just met us, but believe me when I tell you that we know how you feel. We've all been through hell, and are now living the good life. No matter what, you can count on us. Okay?"

Caite wanted to ask about what they'd been through, but instead nodded. She'd ask Rocco later. "Okay."

"Good. Now, Rocco can't keep his eyes off of you. Why don't you go back over there and put him out of his misery," Caroline joked.

Caite turned to look across the sand and saw that Rocco was indeed looking their way.

"He's a good man," Alabama said.

"I know," Caite said. "Thanks again for the conversation," she told everyone.

"Don't forget to let us know about his nickname!" Jessyka called out when Caite started walking back across the sand.

"I will!" Caite replied, and then headed back to Rocco with a huge smile on her face.

When she got close, Gumby asked, "What are you so smiley about? Sometimes I don't trust those women."

It was obvious he was kidding, so Caite didn't take offense. When she got near, Rocco reached out and pulled her onto his lap. Letting out a screech of surprise, Caite giggled when she realized she wasn't going to end up lying in the sand. "Um, is this chair going to hold us both?" she asked as she wrapped her arms around Rocco's neck.

"Don't care. Things go okay over there?"

Feeling warm inside that he was checking to make sure she was good, Caite nodded. "Great, actually."

"Good."

"Come on, Caite, what'cha smilin' about?" Gumby asked again.

"The others told me I've been remiss in not asking Rocco how he got his nickname," she told Gumby, not taking her eyes from Rocco's. "If it's something you'd rather not talk about, it's okay," she said when he didn't immediately start explaining.

Ace burst out laughing. "It's something he'd rather not *remember*, you mean."

"Oh, I'm sorry," Caite apologized. "I didn't mean to bring up hard memories."

"They're hard all right," Rex joked.

"Cut it out, guys," Rocco grumbled. "You're worrying Caite." He met her gaze and said, "It's nothing sensitive, *ma petite fée*. When we were going through SEAL training, I had a hard time keeping my mouth shut when the instructors were grilling us. I always wanted to know why we were doing what we were doing and if there was a purpose. Of course, many of the things we had to do *didn't* have any purpose, other than to tire us out and make sure we could follow orders. One of their favorite punishments was to make recruits carry around a large rock. I had the privilege of carrying that damn thing more than most because I couldn't seem to shut up."

Bubba laughed and took up the story. "I swear to God, that rock was like his baby. He had to take it everywhere."

"Lunch, dinner, and even during PT, he had to lug that thing around," Rex said, joining the story. "He even had to sleep with it in his bunk a few times."

"The instructors started calling him Rocco as a result," Phantom added. Then in a singsong voice, mimicking the long-ago instructors, he said, "Hey, Rocco, how's your rock? Go pick up your rock, Rocco. You named that thing yet, Rocco?"

Everyone laughed, and Caite couldn't help but join them. "You didn't learn your lesson and keep your mouth shut after you had to carry it around a few times?"

"Nope," Rocco confirmed. "And...I've still got that thing too."

Light dawned. "The rock in your workout room in your apartment? You had to carry *that* around? It has to weigh like a hundred pounds!" Caite exclaimed. She'd seen the rock in question and figured it was just a simple decoration or something. A weird one, but who was she to question Rocco's design preferences.

He chuckled. "It's only around forty pounds or so."

"I can't believe you still have it," Caite said, shaking her head.

"When he graduated, the instructors gave it to him, saying anyone as stubborn as him deserved it," Rex informed her.

"You're a nut," Caite told Rocco.

"I'm *your* nut," Rocco corrected her.

She smiled and gave him a short kiss on the lips, thinking about how much the other women were going to love hearing the story.

"Head's up," Phantom said under his breath, "Captain Chambers and Rear Admiral Creasy on deck."

Caite was startled when all six men stood, including Rocco. He put her on her feet, then saluted the two approaching men, as did his teammates.

She wasn't sure what to do, so she just stood there quietly. Rocco and his friends hadn't saluted anyone else since they'd been there. She knew a captain and a rear admiral were above the rank of Commanders North and Hurt, but she wasn't sure how much above.

"Sirs," the six men said practically in unison.

"At ease," the black-haired man said after he'd returned the salute.

The blond man merely nodded at the group in greeting.

"Are you all enjoying yourselves?" the first man asked.

"What's not to enjoy?" Gumby joked. "Sun, surf, and we don't have to roll around in the sand."

"True. Of course, I could always order you to, just for fun," the officer said.

Everyone laughed.

"Sirs, I'd like to introduce you to my girlfriend. This is Caite McCallan. Caite, this is Rear Admiral Creasy and Captain Chambers. They're the men who're in charge of the SEAL units on base."

"It's nice to meet you," Caite said. She shook the rear admiral's hand, then the captain's.

The latter smiled tightly and dropped her hand. "It's good to meet you," he said in a low voice. He had dirty blond hair and dark blue eyes. He was quite tan, and he looked mostly at ease in the beach setting. But even with his somewhat relaxed demeanor, Caite thought he seemed tense, and she figured it was because he was of a higher rank than almost everyone around him. Caite also had the thought that she wouldn't want his job, because it was obviously very stressful, if the lines around his eyes and brow were any indication.

She kind of zoned out when the men started talking about upcoming training and navy business. She stared at the water, where kids were playing in the surf, and she envied them their carefree attitude about the water. She wished she'd learned how to swim when she was young, like them. If her parents had started her lessons just a bit earlier, maybe she wouldn't have been so scared.

SUSAN STOKER

"You don't mind, do you?" Rocco asked, gently nudging her.

Caite looked at him blankly. She hadn't heard anything he'd said.

He gave her a small grin. "Sorry, I tend to forget not everyone is as interested in navy business as we are. The rear admiral needs to talk to us for a second about work. It won't be for very long, five or ten minutes, tops. The captain said he'd stay here and keep you company while we're talking shop."

Not wanting to be a burden on anyone, she said, "I'll just go over and hang with Caroline and the others."

"Looks like they're packing up," Rocco said. "I've know the captain a long time, you'll be safe with him. I promise we won't be long." And with that, he didn't wait for her to agree or disagree. He kissed her on the forehead and squeezed her arm. "I'll be right back," he reassured her.

It was clear that Rocco and the others had a great amount of respect for the two officers who'd shown up late to the party. And even though she'd spent years around higher-ranking officers during her time as a Department of Defense contractor, they still intimidated her. She watched Rocco walk a short distance away so they could talk to the rear admiral without being overheard.

"You're a hard woman to kill, Ms. McCallan," Captain Chambers muttered the second the men were out of hearing range.

Caite looked up at him in confusion. "What?"

"You heard me," he said, reaching out and grabbing her upper arm. He jerked her close to his side. "We're going to take a walk, and you're going to keep your mouth shut and do as I say," Chambers said.

At that, Caite's eyes whipped toward Rocco before swinging back to the captain. His face was blank—but she could see hate burning in his eyes. How he'd been able to mask it earlier, she had no idea.

She tried to jerk her arm out of his grasp, and immediately felt something hard press into her. She looked down, shocked to see the barrel of a small pistol jammed against her side.

"If you don't come with me quietly, right now, I'm going to shoot you, then I'm going to shoot one of these damn brats running around, *then* I'll shoot your precious Navy SEAL boyfriend when he comes over to find out what's going on. Got it?"

Caite met the captain's gaze as he gripped her arm with enough pressure to bruise...

And suddenly, as clear as day, she remembered what one of the Bitoo brothers had said.

"Where are we gonna get a gun?"

"I don't know. Maybe Chambers can help."

"That asshole an American too. He doesn't care about anything but getting those tablets to his buyer."

There was no doubt that this was the man the brothers were talking about—the man who wanted her dead.

Caite glanced again from the cold, lethal look of the man next to her to where Rocco was standing. He was laughing at something someone said and the look of relaxation and happiness on his face was heartbreaking.

He trusted the captain. He never would've left her with him if he hadn't. Somehow the man had slipped under everyone's radar.

"Took you a bit too long to realize who I am," Chambers said with a weird smirk. "Come on, we're going. Keep your mouth shut and no one else will get hurt."

Caite couldn't risk the lives of one of the precious children who were simply enjoying a beautiful day on the beach. And she definitely couldn't risk Rocco's life.

She'd have to play this by ear and take her chance for escape when it came. And it would come. They were on a beach full of Navy SEALs. Surely one of them would sense something was wrong and come to her rescue.

Captain Chambers began to walk her down the beach, away from the picnic and toward a pier sticking out into the water. Caite expected someone to call out and ask where they were going with every step they took. But as they got farther and farther away from the group, and no one said a word, she began to think this man might just get away with killing her after all.

CHAPTER FIFTEEN

They'd walked about three hundred feet when Caite realized she was going to have to take matters into her own hands. If she let Captain Chambers take her out of sight, or get her into a car, she was as good as dead. The man had been trying to kill her for weeks, and the second he got a chance, when there weren't dozens of witnesses, he'd do it.

The beach had narrowed as they'd walked, and they were almost marching in the surf now. To their left was tall grass and weeds and rocks. To their right was the ocean, and in front of them was the pier.

Captain Chambers hadn't said anything else as he forced her down the beach and away from assistance. Caite had tried to look back once, but he'd wrenched her arm so hard, tears formed in her eyes.

He mumbled under his breath about money, smuggling, and how much trouble women were.

Knowing with each step they took away from Rocco, his team, and everyone else enjoying themselves at the party, she was less and less likely to be rescued, Caite made a decision.

Hoping the captain wouldn't immediately shoot her, that he was trying to stay under the radar, she wrenched her arm out of his grasp and threw herself to the side as hard as she could.

She ended up on her hands and knees in the surf, sputtering as a wave chose that moment to wash ashore.

Ignoring the fact that her flip-flops had come off and were washing away with the receding tide, and her shorts were now soaked, Caite quickly stood and backed away from the seething man.

"Come here, Caite," he ordered, pointing at the sand in front of him.

She shook her head and took another step back.

Chambers stalked toward her, stopping when the water lapped at his feet. "I'm warning you," he said, lifting his arm to point the pistol at her.

Caite took another step backward, and she stumbled as a wave hit the backs of her calves.

Someone shouted something down the beach, but she didn't dare take her eyes off of the man in front of her. His face had contorted with rage, and he was glaring at her as if the force of his stare alone could force her to bend to his will. She vaguely wondered how many people said no to this man.

"I wanted to do this quiet and painless," he told her.

"But you're making that impossible. If you don't come back here in ten seconds, I'm going to shoot you right here and now. And I have more connections than you can even imagine. I'll make sure your boyfriend dies a horrible death. He should've died in Bahrain, but you saved him. Do you want to be the cause of his death now?"

Caite shook her head, refusing to give in to his crazy. There hadn't been any other shouts off to their left, but the hair on her arms was standing straight up. Knowing there was only one way to end this standoff, Caite took another step backward. Then another. And another.

The water was up to her thighs now, and every time a wave crashed, she stumbled forward before catching herself and forcing her feet to keep going.

"What the fuck are you doing? Get back here!" Chambers shouted desperately. He took a few steps toward her in the surf.

"Stop right there, Chambers!" a voice rang out from Caite's left.

The second the captain turned to see who had spoken, Caite took the opportunity to do something completely crazy, but hopefully it would take her out of the equation altogether.

She turned and threw herself headfirst into the ocean.

Rocco had no idea what made him turn his head and look down the beach, but what he saw made him blink in surprise.

Captain Chambers and Caite were walking almost arm in arm away from the party.

Interrupting the rear admiral midsentence, he asked, "Where are they going?"

In tandem, the six other men turned to see what he was talking about.

"Maybe the captain wanted to show her something down by the pier?" Creasy mused absentmindedly.

Rocco's brow furrowed. Something about the way they were walking seemed...off. He was trying to make sense of it when Caite suddenly fell to her hands and knees in the surf.

"What the hell?" he muttered, and took a step away —then he saw Captain Chambers raise his arm.

"Holy fuck," Gumby swore, grabbing Rocco by the arm before he could take off sprinting down the beach.

"Let go of me!" Rocco growled, fighting against his friend's hold.

"If you go running toward them, he'll shoot her for sure!" Ace hissed, joining Gumby in trying to hold Rocco back.

"We need to circle around. Surround him so he can't get away," Phantom said.

Rex turned toward where some of the others were packing up and whistled once, long and low.

Immediately, Wolf's head came up—and his entire

demeanor changed when he saw Rex's hand signals. Dropping their beach gear and pointing their women and children toward the parking area, the six retired SEALs made their way as fast as they could toward the group.

"I'll take Wolf and his team behind the dune and cut him off on the other side," Phantom said before running to meet the other men.

Rocco knew with Phantom in charge, the other team would successfully be able to sneak up behind the captain, but that wasn't his concern at the moment. He watched for a heartbeat as Caite continued to back toward the ocean as she and Chambers had words, then he called out after Phantom, "She can't swim!"

He saw his teammate signal in acknowledgment before intercepting Wolf and leading him and the other former SEALs at a fast clip toward the parking lot, so they could get past the captain without him knowing they were there. One man from Wolf's group, Cookie, remained behind and rushed up to where Rocco and the others were standing.

Rocco nodded at the man and turned his attention back to Caite. She stumbled and almost fell when a wave crashed against her legs—and Rocco felt paralyzed for the first time in his life.

He was faced with the worst-case scenario—and he couldn't do a damn thing. Couldn't make a decision about how to save Caite.

"If he thinks he's cornered, it'll pressure him into

shooting," Gumby said quietly. "For whatever reason, he hasn't done it yet. We need to take this slow and easy."

"He's going to kill her," Rocco said, even as his feet started moving, following his teammates toward the woman he loved more than life itself. Caite looked scared out of her mind, but she wasn't freaking out, which was good. He was more proud of her than he'd ever been.

"He would've already done it if that was his intention," the rear admiral said.

Rocco wasn't surprised the man was joining them. He had been a SEAL once upon a time himself, and he had to be pissed that the man they'd *just* been discussing, the man they'd all been looking for this past week, was someone within his own unit.

"He probably thought if he could get her away from the party, he could kill her and no one would know."

Rocco growled once again, the sound vibrating in his chest as he thought of Chambers shooting his woman. He didn't like Creasy's assumption, but knew he was right.

Keeping his eyes on both Chambers and Caite, Rocco walked silently next to his brothers-in-arms. As suddenly as his inability to think had left him, it returned as he watched Caite inching her way backward. He knew exactly what she was planning. And he hated it, wanted to yell at her to stay still, to trust him to take care of Chambers before he could shoot her, but he was still too far away.

"Gumby and Cookie, I need you on Caite. She's not a strong swimmer. At all."

"On it," Gumby said, veering right, toward the ocean.

Cookie took the time to put his hand on Rocco's shoulder. "We've got her," he said. "I give you my word as a SEAL, she'll be safe with us."

Nodding, Rocco watched as Cookie tore off his shirt and followed Gumby into the waves.

The five remaining men continued stalking Chambers, staying behind him and out of his line of vision. They were closing in on him, and quietly talking strategy on how to take him down without letting the man kill Caite or himself, when Caite took a few more steps backward. The water was almost up to her hips now, and she stumbled forward as the waves hit her.

As if just now realizing how far out she was, Chambers yelled something the men couldn't hear and began to walk toward Caite.

"Stop right there, Chambers!" Rear Admiral Creasy yelled.

The captain turned to look at the approaching men, fury clear on his face.

Rocco saw Caite turn and throw herself headfirst into the ocean.

He wanted to go after her, knew she'd be terrified, but he had to trust in his teammates. They'd keep her safe until he could deal with the threat against her.

Chambers cried out in rage, then turned and

squeezed the trigger on the pistol, shooting blindly into the waves where Caite had disappeared.

"You want to shoot someone, shoot me!" Rocco yelled, desperate to get the man to stop.

Abruptly, Chambers turned and aimed the pistol at Rocco. "This is all your fault!" he yelled. "If you'd just died in that fucking cellar, this wouldn't be happening to me!"

Rocco put his hands in the air and stopped about twenty feet from the obviously deranged man. "This can still be fixed, Captain. Just put the gun down and we'll talk."

Chambers laughed manically. "Right. This *can't* be fixed! My life is fucked and we both know it!"

"I'm ordering you to put the weapon down," the rear admiral said.

"Fuck you," Chambers shouted. "Fuck *all* of you! You think I don't know the only thing keeping you from bum rushing me is this gun? The second I put it down, all you fucking SEALs will do your thing and I'll never see the light of day again!"

The man was wrong. The gun wasn't the thing holding any of the men back—it was the fact that they could see Caite. She was still too close to shore, easily in range of the bullets. No SEAL was scared of being shot. Yeah, it hurt like hell, but it would be nothing if it meant taking Chambers down.

Anger simmered inside Rocco. This man had tried

to have Caite killed. Not once. Not twice. But *three times*.

Rocco didn't care about the fact that he'd almost died as a direct result of this man's actions. That was a fact of life in his profession. But the idea that he'd targeted an innocent was unacceptable.

He needed to stall Chambers, give Caite time to get farther away, and give Cookie and Gumby time to get to her.

"What did you think would happen here, Chambers?" he called out. "You'd take Caite away and we wouldn't realize it was you? I *left* her with you, man. Who else was I going to suspect?"

"I had it all worked out!" the captain yelled back, gesturing with the gun and seeming increasingly crazed. "I was gonna tell you she thought she saw a kid by himself on the pier. I escorted her down here and someone jumped us. He got off a shot before I could do anything. It was gonna work, damn it! But that stupid bitch decided to be a hero!"

The captain started to turn toward the ocean, but Rocco quickly took a few steps forward and said, "And then what? The bullet inside her would be traced back to *you*. I thought you were smarter than that, man."

Rocco knew Ace and Bubba were spreading out to his right, and Rex and the rear admiral were doing the same on his left. They'd formed a line and could jump the captain, just as the man himself had feared. Rocco could also see Wolf, Phantom, Abe, Mozart, Dude, and Benny coming up fast and silent behind Chambers.

It was his job to keep the man's attention on him, and not on Caite or what was happening behind him.

"I *am* smarter!" Chamber raged. "I'm a fucking *genius*! I was the one who figured out there was big money in those stupid artifacts. I'm the one who found Andy Edwards and made him funnel information to me! No one cares about Iraq! They fucking bombed our country! Why should they get to keep all those pieces of hardened dirt? They'll just end up breaking them or blowing them up. I was *saving* them!"

"Saving them?" Creasy asked incredulously. "You were selling them to the highest bidder."

"Right! Who are putting them in museums and treating them with respect, which is more than the fucking Taliban would do!" Chambers screeched. "The navy pays us *peanuts*! Why should everyone else profit from those fucking tablets and not me? I've put in my time for my country, and I'm not gonna get *nearly* what I deserve when I retire!"

"What makes you better than the Bitoo brothers?" Rocco asked, having no idea who Andy Edwards was, but making a mental note to find out as soon as possible. "What makes you better than the terrorists looting sacred burial sites and museums in Iraq?"

"I *am* better than them!" Chambers screamed.

"Put the gun down. Now, Chambers!" the rear

admiral ordered again. "Seriously, Isaac...as of now, you haven't hurt anyone. We can work this out."

Chambers laughed. It was a high-pitched, insane sound, but when he spoke, his words were modulated and clear. "There's nothing to be worked out. I'm done. If the thugs in the federal prison don't kill me, my clients will find a way to get to me. All I had to do was make sure she kept her damn mouth shut. I knew if she blabbed, everything was over."

"It *is* over," Creasy told him. "We're friends, Isaac. Let me help you."

"You can't help me," Chambers said, his tone eerily quiet now. "Tell my wife I'm sorry."

Even as Wolf and Phantom dove toward the man from behind, the captain raised the gun to his head and pulled the trigger.

"No!" The rear admiral leaped toward the man he'd worked with for several years.

Within seconds, the SEALs were doing first aid, but Rocco's attention wasn't on the man who had gotten off easy—it was on the ocean. He ran to the place where he'd last seen Caite and squinted, blocking the sun from his eyes with a hand.

But all he could see was water. Miles and miles of water. No Caite.

Caite held her breath and kept her eyes squeezed shut

as she threw herself into the ocean. For a second, she panicked when she couldn't figure out which way was up, but then she let her body go limp, like Rocco had taught her, and felt herself float up to the surface. She immediately turned on her back and tried to calm down.

The waves were trying to push her back toward shore, which was the last place she wanted to go. If she could take herself out of the equation, she had no doubt Rocco and his team could take out Captain Chambers.

Caite kicked her feet and move her hands back and forth, tying to propel herself through the water. Coughing as waves crashed over her head, she kept going as best she could.

When she heard gunshots, she braced herself, waiting for pain to hit her—along with a bullet. But nothing happened.

Picking up her head and trying to look back at shore was a mistake, as she immediately sank under the water. Sputtering and coughing, she forced herself to relax and put her head back, to stare up at the sky as she tried to move through the water.

"When this is over, I'm going to insist on Rocco showing me the right way to swim," she said out loud. Her words were muffled and sounded weird in her head, but somehow talking to herself made her feel better.

"I'm sure I look like a beached whale, but I don't care. Thank God saltwater makes me float, because this is a lot harder than being in the calm cove Rocco took me to."

She coughed as water went in her mouth once again, and she decided that maybe it was better to concentrate on floating and moving away from the beach rather than talking. Caite felt as if she was undulating weirdly, but a glance downward showed she was indeed moving in the right direction.

Caite finally stopped paddling with her hands and kicking with her feet. She didn't want to swim her way to Hawaii, she just needed to get far enough away so she was out of the line of fire. She lay still and continued to stare upward. Everything seemed quiet and serene out in the ocean. She wanted to tread water, to see what was happening, but she didn't know how to do that and not sink.

How long she lay on her back, Caite had no clue, but the second she felt something brush against her, she panicked.

Flailing as if her life depended on it, Caite's head went under once more and she inhaled a huge swallow of seawater before her head popped back above the waves, an arm tight around her waist.

"Easy, Caite. I've got you."

Surprised at the deep voice right next to her, Caite turned to see Gumby. Still coughing and gagging on the water she'd swallowed, she managed to say, "Fancy meeting you here."

The lines next to his eyes crinkled as he smiled at her. "You okay?"

Caite started to nod when she felt something against her other side. She shrieked and threw her arms around Gumby, sure she was about to be eaten by a shark.

A chuckle to her right made her open her eyes and glare at the second man. Cookie, if she remembered right.

"Sorry," he said. "Didn't mean to scare you. Usually women are glad to see me when I appear next to them in the middle of the ocean."

"You do this a lot?" Caite asked snarkily.

"More than you'd think," Cookie responded.

"Are you hurt?" Gumby asked, bringing her attention back to him. "Did you get shot?"

Caite shook her head. "No. I'm okay." Water got in her mouth as she spoke and she sputtered some more.

"Why don't you lie back again," Gumby suggested. "Cookie and I are here, we'll make sure you get back to shore."

"Not yet!" Caite cried. "It's not safe."

"Rocco and the others have things under control," Gumby told her. "He said you weren't a strong swimmer, but I'd say he was wrong. You did just what you should've."

His praise went a long way toward making Caite feel better about her rash decision to dive into the ocean. "They aren't going to let him get away, are they?" she asked. "He's the one who's been trying to kill me."

"He's not going to get away," Cookie said, and Caite glanced at him once more. "Trust us. We'll get you back to Rocco safe and sound."

"Lie back and relax," Gumby urged, peeling her hands from his neck. "That's it. Good girl."

Caite forced herself to let go of Gumby but remained stiff until she felt both Cookie's and Gumby's hands under her back. They easily helped keep her afloat even while swimming with their free hands. She could tell they were swimming parallel to shore, and not directly toward it, and that was okay with her. She was worried about Rocco, but knew deep down that Captain Chambers was no match for him and his team.

Something occurred to her then. "I thought you guys were leaving," she said as she glanced toward Cookie.

"We were. But Wolf heard Rex whistle and saw him signal that they needed help."

"Oh." She really didn't have much more to say after that. She wanted to know what was happening, where Rocco was, but she also didn't want to be *that* person. The needy damsel in distress. She'd gotten herself away from the captain all by herself, thank you very much, she couldn't fall apart now.

"I guess we're even now," she told Gumby as they swam with her through the waves.

"What's that?" he asked.

"We're even. I saved you and you saved me."

He grinned. "I guess that means we have to name our kids after each other then."

"I'm not naming any of my children Gumby."

"Decker."

"What?"

"My name is Decker."

Caite turned her head slightly so she could see him. "Really?"

"Yup."

"I like it."

He grinned again.

"Okay. Done."

"Hey, what about me?" Cookie teased from her other side. "I saved your life too!"

"Fine, what's your name? Your *real* name?" Caite asked.

"Hunter."

"Good lord," Caite mused. "Hunter and Decker. I'll have the most badass little boys around. The little girls at school will throw themselves on the ground in adoration when they walk by."

Both men laughed at that.

Caite sobered. She took a chance that she was safe and secure with their hands under her, and she reached up and touched both men on the shoulder as they swam. "Thank you."

As if they could speak telepathically, both Cookie and Gumby stopped swimming to tread water next to her. They helped her move upright, both holding on to an arm so she didn't sink.

"You don't have to thank us," Gumby said, with no trace of the humor that had just been in his voice.

"Yeah, I do," Caite argued. "When I went into the water, I knew there was a fifty-fifty chance I wasn't going to make it out. I mean, Rocco helped me learn how to float, but that was in a nice smooth cove with no waves...and no crazy men shooting at me. All I knew was that I couldn't let him take me out of sight of the party. If he did, I knew he'd kill me. The ocean was my only shot, and I took it."

"Beautiful *and* smart," Cookie mused.

"Caite, listen to me. You might be dating Rocco, but you belong to all of us. Ace, Bubba, Rex, Phantom, me...*all* of us. Just as the woman I end up with will be, and Ace's woman, etcetera. If Rocco lost you, we'd all suffer. I may not love you quite like *he* does, but I sure as hell still love you...if that makes sense."

Caite could only stare at him in surprise.

"You met my wife today. You saw how close everyone is in our group. Every one of us would do whatever it takes to protect each other's wives and kids. Me and Fiona might not have children of our own, but you better believe that I'd die for Alabama's, or Jess's, or Cheyenne's. And Caite...when a SEAL decides a woman is it for him, she's *it*. Period. So be sure about Rocco. You can hurt him worse than any bullet ever could."

Caite swallowed hard. She didn't want to hurt

Rocco, but hearing from his friends how much she meant to him, to *all* of them, meant more to her than almost anything she'd ever heard in her life.

She opened her mouth to speak—but just then a single shot rang out from the beach.

Moving as one, Cookie and Gumby eased her onto her back and began swimming in earnest away from the area.

Caite wanted to ask what was going on. If Rocco had been shot. If Captain Chambers was still shooting at her...but all she could do was hang on as she moved through the water much faster than she'd ever be able to move on her own.

Closing her eyes, Caite gave her safety over to the two men at her sides. They'd get her to Rocco. She had no doubt.

CHAPTER SIXTEEN

Rocco stared in frustration and fear out at the waves. All he saw were whitecaps. Just as he began to strip off his shirt in preparation for heading out to search for Caite himself, he heard Ace say, "Two o'clock!"

Turning to his right, Rocco saw three figures emerging from the surf.

Taking off at a run, Rocco ignored the shouts from the local police who had just shown up on scene. Knowing his team would have his back, not to mention the word of a rear admiral, Rocco didn't take his eyes off of Cookie, Caite, and Gumby as they struggled to stay on their feet in the strong surf.

Wading into the water to meet them, the second he could, Rocco grabbed Caite and lifted her into his arms. Feeling Cookie and Gumby steadying him on either side, Rocco buried his nose in Caite's hair and held on as tightly as possible.

Neither said a word, simply held on as he walked them to the beach. Once there, Rocco didn't want to let go. Sinking to his knees, he couldn't get any words out. He was overwhelmed with gratitude that she was alive and well in his arms.

A thought struck him then, and he pulled back. "Were you hit, *ma petite fée?*"

Caite immediately shook her head.

"Thank God," Rocco groaned, then let out the breath he hadn't realized he'd been holding.

"Are you okay? We heard a shot," she said, putting a hand on the side of his face.

"I'm fine. We're all okay."

"Then who was shot?"

Rocco exchanged a look with Gumby then turned back to Caite. "Chambers."

Her eyes got wide. "Did you shoot him? Are you going to be arrested?"

Rocco shook her head. "No, *ma petite fée.* He shot himself. None of us were armed."

Instead of being shocked at hearing about Chambers, she fixated on the other thing he said. "You weren't armed? How were you going to take him down then? He had a *gun!* He could've shot you! He said he was going to kill you or one of the kids if I yelled out."

"I'm a SEAL. We're all SEALs," Rocco said matter-of-factly. "We don't need weapons because we *are* weapons, Caite."

She rolled her eyes, and Rocco was just extremely

relieved she wasn't hysterical. "Save me from macho navy heroes."

"She swallowed a lot of water," Gumby said from above them. "She's probably gonna be dehydrated."

"I'm fine," Caite mumbled as she buried her face back into the side of Rocco's neck.

"Help me up?" Rocco asked his friends, and easily stood with a little boost from each of them when they grabbed his arms.

Then, holding Caite as if she were made of glass, even though he knew from experience she had a core of steel, Rocco carried her down the beach toward where they'd left their chairs. He knew they'd have to talk to the cops, and they wouldn't be leaving for a while, but he needed to make sure Caite was good. She came before everyone and everything else. Always.

Caite was a little surprised that Rocco refused to leave her side. She figured he'd have to talk to the navy bigwigs who had descended on the little beach like a plague of locusts. Not only them, but the navy investigators, and the local cops and detectives who had shown up as well. Within thirty minutes, there were more law enforcement personnel on the beach than there had been people enjoying the navy party.

Caroline and the rest of the women had given their statements to the police as to what they'd seen from their vantage point, and had been shooed off by their husbands. The other guests had been questioned and politely asked to leave as well.

Caite was the only woman left on the beach, other than the female officers and detectives. She shivered, both because she was chilled and in reaction to what she'd gone through. Now that she'd had time to really think about it, she realized how lucky she'd been.

"You're okay, *ma petite fée*," Rocco said softly. They'd both been interviewed several times by both NCIS and the local police. Rear Admiral Creasy had been a godsend, as he'd taken charge of the scene and just about everyone seemed to defer to him.

"Hang on just a few more minutes and we'll be out of here," Rocco told her.

She nodded.

"Caite?"

"Yeah?" she said, looking up at him.

"What you did was incredibly stupid, you know that, right?" Rocco asked.

She immediately felt her hackles rise. She'd done the only thing she *could* do at the time. Unlike Rocco and the rest of his buddies, *she* wasn't a walking, talking weapon.

She'd recently watched a clip on the internet of a Navy SEAL guy demonstrating what you should do in a knife fight. The camera panned away from the buff, hot SEAL to a fake attacker with a knife, and when it panned back to the SEAL, the only thing left to see was the back of the man as he ran as fast as he could away from the fight.

That had stuck with her. She couldn't have fought the captain. He was bigger than her, meaner, and a lot more desperate.

Rocco's words hurt, and she tried to pull away from him, no matter that she was still cold. But he wouldn't let go.

Caite opened her mouth to defend herself, but he spoke before she could.

"It was also the bravest thing I've ever seen in my life...and I've seen some incredibly brave shit. I'm so proud of you, *ma petite fée*. You did the one thing that would make sure this ended the way it did, without you or any of the good guys being hurt. You took yourself out of the equation."

The tears that had hovered at the surface of her eyes spilled over. "Did he say why?" she asked between hiccupped breaths.

"Nothing that made sense," Rocco said. "I'm sure NCIS will find out a lot more once they delve into his financial situation. He babbled about money and retirement, and some guy named Andy Edwards, but the bottom line is, I don't give one little shit. He dishonored the navy and the SEALs. Not only that, but he tried to kill you. Several times. I hope he rots in hell."

Caite couldn't help but grin. Her man was blood-thirsty, but she liked it. But then something else registered. "Petty Officer Edwards?" she asked.

Rocco's eyes narrowed. "I don't know. Who's Petty Officer Edwards?"

"He works in IT in Bahrain. Whenever we had computer issues, he'd come and help us. He's kinda quiet, and I got the impression he was happiest when he was in the barracks playing that video game, *This is War*, with his buddies, but he was always really nice to me. And helpful."

"Shit," Rocco said, shaking his head.

"What? Was he in on this too?" Caite asked with a frown.

"Looks that way," Rocco said. "I'll get with Creasy and Commander Horner and let them know. But it makes sense. That's probably why the fingerprints from that kid who tried to carjack us never showed up."

Turning in his arms, Caite wrapped her own around his waist. Rocco looked pissed. "Is it over?" she asked.

"Yeah, you're safe, Caite."

Rocco tipped his head down and ran a hand over her hair. It was mostly dry now and probably sticking out in a million different directions, but Caite didn't care about her hair at the moment.

"I love you, Blake Wise."

She saw the anger leach out of his eyes, and tenderness replace it. "Yeah?" he asked.

Smiling, Caite nodded.

"It's a good thing, since I love you too, *ma petite fée*. It'll make you moving in a hell of a lot easier if you love me back."

She chuckled. "You were still going to move me in if I *didn't* love you?"

"Yup. I figured if I gave you enough time, you wouldn't be able to resist me."

Shaking her head, Caite smiled at him. "If you screw up, does that mean I can order you to carry that rock around the apartment for punishment?"

His face lit up when he smiled. "You could order me to do just about anything, Caite, and I'd move Heaven and Earth to make sure it was done."

His words melted her heart. "Thank you for sending Gumby and Cookie out to get me."

"I would've gone myself, but I had to make sure Chambers wasn't going to be a threat to you. I had to see it done. I wasn't going to let him continue to terrorize you."

"I know." And she did. She wasn't upset that it wasn't Rocco who was in the ocean with her. He'd sent men he trusted and respected and had stayed behind to eliminate the threat. She knew he would've done whatever was necessary to make sure she was safe.

"I love you, Caite. I don't know what I'd do without you in my life," Rocco said solemnly.

"Good thing you'll never have to find out," Caite returned.

He hugged her to him then, and Caite had never felt more secure. The way she felt in Rocco's arms was so different from any man she'd ever been with. It was as if his arms were bulletproof shields, making sure nothing could get through to hurt her. She knew it was fanciful, and there was a good chance they'd fight in the future—she was too independent, and he was too bossy and protective for them not to fight—but she also knew without a doubt, at the end of the day, when they settled in bed for the night, she'd be snuggled deep in his arms, just as she was now.

* * *

"How's the new job?" Gumby asked, leaning against edge of her desk. He smirked when Caite glared at him and shooed him off with her hands.

"It's fine, except for you and everyone else coming by to check on me every five minutes. My boss is gonna think I'm out here socializing instead of working," Caite protested.

"Never," Gumby reassured her. "He knows he lucked out when he hired you."

Caite rolled her eyes. "As if he had a choice. After Slade and Rear Admiral Creasy recommended me, there really wasn't anything he could do *but* hire me."

"Wrong," Gumby told her. "Your past work spoke for itself. Just because that asshole in Bahrain couldn't see what an amazing employee he had, doesn't mean others couldn't. Besides, you speaking French was the tipping point. You know how badly they needed someone to help transcribe the hundreds of hours of surveillance tapes they have. You're a godsend to the Naval Criminal Investigative Service."

Caite nodded. "I guess this is what I get for complaining about being bored, huh?" she quipped.

Gumby chuckled. He knew all about how bored Caite had been, as Rocco had told them she'd cleaned his apartment from top to bottom several times.

She'd bounced back from her experience on the beach even as the ramifications of Captain Chambers's deceit continued to reverberate throughout the navy. He'd sucked way too many good men into his schemes, including Andy Edwards, the mole Commander Horner had been searching for in Bahrain. He'd been taken into custody for his role in what had happened in Manama, and for hacking into the FBI database to erase Carter Richards's fingerprints and hindering a federal investigation.

Gumby was thrilled for Rocco. It was obvious he and Caite were meant to be together. He wasn't jealous, not really...but seeing how happy his buddy was just made him all the more eager to find his own soul mate.

"I just wanted to stop by and make sure you were good," Gumby told Caite.

"I'm good," she reassured him. "Rocco's coming by later, and we're going to go out and celebrate."

"Remember, I'm expecting you to name your first-born after me," Gumby teased.

Caite scoffed. "Why do guys automatically think about sex when the word 'celebrate' is mentioned?"

"Are you denying that's what's going to happen tonight?" Gumby asked, grinning.

Caite laughed and held up her hands. "Fine. You win. We're gonna have hot monkey sex tonight, but *after* Rocco takes me out for a nice fancy dinner."

Gumby loved how Caite treated him like an irritating brother. He had an older brother himself, but never had a sister he could tease. "I knew it!"

"Whatever," Caite said. "Now get out. I have work to do."

"Yes, ma'am," Gumby said, saluting her. The second he was out of earshot, he took his phone out of his pocket and clicked on Rocco's name. "She's good," he said when his friend picked up.

Rocco sighed in relief. "I figured she would be, but I appreciate you checking up on her all the same."

"Anytime."

"You headed out now?"

"Yeah. I'm gonna go back to my place for lunch, then I'll meet you guys at the office so we can continue the debrief for next week's mission."

"Sounds good. Drive safe," Rocco told him.

"Always. Later."

"Bye."

Gumby clicked off the phone and headed for his pickup. After growing up in Texas, he found it almost impossible to drive anything but a pickup truck. He pulled out of the NCIS parking lot and headed for his house. He'd bought the small beachside place for a steal when it had been foreclosed. It still needed a lot of work, and he was slowly but surely getting it fixed up in his downtime.

He was a few blocks from home when something on the side of the road caught his attention. Gumby was pulling over before he'd even thought about it. Jumping out of the truck, he raced toward the man and woman having a knock-down drag-out fight in the front yard of a dilapidated house.

The woman was petite, and the man she was fighting was at least a foot taller. And way more muscular. But, amazingly, she was holding her own.

"Stop it!" Gumby yelled as he got close.

The man looked up in surprise and swore before turning and bolting.

Gumby was about to follow to make sure the bastard was held accountable for hitting a woman, when the woman in question grabbed his arm and urgently said, "Help me!"

Gumby was well trained in first aid, as he and the rest of the team had to be ready to give life-saving aid at a moment's notice. He turned, ready to stop some bleeding or set a broken bone—but what he saw shocked the shit out him.

The woman had let go of his arm and was kneeling on the ground next to a badly injured dog. It was a small pit bull, who was alternating growling and whimpering in fright, cowering away from its would-be rescuer.

"I'm not sure you should be that close to him,"

Gumby said in a low voice, trying not to provoke the injured animal any more than it already was.

"Why not?" the woman asked, twisting to look up at him. Her lip was bleeding and her shirt was torn and hanging loosely off one shoulder. Gumby could see her pink bra strap on her nearly identically colored shoulder. She even had a black eye forming, but she didn't seem to notice her own disarray.

"Because he could bite you. He's hurt. Who was that guy? I need to call the cops."

"No! No cops!" the woman said, looking nervous for the first time. "I just need help getting *her* into my car."

Gumby frowned. "Do you know the guy who was hitting you?"

"No," she said a shade too quickly, and Gumby's bullshit meter was spiking.

"What's going on?"

Sighing, the woman sat back on her heels and looked up at him. "Will you help me if I tell you?"

"Yes."

"Fine. That guy is always trying to get pit bulls that people are giving away on social media or Craigslist. I got his address when he stupidly posted it in a group on Facebook, when someone was trying to get rid of a dog. He's had this beauty in his yard for at least a week. As far as I can tell, he hasn't fed her or given her any water. Then this morning, while I was watching, he poured something on her back. Look! Whatever it was, it burned her. It had to be caustic. I need to get her to the vet. Not only that, but check out her paws. Sometime when I wasn't around, she was dragged. Probably behind a car or a motorcycle or something. Assholes were probably using her as a bait dog too. Look at the scars on her beautiful face!"

Gumby looked down at the shivering mess of a dog at her feet. There was a line of missing hair along her backbone that did indeed look like it was from some sort of burn or caustic agent. And the dog's paws were bloody, and still bleeding.

His heart melted. No dog deserved to be abused like this one had been.

Drawn to the pitiful animal as if by a string, he kneeled next to the black dog, who looked way too skinny for her size, and held out his hand tentatively. The dog whimpered and stretched her nose out to his fingers.

Then she shocked the shit out of him by crawling on her belly until she was right in front of him and resting her head on his leg.

Gumby looked up at the woman in surprise. She looked equally shocked. Then she recovered and looked around nervously. "We need to get out of here. I was in the process of stealing this dog when that guy came out of his house and tried to stop me."

"You were stealing her?"

She sat up and put her hands on her hips. Even kneeling on the ground, she was a force. "Yeah. I *was*. He took exception, and we were fighting over her."

Shaking his head, Gumby said, "I'm going to regret this." Then he slowly stood and leaned over and easily picked up the trembling, abused dog.

"Lord, you're big," the woman said, looking up at him. "There's no way I could've carried her like that."

"Come on," Gumby said. "If that guy has friends, I don't think it'll be a good idea if we're standing around chatting."

"Right," she said, gesturing toward the street. "My name's Sidney. Sidney Hale."

"Decker Kincade," Gumby told her.

"Thanks for stopping to help, Deck," Sidney said as she ran ahead to her small Honda Accord, which had seen better days. It was at least ten years old and had several dents and scratches in the black paint.

Gumby bypassed her car and headed for his truck.

"Hey, what are you doing?" she fretted as she shuffled alongside him.

"I'm taking Hannah to the vet."

"Hannah?" Sidney asked.

"That's what I'm naming her," Gumby said, not knowing why he'd thought of that name, just that it seemed to fit the small black pit bull. It was a dignified name for an animal who had been treated with anything but dignity for most of her life.

"But *I'm* taking her."

"Wrong," Gumby said, turning to face Sidney. "But you're welcome to come with me. In fact, I insist."

"Oh, but I... Maybe we can talk about this." She stumbled over her words.

"No time to talk," Gumby said as he opened his door with one hand and placed the injured dog across the front bench seat of his truck. "There's a vet near where I live. You can follow me there." Then, he slowly reached out and touched his fingers to the corner of her mouth and wiped away a smear of blood. "After I take care of Hannah, I can make sure you're okay."

Using her shoulder, she wiped at her mouth with her T-shirt. "I'm fine." The words were said with more bravado than Gumby had seen in a while. He figured the woman to be in her early thirties, but the pain in her eyes hinted at a very hard life.

He was intrigued. Anyone who would physically fight a man obviously stronger than she was, over the life of a dog, was worth knowing in his eyes.

"Come with me," he said gently. "Help me get Hannah settled. It's why you were here fighting for her, right?"

"Right," Sidney said. "Fine. But don't think you can just take off with her. I'll be right on your heels, Deck." And with that, she turned and stomped back to her old car.

Gumby watched her go with a smile. She might be small, but she had curves that went on for days.

Yes, he was definitely intrigued.

He jogged around and got into the driver's seat once he was sure Sidney was safely inside her vehicle. Hannah whined, and Gumby put a hand on her head, amazed when she immediately quieted at his touch. "Hang in there, girl. We'll get you fixed up and get some food in your belly as soon as we can."

As if the dog could understand, she nuzzled his hand and sighed in contentment. Looking into his rearview mirror at the vehicle following his, Gumby smiled. He had a feeling Sidney Hale wouldn't be nearly as docile as the injured and abused dog next to him. Excitement and anticipation raced through his veins.

For the first time in a long time, Gumby had something to look forward to other than the next mission.

Be sure to pick up Gumby's story, *Securing Sidney, coming out soon!*

JOIN my Newsletter and find out about sales, free books, contests and new releases before anyone else!!
Click HERE

Want to know when my books go on sale? Follow me on Bookbub HERE!

Would you like Susan's Book Protecting Caroline
for FREE?
Click HERE

Also by Susan Stoker

Delta Force Heroes Series

Rescuing Rayne

Rescuing Aimee (novella)

Rescuing Emily

Rescuing Harley

Marrying Emily

Rescuing Kassie

Rescuing Bryn

Rescuing Casey

Rescuing Sadie

Rescuing Wendy

Rescuing Mary

Rescuing Macie (April 2019)

Badge of Honor: Texas Heroes Series

Justice for Mackenzie

Justice for Mickie

Justice for Corrie

Justice for Laine (novella)

Shelter for Elizabeth

Justice for Boone

Shelter for Adeline

Shelter for Sophie

Justice for Erin

Justice for Milena

Shelter for Blythe
Justice for Hope
Shelter for Quinn (Feb 2019)
Shelter for Koren (June 2019)
Shelter for Penelope (Oct 2019)

SEAL of Protection: Legacy Series

Securing Caite
Securing Sidney (May 2019)
Securing Piper (Sept 2019)
Securing Zoey (TBA)
Securing Avery (TBA)
Securing Kalee (TBA)

Ace Security Series

Claiming Grace
Claiming Alexis
Claiming Bailey
Claiming Felicity

Mountain Mercenaries Series

Defending Allye
Defending Chloe
Defending Morgan (Mar 2019)
Defending Harlow (July 2019)
Defending Everly (TBA)
Defending Zara (TBA)
Defending Raven (TBA)

SEAL of Protection Series

Protecting Caroline

Protecting Alabama

Protecting Fiona

Marrying Caroline (novella)

Protecting Summer

Protecting Cheyenne

Protecting Jessyka

Protecting Julie (novella)

Protecting Melody

Protecting the Future

Protecting Kiera (novella)

Protecting Dakota

Stand Alone

The Guardian Mist

Nature's Rift

A Princess for Cale

A Moment in Time- A Collection of Short Stories

Lambert's Lady

Special Operations Fan Fiction

http://www.AcesPress.com

Beyond Reality Series

Outback Hearts

Flaming Hearts

Frozen Hearts

Writing as Annie George:

Stepbrother Virgin (erotic novella)

ABOUT THE AUTHOR

New York Times, USA Today and *Wall Street Journal* Bestselling Author Susan Stoker has a heart as big as the state of Tennessee where she lives, but this all American girl has also spent the last fourteen years living in Missouri, California, Colorado, Indiana, and Texas. She's married to a retired Army man who now gets to follow *her* around the country.

She debuted her first series in 2014 and quickly followed that up with the SEAL of Protection Series, which solidified her love of writing and creating stories readers can get lost in.

If you enjoyed this book, or any book, please consider leaving a review. It's appreciated by authors more than you'll know.

www.stokeraces.com
www.AcesPress.com
susan@stokeraces.com

Made in the USA
Middletown, DE
11 January 2019